NOT ALONE

BOOKS BY FREDERIC MARTIN

The Vox Oculis Series

Not Alone

The Innocence of Westbury

Forest

NOT ALONE

A VOX OCULIS NOVEL: BOOK ONE

FREDERIC MARTIN

NthSense Books

Published by NthSense Books
Richmond, Vermont
www.nthsensebooks.com

NthSense, NthSense Books, and the NthSense Books logo are trademarks of NthSense, LLC.

Cover images used under license from Shutterstock.com.

ISBN: 978-1-7340240-6-7 (hardcover)
ISBN: 978-1-7340240-0-5 (paperback)
ISBN: 978-1-7340240-1-2 (ebook)

AUTHOR'S NOTE

Welcome to "Not Alone," the first book of the *Vox Oculis* trilogy! I am honored and thrilled that you selected this book over the many other fine books available, especially considering the mind-numbing ocean of books you had to choose from. However, there is something I feel compelled to tell you before you dive into the first chapters: This is not going to be your typical coming-of-age tale.

Let me explain: When I was faced with the requirement (on many websites) to plug this series into one of the well-known pre-defined genres, I was at a bit of a loss. I had never really thought about genre as I was writing, I was just putting the story down as it came to me. But I had no choice—selecting a genre is a gateway to many a book site, so I did my best.

At first, I tried "sci-fi" and quickly discovered that my storyline wasn't even close to the high fantasy world-building style that dominates that genre, even though there is a sci-fi element to this story. Then I tried "YA" and discovered that YA is dominated by angsty teen romance novels. (Okay, tiny spoiler: There is an element of romance in books two and three, but I wouldn't call it angsty or even awkward. I'll leave it to you to decide what flavor of romance develops and how it affects your dopamine levels. Romances, plural, I mean. Okay, TMI already.)

Next, I looked at "coming-of-age" and, *of course* it is coming-of-age: The main characters are fourteen and fifteen going on fifteen and sixteen so it is unavoidable to deal with coming-of-age issues. A bigger component, however, is the mystery surrounding our main character's background. That makes this a mystery, right? Maybe, but what about the nail-biting life-threatening event that happens in the second half of the book? Does that make it a thriller? Well, I think you will find, as you read the first half of this book and experience its relatively mellow pace, (after all, isn't early adolescence a magical ride down the lazy river?) I could hardly claim it was a hang-on-to-your-hat-here-we-go Jack Ryan style thrill ride. So, not *really* a thriller. Instead, perhaps it is . . .

Okay. Forget traditional genres. This is what I decided the *Vox Oculis* trilogy really is: A contemporary YA coming-of-age mystery thriller with a touch of sci-fi and romance. A new genre: CYACOAMTWATOSF&R. Think it will catch on? Well . . . something tells me you will never see that genre on Amazon.

In the end, I concluded that genres are just boxes, and *Vox Oculis* doesn't fit in a box, so forget about genres. This is just a great story and I feel privileged to have discovered it and hope that you will be as intrigued and enthralled by it as I was. And continue to be.

-fm

AUGUST, 2031

"As humans, we perceive the world through our wonderful senses of taste, touch, sound, smell, and sight. All these senses combine in our brain to create this rich, beautiful reality that we live in. It is these senses that allow us to not only perceive, but to interact with the world.

As humans, we naturally tend to believe that the world we perceive is the only reality. But consider for a moment a dog's world. Dogs can only discern two basic colors, and yet can see in five times less light than we can. Their ears have a range of hearing that is three times higher than ours, and their noses have a sense of smell that is forty-four times more sensitive than ours.

What is their reality? Imagine if you had the senses that a dog has. Think of how your brain would have to rewire itself to handle these different senses. Can we even imagine it?

I ask this question because I am here today to tell you about some very, very, very rare people that have senses, in particular eyes, that perceive the world much differently than the rest of us. Their eyes can perceive twice the range of color and actually radiate a light we can't even see.

Their eyes have several other amazing features that I'll tell you about later in the talk, but the point I want to make now is this: reality for these rare individuals is so different from ours that it is unimaginable and incomprehensible to most of us. So incredible and incomprehensible, it is magical. But like so many magical things, to some, it is threatening . . ."

— FROM THE INTERNATIONAL SYMPOSIUM ON GENETIC VARIANCE, CASTLETON UNIVERSITY, AUGUST 14TH, 2031

JUNE, 2011

1

ANOTHER YEAR OF SURVIVAL

Blue's eyes were closed. She had closed them so she could open her mind to the familiar sounds that surrounded her now. There was the whine of the car tires on warm asphalt, the muffled hum of the motor that was buried somewhere behind the dashboard in front of her, the occasional rush of a car racing by in the other direction. And over it all was the soothing soft rumble of the rushing wind just above her head, coming from a slot formed by the slightly rolled down window. Blue felt the pressure of the seat gently pushing her about as the car followed the lumps and rolls and curves of the road. She felt the warmth of the sun as it moved to different places on her body mirroring the movements of the car like a solar compass. Shadows of passing trees created a pink-orange pulsing light show on the inside of her closed eyelids. The shadows gave the illusion that instead of being inside a car, she was in the middle of a stampede of giants who were racing the opposite direction and rocking the ground with their massive strides. She felt a kinship to the tree-giants because she wished she was racing the opposite direction, too. She didn't know the destination of the giants but it had to be better than where she was going.

She had made trips like this before. Many times. Each one was supposed to be the last, the one that resulted in a permanent situation. Instead, each one resulted in a return trip. Return to what? Brookhaven Shelter, that dismal holding tank for the unwanted, or a respite house where there was at least someone who was trying to be helpful, or wherever else they had room to keep her until the next family who might take her came around. And then off she went again. She had long ago abandoned hope that the next place would be the one that actually worked, where she could create some sort of normal stable life like the one every single kid around her seemed to have. For Blue, this car and the woman who drove it, Mrs. Jamison, were the only stable parts of her life.

Blue had started to fantasize that instead of stopping, they could just keep going. They could live in this car, driving and driving forever, visiting a hundred new places each year. They would never stay for long—just long enough to experience something new but not long enough for something bad to start happening. Then they would hop in the car and take off for another new place. They would never need to get to know anyone else. Blue would never have to pretend to be someone she was not. She would never again have to stand by her familiar beat-up old duffel bags and watch as Mrs. Jamison drove off, carrying hope and stability with her. Blue sighed. She was going to have to go through the ritual again. There was no driving off into the sunset for her.

She concentrated on the sounds again to stop these uncomfortable thoughts from rattling around in her brain. The rumbling wind was soothing and she eased the window down a tad more to make it louder. The distraction worked for a while, but the thoughts managed to elbow their way back in and circle round and round. It was impossible to stop her brain sometimes, but she managed to at least guide it to thinking about less stressful things, like some of the things Mrs. Jamison had said earlier in the trip. Well, not "said" exactly, more like what she thought. What Mrs. Jamison had said out loud were the details of the new situation, which Blue had listened to politely but wasn't interested in processing just then. She caught the gist of it, there was a lot of blah, blah, blah about the new family, and something about Mrs. O'Day and blah, blah. Blue tucked the words away for a later time when she could control her reaction to them. She didn't want to deal with them just then. Thankfully, Mrs. Jamison didn't rattle on and on. She only gave Blue the essentials and then stopped. It was like she knew how much Blue could handle at a time, and then she knew when to be quiet.

When Mrs. Jamison was quiet, Mrs. Jamison was thoughtful. Blue paid more attention to Mrs. Jamison's thoughts than her words, because they were more than just the monotonous drone of pointless information about Blue's new situation. They were the deep thoughts of the true Mrs. Jamison, and they comforted her.

"I DON'T KNOW HOW THIS GIRL MANAGES TO SURVIVE ALL THESE CHANGES . . . THREE FAMILIES AND A GROUP HOME IN FOUR YEARS," thought Mrs. Jamison. She looked at Blue and Blue gave her a small half-smile. *"AND THE TROUBLE SHE'S SEEN, AND LOOK AT HER. HERE SHE SITS, AS CALM AND PEACEFUL AS A SAINT . . . I HONESTLY DON'T THINK I COULD DO IT . . . SHE MUST HAVE SOME INNER STRENGTH I DON'T HAVE . . . WHY CAN'T THERE BE MORE FAMILIES OUT THERE WILLING TO TAKE THESE OLDER KIDS . . . ALL THEY WANT IS THE YOUNGER ONES . . . I GUESS I CAN'T BLAME THEM . . . IT'S HARD TAKING IN THESE KIDS WHO HAVE SEEN SO MUCH TROUBLE . . . THANK GOODNESS WE GOT THE O'DAYS THIS TIME."*

Blue couldn't hear everyone's thoughts, and some people's thoughts she didn't want to hear, but Mrs. Jamison was a rarity, a truly good soul, so she didn't mind listening in on her thoughts. They had a musical, lyrical quality to them. They were the sounds of a thoughtful person. They were a far cry from the bitter, spiteful thoughts of truly vicious people, people Blue sometimes couldn't ignore, people she sometimes couldn't control her reactions to. Sometimes those people's thoughts just crossed a line, and Blue couldn't let them get away with it. And that is one of the reasons why she was sitting in this car. Again. Another year, another new foster family, a new school, new vicious kids, new idiot teachers, new trips to principal's office, new breakdowns, new violent outbursts, new counselors, new therapists.

Another year to survive.

The car slowed down and Mrs. Jamison pulled to the curb next to an old Victorian-style house. It had gray shingles and white trim, which gave it an ancient, wise look. A small yard was surrounded by a low white fence, and lilacs were tucked about the foundation of the house like a fragrant and colorful scarf around an old lady's neck. From the front door came a solidly built woman whose age was hard to determine but whose face showed a lot of experience. Mrs. O'Day, no doubt. She had a nice smile, Blue thought. It was a comforting smile, even to Blue's hardened eyes. Not overdone, not forced, not artificial. It was very natural. She noted it, but took no encouragement from it. Never get optimistic, it will just make it worse later when you get let down. Again.

She closed her eyes and took one last note of the pressure and warmth of the car seat on her legs and felt the vibration of the car stop as Mrs. Jamison turned it off. Blue sighed, took a breath, opened her eyes, and opened the door. As she got out, she put on her practiced act of being an ordinary girl joining an ordinary family looking forward to an ordinary year. It was like putting on an old well-worn sweater. But underneath the sweater, her heart was empty.

2

WILL

Will was awake and had been for some time, but he kept his eyes closed just for the pleasant sensation: no more school. He didn't have to jump out of bed onto the cold floor and struggle into his clothes while stumbling down the hall. No more squinting into the glare of the brightly-lit bathroom only to have the door slammed in his face by his little sister, Rose, as she slipped in ahead of him.

No, those mornings were gone for a while, replaced by the luxury of sleeping in—letting the sun warm him in bed. He knew it would end all too soon, in a couple of weeks when his summer job started. But now it was nice to just bask in the glory of having gotten through 9th grade and looking forward to being in 10th without having to deal with being at the bottom of the pecking order anymore.

Being a freshman sucked. He had no idea it would be so sucky. The only decent part about it was that he managed to squeak onto the JV basketball team. For once he actually thanked God for living in a small Vermont town with only a Division 2 high school team. There was no way he would have made it on a Division 1 JV team. And now he was a sophomore! That word had such a delicious sound to it, Will thought. It sounded like freedom. It was like getting released from prison.

It was so pleasant just lying there with that thought that he didn't even mind when Rose came in and plunked herself down on his bed with a bowl of cereal in her hand and a significant look on her face. She looked away and munched thoughtfully for a while, glancing at Will from time to time, waiting for him to get annoyed. It wasn't working. There wasn't much that could knock Will out of his good mood. She leaned over toward him, close to his face, and slurped a spoonful of cereal as long and slow and as annoyingly as she could. Then she chewed it open-mouthed, smacking loudly. Will just laughed.

"Wow, are you in a good mood today!" she said, trying to sound disappointed. Will could tell she wasn't really. She could be ridiculously annoying sometimes but today it was just an act. She was glad school was over, too.

Rose leaned back and sat cross-legged, concentrating on her breakfast. "I heard the O'Days took in another kid," she said as she sucked down another spoonful and glanced slyly at him.

That *did* catch him by surprise, but he wasn't about to let on. "Oh my goodness!" he said. "The O'Days took in a foster child! What a shock! What will the neighbors say!"

Rose snorted and laughed.

The O'Days were the neighbors across the street and down the block. They lived in a huge old Victorian house. The whole neighborhood had always treated "Ma Beth" and "Pa Bill" O'Day almost like second parents. A new foster kid at their house was as normal as a March snow storm.

"Have you seen him … her … IT … yet?" asked Will.

Rose snorted again. "No, but I know it's a girl. Fourteen I think." Rose frowned. "Why can't they ever get a girl who's closer to my age?"

"Well, I think it's because they keep most girls your age in a cage at the zoo," said Will, "or they should."

Rose stuck her tongue out. It was all milky and covered with granola crumbs.

"Gross! See what I mean? You animal," Will said. But Rose had succeeded in getting his attention. A girl. Fourteen was only a year or two younger than he was. Probably an eighth grader, he thought. Make that ninth grader now. An incoming freshman. Lucky her.

"I don't suppose you heard what grade she's in?"

"Nope, and we zoo animals would never tell you if we did. We stick together," said Rose. "Sam said her nickname is Little Fox." Sam was the youngest O'Day and the same age as Rose. "Perfect for being in the zoo. I think I'll call myself something zoo-ey—maybe Meerkat!"

"Little Fox? That's not her real name."

"So . . . that's even *more* interesting," said Rose. "Sam said her actual name is Blue. Don't you think that is a cool name? I wonder if it is short for something else, like Blooo . . . oom? Blossom?"

"How about Blueberry? Or Blooper, or Bluto?"

Rose laughed. "That would be really biz-arre." She had recently locked onto the word 'bizarre' and used it every chance she had, as only a nine-year-old sister can, with a long buzzing "bizzzz" and a slow, dangling "aarrr."

"Anyway, that's all Sam knew except that he says she doesn't talk much and just stays in her bedroom a lot."

Not unusual for a new foster kid at the O'Days, thought Will. "I bet I would hunker down in my room for a while if I were a newbie in that house."

"Yeah, or if you did something wrong." She looked at Will with a sly grin.

"And . . . that would be?"

"She had an 'incident' the second day she was in the house."

"An incident? The second day?" said Will. "How long has she been there?" He thought his good friend Wu would have told him about it at school, but come to think of it, Will had been concentrating so much on final exams, he really didn't see Wu much in the past week. Wu was another foster kid at the O'Days. His full name was Ben Wu, but everyone called him "Wu."

"Since last Wednesday, I guess," said Rose.

Right in the middle of exams, thought Will. "Huh," he said. "So what was this 'incident'?"

Rose picked up her empty cereal bowl and started heading out of Will's bedroom. "Uh, I think I hear Mom calling..."

Okay, thought Will, now she is starting to be my familiar annoying sister. "So are you going to tell me?"

Rose turned and said limply, "Tell you what?" And then she started accelerating out the door.

He jumped out of bed and chased her squealing down the hall. He caught up to her, grabbed her around the waist and started tickling her until she finally yelled "Stop ... stop ... stop!" between gasps of laughter.

Rose finally managed to get out the answer. "She ... killed ... the screamer!"

"What?" He stopped tickling her. Rose was still trying to get her breath. "She killed the screamer?"

"Yeah!" said Rose.

The screamer was a relic of technology that survived at the O'Day household because they got by on a lot of second-hand stuff. It was a remote control for their ancient cathode-ray tube television. Will and Rose and their parents had a peculiar reaction to those older remote controls that no one else had. Some caused a slightly annoying ringing in their head, but the O'Day's TV remote created an excruciating, high-pitched screech. It was almost unbearable to Will and Rose, so they had christened it 'the screamer' and had often thought about putting it out of its misery themselves. But it appeared that Blue had beaten them to it.

Will looked at Rose. In his head, he formed words, *"YOU DON'T THINK..."*

Deep in the cortex of Will's brain these words generated an electrical impulse that filtered through an intricate web of neurons that were as rare as they were ancient in humans. All Will felt was a slight tingle at the back of his eyes that was as familiar as breathing to him. What he didn't feel was the invisible stream of photons that resulted from this tingle and went straight into the eyes of his sister.

"*I don't know!*" she replied. Her words formed in his head as if he were thinking them to himself. She continued, "*Sam said she threw it out the door and bolted right up to the third-floor bedroom the rest of the day!*"

"*Wow, she took the third-floor bedroom?*"

The third floor was more of an attic than a regular floor. It was usually the last choice for anyone living in the O'Day's house. With the summer coming on, it was also the hottest, most miserable place in the house. He wondered how long 'Little Fox' would last up there.

Will looked away from Rose, but she continued out loud. "Sam says she chose it! She could have had Nate's room, and Nate would have had to move to the third-floor bedroom, but she wanted it."

A name of 'Blue', a nickname of 'Little Fox', the third-floor bedroom, and the apparent executioner of the screamer. Will didn't know what to think. He knew why he and Rose wanted to destroy the screamer, but he didn't know if that was the same reason Blue actually did it. On the other hand, what else could it possibly be?

"Well, wouldn't be summer if we didn't have a crazy story from the O'Day house."

"I know, right?" said Rose with an impish grin.

"Ugh! Don't say that stupid phrase. You sound like a valley girl," he said, knowing exactly where this was going.

"I know … right?"

"Okay, now you're just trying to be irritating."

"I know … … right?"

"You're asking for it."

"I know … … … RIGHT?"

Will lunged for her but she was ready and had a head start. She ran down the hall, lobbing "I know, RIGHT?" over her shoulder until she ducked into her room and slammed her door behind her with a final squeal.

"You crazy animal!"

From behind the closed door came, "I know, RIGHT?" followed by hysterical laughter.

He stood in the hall. Yeah, right, goofball. You win. He laughed to himself. He liked his sister, she was fun. But his mind was distracted. This incident with the screamer and the new girl—there couldn't be any other reason for it, could there? Then again, a lot of crazy characters had come through the O'Day's house. He was just hoping that this might be the kind of crazy he had been looking for his entire life.

3

THE PARK

It was past noon by the time Will got dressed and ate some breakfast. His mom was already out of the house, his dad was at work, and Rose was next door with a friend. Will decided it was time to ride down to the park and see if Wu was at the basketball court.

Will hopped on his bike. His route took him right past the O'Day's house. Just as he was passing by the gate at the end of the O'Day's side yard, he glanced to his right and up at the third floor of the O'Day's house. He caught a glimpse of a face in the single gable window that was near the peak of the steep roof. It was the face of a girl with long dark hair. She was looking straight out as if seeing something on the horizon. It had to be the new girl.

The third-floor bedroom was a familiar room. When it was vacant, and it often was, he and Wu would go up there. From that gable window, you could look out over the tops of the neighbor's trees all the way across the valley to the countryside on the other side of the river. He couldn't blame her for wanting it. It may have been a small room and hot in the summer, but it had the best views of any house on the street.

Will got to the park and, as he expected, Wu was there. Wu spent a lot of time on the basketball court at the park, by himself or with whoever showed up. He was alone today, just dribbling intricate patterns on the court and working on his shooting.

"Hey, Wu," Will said as he hopped off his bike. "I hear you have a new foster sister."

Wu set himself for a shot and let it fly. The ball soared gracefully and went through the hoop. Nothing but net. "Yeah, first one in a while. First sister that is."

Will joined Wu on the court, grabbed the ball, and passed it back to Wu. "So an older sister, younger sister? Has she got boobs yet?"

Wu chucked the ball at Will. "Watch it there, that's my new sister you're talking about. She's younger and no, not really. At least none to speak of."

Will chased the ball, grabbed it and made a layup. "So must be weird having a girl in the house. What's she like?"

Wu retrieved the ball and dribbled it thoughtfully for a moment or two. "Hard to say. She hasn't said a word to me yet, but I think she's okay." He paused. "She is . . . different." He took another shot. "Kind of serious-looking all the time."

Will retrieved the rebound and tried a layup. "So in other words, pretty much as disturbed as the rest of you."

"Maybe, but I'm sure she's a better shot than you." The ball bounced off the rim. Wu and Will fought for the rebound, and Wu came down with it. "After all, I don't think there is anyone who could be worse."

"Very funny, Mr. Freakishly Tall Asian Orphan Boy."

Wu just smiled and swished another pretty shot from the foul line. Wu had been with the O'Days longer than any of the other kids. He was abandoned as a baby, probably because he had a severe cleft palate, and a state agency picked him up. The O'Days took him in when he was four years old and found funding to fix his cleft palate with plastic surgery. Now Wu was fifteen, six feet tall and still growing. He was also the star on the JV basketball team, and the Varsity coach was eying him hungrily. Wu was far from handsome, but he wasn't ugly either, and he definitely had his head on straight.

"So, what's different about her?" asked Will, ". . . besides the fact that she hasn't said anything to you, which I don't find a bit strange."

"Oh, you are just so hilarious today!" Wu dribbled the ball as he walked toward Will but then he got serious. "Well to start, she has a pretty interesting name: Blue. I've heard of dogs named Blue, but never a person." He stopped dribbling and held the ball. "And clearly she is a hard case, or she wouldn't have been admitted to the hallowed hallways of the O'Day insane asylum. And speaking from experience, I think this is a head-hard case."

"A head-hard case. What a surprise. Are any of you not head-hard cases?"

Wu bonked him in the head with the ball. "Looks like your head's pretty hard, smart ass."

Will laughed as he snatched the ball out of Wu's hand and did a fast break layup. "So what does the head-hard case have against your remote control?" Will looked back to see how Wu would react to the question.

Wu snorted and said, "Yeah, that was really something. I mean, remember Sean, when he first came? First thing he did was punch a hole in the wall and scare the crap out of all of us!"

Sean had been an interesting member of the O'Day household, and pretty harmless, unless you were a wall. He never hit anyone but had a compulsive self-abuse problem.

"Well, this came out of the blue," Wu said smirking and giving Will a sidelong glance. Will grimaced. Yeah I get it, thought Will. Blue came out of the blue. He didn't even have to say it out loud. He just rolled his eyes at Wu.

Wu went on. "I mean the caseworker warned us that she was kind of prone to compulsive behavior, whatever that means, but she didn't say anything about something like this. You know she moved into the third-floor bedroom?"

"Yeah, I heard through Rose through Sam."

"Well, she's just been staying there almost all the time so far. And we've been leaving her alone. Ma Beth figures she'll come out when she's ready. Somehow she slips out of her room when no one is looking and sneaks down to the bathroom or down to the kitchen to, you know, eat and wash and go to the bathroom. She doesn't eat with us at the table, she just sneaks down sometime at night and grabs food from the refrigerator and sneaks back to her room."

"That's wild. Kinda cool, actually. Of course, I can't blame her for not wanting to eat with you animals."

"Yuck yuck Mr. Comedian. So anyway, last night I was in the rec room, you know next to the kitchen. I made a snack and was watching TV. Nothing much was on, and I was kind of mindlessly running through the channels using the remote control. Then the next thing I knew, she was standing right in front of me with the remote in her hand. I had no idea she was around and then *boom*—there she was. I didn't even feel her grab the remote out of my hand! It was like she materialized out of nowhere. Well, she looked at me. I tell you, she had a weird look on her face. It wasn't wild, or angry, or sad, it was just kind of..." Wu had to think for a moment, "... well it was like 'here we go all over again.' Then she threw the remote out the back door smack against the patio wall and ran up to her room. Man, she is quick and very quiet." He had a touch of admiration in his voice and he cracked a little smile.

Will ruminated on this. She was quick. Quick as a little fox. "That's pretty wild. But not the wildest story to come out of your house," he said.

"True," said Wu. "Never a dull moment with the O'Days, right?"

Will said, "You got that right." He grabbed the ball from Wu and took off down the court. The conversation was over for now. They got down to the business at hand which was playing basketball. They played "horse" a few times and Will managed to actually get up to "h-o-r" once but only because Wu was going easy on him. Some other kids showed up and they pretty much used up the rest of the afternoon playing basketball.

As it got close to dinnertime they both headed back home. Will walked his bike back with Wu, and Wu told Will more about Blue's background. Turns out her real first name really was just Blue, not short for anything else, and she came from a long string of foster homes.

"Apparently nothing has worked out yet," Wu said. "No details, just nothing worked out. She doesn't have any family, so if she doesn't settle in somewhere she'll just wind up aging out."

Will knew that most orphans who go through foster homes wind up either back with family members or getting adopted. Unfortunately, a lot of them never find a permanent home, and they wind up "aging out"; they turn eighteen and leave the foster system and out on their own without ever having had anything they could call a family. Will knew all this because of all the O'Days he had known. He spent many hours in their kitchen, and Mrs. O'Day would tell him all about the foster system and how it works.

"So how did she become an orphan?" asked Will.

"Her family died in a house fire when she was ten. She was the only survivor," said Wu. He looked at Will. "Can you imagine that? Losing your whole family when you're ten? Man, that sucks."

"Yeah, but you lost your family when you were a baby."

"But I didn't even know them. I can't even tell you what they looked like." Wu paused and then continued. "They said she had a lot of trouble at first. I mean, who wouldn't after that! They didn't give a lot of details, but I guess it was a long time before they even tried her out in a foster home. It must have been a disaster if we're the fourth home she's been in. They told us that she was very reclusive and hard to communicate with, and moody. I don't know. She seems pretty okay to me. I think she just likes being left alone."

They both walked thoughtfully the rest of the way to the O'Day house. Will broke the silence as they arrived. "Well, good luck with her. You better lock up the rest of your remotes, though, if you want them to survive."

Wu gave him a shove and said, "Hey, don't diss my sister." He wasn't smiling. That's the way Wu was. Blue wasn't even there for two days, hadn't said a word to Wu, and he was already protecting her.

"Hey, sorry, man. I think it's great you got a sister. She sounds a lot less boring than you other zombies." He held up his fist.

Wu's severe look faded. He wasn't exactly smiling, but he gave Will a fist bump and said, "Tell me about it, stiff."

Will watched as Wu went in the house, but didn't move to get on his bike and head home. Instead, he looked up to see if Blue was still there in the window. For some reason, maybe because of what Wu had told him, he wasn't surprised to see her in almost the same spot as she had been earlier. Her face was a little pinker now because of the light of the early evening. The darkness of the room behind her, combined with her dark hair, made her face almost luminescent, but her expression was just as wan and distant as it was before.

Will looked back down and started to get on his bike, and then stopped. From what Wu had said, it wasn't likely. Blue was probably more of a troubled kid with a compulsion to destroy things. That was more the mold of the O'Day orphans. But, still, he had to try it. He looked up at the window again. She was still staring, clearly lost in thought. Was it too far to try? It was still pretty light out. He knew *he* could pick it up from that far, even during the day, but he was not sure how sensitive she was, if she was at all. What the heck, it wasn't like anyone else would hear it, at least no one he'd met in his lifetime, outside his family.

He gave it a try. He started with a "*CLICK, CLICK, CLICK,*"—something he used to get his sister's or parent's attention. Everyone in his family had a different way of getting each other's attention. His father's sounded like he was clearing his throat. Will liked to click. The click was easy to project and would bounce off of reflective objects better than other sounds.

She didn't respond. He felt the familiar disappointment rising in his gut. Still, he kept his eyes on her and clicked a few more times, and then he saw her move. Her head turned to one side, and then the other. She looked puzzled and then startled. Then she looked down straight at him. As soon as her eyes were on his, in his head he said, *"HEY,"* like when you met a friend on the street. She instantly froze and her mouth went slightly open and then, as if she realized she had let some surprise show, she snapped it shut again. Then, with just a moment's hesitation, she slapped the curtains closed and disappeared.

Will stood there, just a little bit dazed. He was not sure that that had really happened. He had been hopeful, because of the story about the screamer, but he honest-to-god had not expected a reaction. He had been disappointed so many other times in his life that he had pretty much given up hope of finding anyone outside his family that could communicate the same way they could. He had tried a thousand times with a thousand different people. The result was always the same. A thousand failures.

Oh, he had gotten reactions that he *thought* could have been real, but they always turned out to be just false reads. Mirages. Wishful thinking. Was this a mirage? Was he just imagining it because he wanted it to be true? She had reacted to his *"HEY,"* hadn't she? Or had she? It could have been coincidence. Maybe she was reacting to something else and happened to look down and then, when she saw him, was surprised. What girl wouldn't react like that if a boy was staring at her?

No way. No one had ever reacted like this before.

He looked back up. Curtains still closed. Damn it! He waited, but just for a moment. He wanted to try again, see if he could find out for sure, but he didn't want the O'Days to spot him and wonder why he was still hanging around. "Oh just standing here staring at Blue." Right, you weirdo. He took one last glance. Closed curtains. Damn.

He started walking his bike home, thinking. It had to be true. It needs to be true. For once in his life, it needed to be true. He pounded his handlebars with his fists. He needed to do something else to find out for sure. This was going to drive him nuts until he knew the answer. He stopped. Just go back to the O'Days, he thought. Go up to the third-floor bedroom, hammer on the door until she opens up and confront her face-to-face. Why not? Screw the consequences. Just do it, he thought. For once in your life do something off the straight and narrow. Why the hell not? He turned his bike and took a step and then his irritating brain monitor woke up. *"Whoa, there, don't you think that would be a bad start, Will?"* Who cares! *"What about Wu and his family, wouldn't they find that rude?"* Oh shut up, dammit, you sound like my mother! *"Now now, watch your language!"* Oh God. He was his mother. Damn.

Problem was, his annoying brain monitor was probably right. If Blue was what he was hoping she was, he should be careful about it. No one knew about their family trait and they were careful about that secret. She was probably keeping it secret, too. It's not exactly something you would advertise if you were alone and on your own.

He would think about it overnight. Come up with some approach. He just wasn't sure what it would be. Just as he came to this conclusion, he realized he was standing in front of his house. He must have just kept walking while he was thinking. At that exact moment, his mom stuck her head out the front door and said, "Hey there Mr. Heavy Thinker, why don't you put away that bike and wash up for dinner?"

A lone figure stood under the trees watching the two boys as they left the basketball court. A hand raised a cigarette to lips buried in a tawny, well-trimmed beard. A tiny red ember glowed as the man took a long pull. After a pause, a plume of gauzy white smoke streamed out, piling into a confused cloud that rose in a lazy swirl that partially obscured the pensive face behind it.

The man followed the boys with his eyes as they walked away. The tall lanky one had a ball under his arm, and the shaggy, scrappy one pushed a bike. Nice bike, the man thought. He took another pull on his cigarette and gazed at the deserted court. It was lumpy with age and had cracks and low patches where accumulated dirt created treacherous footing. Stubborn bits of grass poked out here and there, but the kids had made the most of it. They had danced lightly over the slippery dirt patches and instinctively adjusted for the odd angle of the ball whenever it bounced off a jagged crack. They actually weren't half bad—might even hold their own in the upper east side, he thought. He was glad they'd left, though. It was getting towards business time and the fewer non-customers around, the better, and these boys weren't customers. At least not yet. You never knew in these little rural towns.

He took a last pull from the cigarette before dropping it to the ground and grinding it into the dirt. He exhaled a last swirl of smoke and watched as it danced with the breeze before finally dissipating into the cobalt blue sky. He was getting to like it here. Business was good, law enforcement was lax, and there was no competition. And now he had a new kid to help him—meaning a lot more money for him for not a lot of work—as long as this kid panned out. They didn't always, but it seemed like this one would. Had the right hard-luck background and fly-under-the-radar attitude, plus a strong motivation to make a quick buck and stay out of jail. All good qualities. But most importantly, this kid would keep his mouth shut. He had made him keenly aware of what would happen if he didn't.

But right now, it was a beautiful sunny late afternoon, the park was quiet, and the sight of his first customer walking into view made it perfect. It was a reliable customer that didn't freak out and make a scene. Just a quick swap and everyone was happy.

Yeah, he liked this town. Maybe he would stay longer than he had originally planned.

4

BLUE

Blue sat on her bed and gazed out the open gable window. Puffs of early summer air carried in the rich aroma of rapidly unfolding foliage as it made its urgent push to take advantage of the short summer season. She could see high out over the last few streets on the edge of town and across the river where soft green hills were decorated with the little red square of a barn here, the bright shingles of a house there, all nestled in a patchwork of freshly mowed fields chiseled into the shaggy carpet of maples and pines. She put her elbows on the window sill, rested her chin in her hands, and took in the panorama for a long time. It was spectacular, really. She had never had a view like this, or a room like this, or even a room all to herself for that matter.

As she let her eyes wander across the landscape, she made a mental list of all the other benefits of her room. Strategically speaking, the location couldn't have been better. It was at the top of the house on the third floor. Outside her door was a tiny landing at the top of a narrow stair. Across from her room was the door to the storage attic, the only other room on the third floor. The stairs to her landing were completely creak-free except for one step at the bottom, and as long as she stepped on the part right next to the wall, she could slip down the stairs in complete silence. There was a half-bath under her stairway and she could actually hop over the tiny banister and get to the bathroom without setting foot in the hallway. The second-floor hallway led to two stairways, the main stair that went from a balcony down to the living room and a steep back stairway that led down to the rec room off the kitchen. There was a patio door off the rec room that led out to the back porch and back yard.

The boys, because right now all the other O'Day foster kids were boys, all used the big bathroom at the end of the second-floor hall. There were three bedrooms on the second floor. There was the main bedroom for Ma Beth and Pa Bill at the other end of the hallway. They had their own master bathroom. The three boys split the remaining two bedrooms. Wu and Sam shared the big room, and Nate, the oldest, had his own room at the end of the hall across from the big bathroom.

Not a bad setup. Except for the open landing onto the living room, she could pretty much slip anywhere in the house with a minimum of contact—like a little fox, moving undetected through the woods.

Little Fox. She smiled at that. It was Julian Hilbert, the ass from foster family number two who came up with that name. Julian Jackass Hilbert. Jerk. He was an expert at hitting you just hard enough that it hurt like hell but didn't leave a bruise. He never missed a chance to practice on her when no one else was looking— that is until she'd decided she'd had enough. That was the time he cornered her as she was leaving for school, grabbed her arm, and tried to jab her shoulder but wound up punching the wall instead, because with a quick twist she had managed to get out of his grasp and duck under his arm. He yelped with pain and then threw out his leg to try and trip her, but she stepped nimbly over it, shoved him into the wall, and dashed out the door. It all happened in an instant, and Julian was left cursing and shouting after her, "I'll get you back, you little fox!" Get her back for what? For him being an idiot? What an ass. He never did get her back, she made sure of it. But she did like the name.

A loud squawk and flapping shadow startled her back to reality as a huge black bird flew out of a nearby tree. She watched as he pumped his powerful wings and sailed off on some suddenly urgent bird errand. Her eyes followed his flight, and she tried to picture what he was seeing. She imagined looking down and watching as the ant-like humans scurried around in their little cars and ran in and out of little boxes in their busy little pointless errands. It must have been puzzling to a bird, but she imagined he didn't care. He was flying above it all, nothing but a casual observer. She envied him. If she could fly, she could float high over all those ants and never have to interact with them or listen to their constant *chiss*—the constant whisper of their private thoughts, leaking out of their eyes and into her brain. But here she was, stuck on the ground, forced to figure out how to fit into this ant farm and live a normal ant life.

She sighed. What was a normal life, anyway? Normal for her was avoiding all but the most necessary contact—just enough that she came off as a quirky introvert but not so much that they would call in the shrinks. But what else could she do? She never knew when some ridiculous unfiltered *chiss* would catch her off-guard, like a rabbit-punch, and set her off. She would overreact, they would yell at her, she would go even more ballistic, then out would come the benzo, and . . . . . . yeah.

Being alone was so much easier for everyone.

At least the O'Days seemed to be rolling with it. All the other foster families, wanted to try and "connect" with her and "draw her out." All she wanted was for them to fucking leave her alone! For the past two days, that was what she had been waiting for, the attempts to draw her out. But they just left her alone—not ignoring her, but certainly giving her a lot of space. It was a relief, really. She wasn't sure how long it would last, but so far, it had been way better than she expected. Amazingly, even what happened last night didn't appear to derail anything. At least, not yet.

It wasn't *chiss* that set her off last night. It was a *klax*. The night had started out fine—meal time came around, and one of the boys called up to tell her dinner was ready. She replied that she wasn't very hungry and could she please skip the meal. So far, the answer was always yes. She would just slip downstairs later and grab some leftovers, taking them up to her room to eat by herself. After the third 'skipped' meal, it was clear they picked up on what she was doing, but they just acted as if it was the most normal thing in the world. Pretty soon, leftovers were showing up in the kitchen in fairly convenient locations for post-meal vulturing. Blue was a little wary of it, wondering if there wasn't some sort of catch, but so far so good, and she sure wasn't going to squander the opportunity while the going was good.

Last night she did the usual skip request and then she slipped downstairs later and discovered a half casserole of lasagna on the stove, still warm. God, she loved lasagna. She scooped up a big slice and put it on the plate she'd brought with her. She was just about to slip through the rec room and up the back stairs when she heard loud footsteps clattering down. She stood behind the wall separating the rec room and the kitchen and waited. It was Wu. He came clumping into the kitchen and headed straight to the lasagna, clearly hunting for leftovers just like Blue. She stayed hidden, waiting for a chance to skip across the rec room and get upstairs unseen. She didn't get the chance because he brought his plate of food straight into the rec room, flopped onto the couch, and grabbed the TV remote.

He must have been oblivious to her standing there as he passed. He was faced away from her now, towards the table and TV, and the back stairs. She started to inch her way to an alternate escape when a piercing screech started pounding her brain like a fire alarm: "*EEEE . . . EEEEE . . . EEEE!*" She nearly jumped out of her skin and before she could completely recover, it came again. *"EEEE . . . EEEEE . . . EEEE!"*

She looked at Wu's hand. Every time he hit a button on the remote, the screeching came again. She should have just gotten out of there, but there was something so irritating about that remote that she couldn't let it go. It was a *klax*. Stuff that no one else could hear but created an obnoxious explosion of sound inside her head. She'd never encountered a *klax* that was so frigging loud! And obnoxious! The next thing she knew she was standing in front of Wu with the remote in her hand. Her head was still ringing as she stood there for a moment in the welcome release from the excruciating sound. She looked up at Wu for a second and then without even thinking ran to the door and chucked the remote out of the house. It smashed into a wall and transformed instantly into a most satisfying and clearly irreversible pile of shattered plastic. Blue stood in the door and looked at the wreckage. She experienced a brief euphoria until it dawned on her what she had done.

Damn. There it was, one of those overreactions. Her reflex action to stuff only she could hear in this private little hell she lived in. She took another look at Wu, who was standing there looking completely puzzled, and then she turned, grabbed her lasagna, and dashed back up to her room. Her sanctuary.

Blue had stayed there and waited. Soon she got the expected knock at her door, but instead of an angry demand for her to come out and explain what she had just done, a soft voice merely said, "Blue, are you okay? Do you need anything?" She hesitated a moment. This was so unexpected, she wasn't quite sure how to react. She decided to pretend it was the door talking and not Ma Beth. That made it easier. Addressing the door she said simply, "I'm fine."

The reply from the door was: "It's good to hear that. We're here if you need anything. If you don't want to talk, you can just leave a note downstairs on the counter." And like magic, a pad of paper and a pencil appeared under the door. Blue already had plenty of writing supplies, but she thought the pad and pencil were a very professional touch on the part of the door. She decided that this was a door she could reason with. The door said one last thing. "Blue, it's nice to hear your voice." Very unexpected. Nice, but unexpected.

A distant squawk from the black bird brought her out of her reverie. The sun was getting lower in the sky. She realized she had lost all track of time just sitting there, looking out the window, engrossed in her thoughts. A movement down below caught her attention. It was Wu walking up the street.

She had gotten a good look at Wu when they had their encounter last evening. She had felt his shock and surprise, but he didn't seem angry, just puzzled. You could read a lot about people when they are shocked. It's like their mask comes off for just a moment. Wu, unmasked, was not scary, he seemed like . . . well . . . like he was going to be a real good father when he was older. Blue kind of shocked herself with this judgment. It didn't seem like her to think something like that, but the idea did seem to suit Wu perfectly.

She saw that Wu was walking with another kid, a boy. Compared to Wu's tall, lanky frame, this kid looked solid, like he wouldn't blow away in a strong wind. It was something more than solid, too. Something more . . . athletic. His head was covered in thick, wavy hair and he was wearing a tie-dye shirt. The corner of her mouth twitched up a little. Not what you'd call trendy style with in-crowd these days.

Watching them walking along like that, free to roam on their own, go where they wanted—it suddenly put a damper on her mood, an unwanted reminder that she'd been confined to the house and the yard for her first week—payback for her history of unauthorized meanderings at previous homes, she was sure.

Wu and his friend stopped at the gate and were talking. Wu seemed a little miffed—about what? She was too far away to catch his *chiss*. Wu came into the house, and the boy turned and started to leave. She glanced away. She didn't want him to look up and see her staring at him, but she didn't leave the window.

What happened next knocked Blue completely out of orbit.

It started with a noise inside her head. It was a "CLICK, CLICK, CLICK" sound. It seemed to come from several places at once, a lot like how she heard *chiss* or *klax*, but she had never heard anything quite like this before. She looked around to see if she could focus on where it was coming from. Her eyes finally settled on Wu's friend. He was looking straight at her. The clicking stopped. And then, a voice that wasn't hers sounded a single word in her head . . . "HEY."

Blue gasped. She gaped at the boy for a moment and then jerked back from the window and slapped the curtains closed. This was not just someone's aimless *chiss* drifting like background noise into her brain! This was someone who just said "HEY" to her. On purpose. Deliberately. Right in her head! This was a *vox!* She didn't think she would hear anything like that again in her life! Could it be that there was still someone else like her out there? She peeked out of the curtains and looked for the boy. He was gone.

Had that really happened? Was she just dreaming? Dammit, this had better not be a hallucination. She had just started to get her life under control. She had stopped looking for people like her. It was when she stopped pleading to people with her vox, and looking for responses that were never coming, that people had stopped treating her like she was crazy. She didn't want that to start again. If she freaked anyone out it would be back to therapy, back to psychiatrists. She was done with that. But what if it was real? It was the most real thing that had happened to her in four and a half years!

Crap, she wasn't sure what to do. She had an unbearable urge to dash down the stairs and chase after this kid and stare him in the eyes and find out for real. But if she was wrong and she freaked him out, that, on top of staying holed up in her room, not eating with the family, destroying stuff, could turn this promising start at the

O'Days into something all too familiar. Another round through the foster grinder.

Shit.

Shit, shit, shit. She instinctively grabbed a pencil and pad of paper and did what she often did at times like this. She started drawing. Drawing was about the only positive thing that came from all her otherwise useless therapy sessions. The sound of a pencil lead scritching across the smooth texture of paper quieted the clamor of confusion bouncing around her brain. She made her eyes focus on the line trailing out from the pencil tip as her hand made delicate adjustments of pressure to guide the line in just the right arc until it was time to lift the point and start the next arc. Again and again went the scritch, scritch, scritch of the pencil until forms started revealing themselves. They were animals, like Fiver from *Watership Down* and Martin, from *Redwall*—creatures that lived in a different world, one that was not confusing, one that she could control.

She drew and drew and drew until she started having a hard time following the pencil. She looked up. The sun was down. Next to her in the darkness were a dozen scattered pages filled with drawings and a small pile of dull pencils. She put down her pad, closed her eyes, and just sat, relaxed, in the darkness. Her brain had found the quiet time it needed to chill out and reset, and now it was time to fire it back up. She took in a deep breath and let it out slowly. Before the last bit of breath was out, she knew what she needed to do. She had to find out who this boy was. Clearly, he was Wu's friend. She felt she could trust Wu.

She grabbed a piece of paper and wrote a note, folded it, listened carefully at her door, slipped downstairs and taped the note to Wu's door.

5

———

CONTACT

Will couldn't sleep. Did she really hear his vox or was it coincidence? Vox or coincidence? Vox or coincidence? God, he couldn't stop his head from see-sawing back and forth. He drifted off into a weird half-asleep dream. In the dream, he discovered that she was some long-lost sister and that she had inherited millions of dollars and she was going to share it with her rediscovered brother and sister. That somehow morphed into an angry pack of O'Days all wearing animal skins and chasing him through a field of boulders calling him a perv and throwing stones at him. His legs flailed away trying to run but his feet couldn't seem to get any traction. And he was naked.

He woke up in a sweat, completely entangled in a pile of twisted bedding. He looked at the clock. It was only one o'clock. Jesus! Was this night ever going to get through? He just wanted it to be over so he could get up and go talk to Wu and figure out some way of meeting this girl face-to-face. That made it even harder to get to sleep. By about 2 a.m. he was despairing that this night would ever end, and then the next thing he knew someone was banging on his bedroom door. Will looked at the clock. 9 a.m.! The banging on the door started again. "Who is it?" he said.

Wu didn't answer, he just opened the door and bounced in. "Man, you lazy bum!" said Wu. "Some people live in luxury, being able to sleep in all the time. Do you know what time it is?"

"Yeah, yeah, yeah," said Will. "I just couldn't get to sleep last night."

"Well maybe you shouldn't be up partying all night," said Wu. "But hey, it seems my new little sister is suddenly interested in you. She taped this to my door last night." He handed Will a folded piece of paper. On the outside, it said "Wu." Inside it said simply—

Who is your friend

"I assumed she meant you, but maybe she meant it as an existential question?"

Will rolled back on his bed and tried to act surprised. "Huh, she must have seen us when we got back from the park." Will knew very well that "who" was him, but he didn't tell Wu as much. "Well, it looks like she at least knows English and can write."

Wu sat on the floor and said "Yeah, and that's not all. She also left a note for Ma Beth in the kitchen. She said she was sorry for breaking the remote and wanted to know what she could do to make up for it."

"And she seems to have a sense of right and wrong," said Will.

"Yeah," said Wu. "And at least she is communicating now. She still waited until after breakfast to sneak down for leftovers, though," "*And she did clean up after herself which is more than can be said of me.*"

Will picked up on Wu's *chiss*. Wu was a "leaker." That's what his family called normal people whose *chiss* was easy to pick up. Of course, most normal people leaked *chiss*, but some people's *chiss* was so quiet you couldn't make out the words. It was more like a murmur. Others were like loud whispers that you could pick up clearly if there wasn't a lot of other noise around. Wu's were easy to pick up. Sometimes too easy.

"So did you reply to her?" Will asked.

"I put a note under her door. That seems to be how she likes to communicate. I just wrote one word—'Will.' I figured she likes short and sweet, and that is about as short as it gets." Then Wu snorted. "Who. Will. Who, will, what, when, where? Maybe that will be her answer 'what?'" He started chuckling.

"So this is how she communicates with everyone? Even Ma Beth?" Will asked, ignoring Wu's chuckling. "Why doesn't she text or email?"

"She doesn't have a computer yet, and you know we don't have phones except the two prepaid phones we share. Pa Bill lives in the Stone Age. God, it's 2011, you'd think we'd at least get to have our own phones. We're lucky we even have laptops, and the state helps pay for those. So just notes for now, except Ma Beth actually talked to her through the door after smashing the remote."

"Well that's a start, I guess," said Will.

So now at least she knew his name. He wasn't quite sure what should come next. Since she showed some curiosity about him, maybe he would just wait and see what she did next.

He didn't have to wait long. That very afternoon when Wu stopped by to meet Will for a game of basketball down at the park, he handed Will an envelope. On the outside was written,

Wu, give this to Will

"I'm impressed," said Wu. "She is here only four days, sees you from her window only once or twice and *boom!* you are part of her inner circle. She needs to work on her etiquette, though. I almost gave it back to her, asking for the 'magic word', but Ma Beth said to go easy on her these early days. So here you go. In a sealed envelope no less."

Will opened the note. There was one word,

Hey

The word flashed through him like a wave of hot flame. He couldn't believe it. All the doubts evaporated with just that one word. She was *real*. Will suddenly felt very light and alive. He wanted to shout and pump his fists but Wu was standing right there. Wu knew nothing about his family's particular talent, no one did, but Wu was his best friend, and he couldn't just blow him off.

"It just says 'hey'," said Will and he showed Wu the note. He barely kept a quiver out of his voice. He did his best to sound honestly puzzled, "What do you suppose that means?"

Wu shrugged. "I don't know. Weird. Just 'hey', huh?" He looked thoughtful for a moment and then said with conviction, "Head-hard case. She's one of the family."

Will did his best to hide his sigh of relief. Wu had just taken it in stride. It struck Will how brilliant the note was. Blue must have known that Wu might see it, but it gave nothing away, and yet it told Will everything.

Will knew he should say something. "How about I just write her a note and say 'hey' back, and see where it goes? It seems that she wants to communicate with notes. The only question is—can she put more than two words in one note?"

"Hah hah. The question is, can you? It's a wonder you even made it to high school. Maybe you could write 'hey hey.'"

"Very funny." Will gave Wu a shove.

What Will actually wrote that evening was this:

> Hey.
> If you need to talk to someone who
> knows what it is like to hear things
> other people don't, just ask.
> No one else knows including
> Wu. By the way, Wu is
> a great guy, you can trust him.

He would give it to Wu in the morning to slip under Blue's door. In a sealed envelope.

6

IS IT POSSIBLE?

Blue read Will's note and sat down on the bed carefully. She was not sure what pot of emotions had just been stirred up, but she had difficulty keeping a cap on the pressure that she felt pushing up from her chest. It was that feeling of hope and optimism that had been beaten into submission so many times in the past. This was someone who *knew!* She couldn't believe that there was actually someone else out there who knew! Knew what it was like to be disbelieved, knew what it was like to hear things no one else heard, to be enveloped with *chiss* all the time, to hear other people's thoughts and emotions and not able to express her own!

She wasn't sure what to do next. Part of her was waiting for the inevitable drop of the 'other shoe', the fly in the ointment, the 'catch.' It always happened. Something good would come to her, and then it would get taken away, or broken, or followed immediately by something bad. It was like a rule, and if she broke the rule, like relaxing and enjoying the moment and being happy, then the disappointment that followed would be doubly painful.

She didn't want to break the rule. This was way too good to spoil. She decided to pre-empt the rule. She was going to be careful. What was the flaw, what was she missing? Maybe this kid would turn out to be a jerk. Like Julian. That would figure, just when she finds the first person of her own kind, a boy no less, he turns out to be an ass. But he was friends with Wu, and Wu was a good person. She had already determined that. The flaw had to be something else. Well, she would just have to wait and see what that was, but she was not going to let it catch her off guard. Oh no, those days were behind her.

Next day, Will slept in again—this time, it was for real sleep. As he sat there awake with the warming summer breeze coming in his window, he thought about what was going to happen next. He had no idea what to expect. This girl could be a psycho. After all, she's gone through four foster families, went berserk on a remote control, and holes up in her room all the time. Yet with just the contents of those few notes, he could tell there was a sharp intelligence there. She was clever. She communicated a lot with just the few words she had produced. But there wasn't much more he could do, with her secure in her little tower up there on the third floor—Rapunzel unwilling to let down her hair. Just notes.

Someone knocked softly on his door.

"I think 10 a.m. is a safe time to knock on your door," came his mother's voice. "Are you awake?"

"Yeah, I'm awake," said Will trying to sound like he had just woken up.

"Can I come in?" asked his mother.

"Sure," Will replied.

She walked over to his bed and said, "I can see you are taking full advantage of your week off!" "*Good for you!*" She handed him an envelope. "Wu dropped this off, said it was from the new girl over there. Blue is her name?"

"Yeah," said Will.

His mother looked thoughtful for a second and then asked, "So what is with the notes?"

Will decided to confide in her a little bit. "Wu says she just holes up in her room and will only communicate in notes. She doesn't even come down for meals"

"Goodness," said his mom. "How does she eat?"

Such a 'Mom' thing to say, thought Will.

"She sneaks down and grabs leftovers from the fridge. Wu says she always manages to do it when nobody notices. They say her nickname is 'Little Fox'. Wu actually kind of thinks it's cool how she manages it."

"Well," said his mom, "I just hope she is getting enough to eat."

She handed him the envelope, and written on the outside it said,

Wu, please give this to Will

Will noted the "please" this time. His mom hung around hopefully. Will looked up and gave her a "*FAT CHANCE*" and his mom responded, "*WORTH A TRY* . . ." over her shoulder as she left, closing the door behind her.

He opened the envelope envisioning Blue's room stacked to the ceiling with blank notes and envelopes. He read:

What is your M.O. ?

What is that supposed to mean? 'What's your M.O.?' There went his pleasant, late sleep-in mood. Why can't she be a little more explicit? He knew it meant *modus operandi*. Blue was asking him what he was up to. What was he up to? He was just trying to be friendly, especially to someone he now knew was, well, one of his 'kind.' He also wanted to let her know that she wasn't the only one that was holed up all the time, that he had been craving someone outside his family that he could fully relate to.

But at least he *had* a family. Jesus. He couldn't imagine what it would have been like to lose your family and be this way with absolutely no one knowing what was going on. He tried to think about what it was like when he was ten years old. All he could remember is that he relied completely on his parents for everything. How would he have handled losing his parents at ten years old? He didn't have a clue.

This was getting frustrating. He wanted to talk to her. He meant real talk—with words and thoughts, not just notes. He wrote a note, got up, got dressed and headed to the O'Days. This note he was going to deliver himself.

———

"Hello Mr. Will Woods," said Mrs. O'Day. "I suppose you'd be looking for Wu?"

"Hi Mrs. O'Day," said Will. "Yes, is Wu around?" Will had come to the O'Day's back screen door which opened straight into the kitchen.

"Well, he went down to the park just after breakfast, as usual. I am sure he would like some company," said Mrs. O'Day. "Have you had breakfast yet? Would you like to come in for a bite before you go down?"

"No thanks, Mrs. O'Day. I just ate. I came over to give this note to Blue. She asked me a question with a note Wu brought over, and I wrote her an answer. Seems like that's how she likes to communicate." He didn't know why, but he felt a little shy and nervous about talking to Mrs. O'Day about Blue.

"Well, you go right on up. She's on the third floor. Don't bother knocking. Just slip the note under the door. She likes to be by herself, but I think she'll come out of her shell by and by."

Will hesitated but then went through the kitchen to the rec

room and up the back stairway. It was odd that he felt out of place delivering this note in a house that was so familiar to him. He always felt like it was a second home, but now it seemed like a stranger's house. He saw Nate coming down the stairs and said, "Hey, Nate," as usual and Nate replied, "Hey, Will," as usual, but Will still felt awkward.

He climbed up the attic stairs and stood in front of the familiar door. What was once a vacant hideout for he and Wu now belonged to Blue. He raised his hand to knock, but hesitated. Should he talk to her now? Or just let her read the note and wait until she responded? His earlier resolve to talk to her had evaporated. He was actually nervous. Why? She was just a girl. Not even fifteen. There was no reason he should be nervous, but he was. He quickly slipped the note under the door. He would just wait for her to send a reply note through Wu. As he turned to head back down the stairs, he heard a movement behind the door. He stopped. Even though he really didn't want to be there now, he waited. There was a sound of paper being picked up, then unfolded, and then a pause.

The door opened and there was Blue. It was the same girl he had seen in the window, but now it was associated with the rest of her. The girl that stood in front of him now had a face with a small nose, dark eyebrows, well-defined jawline, prominent cheekbones, and long dark hair. She was smaller than he expected. And younger looking. The expression on her face was hard to read. She looked him in the eye for a moment and then a single word formed in his head. The tone of it was fresh—light and melodic, almost foreign. The word was: "*OKAY.*" Blue stood still for just an instant, and then she shut the door.

Will stood there for a moment. The eyes were eyes he knew. There was absolutely no doubt now. She had actually voxed him. Vox oculis. Eyes speaking to eyes. This was the first real vox from someone who was not his family that he had ever heard.

What the next step was, he wasn't sure. Should he knock on her door and see if she wanted to, what . . . talk? Vox? Play basketball?

Hug? Cry? He wanted to knock but wasn't sure what to say. Maybe this was enough. His legs seemed to agree. Without him even thinking about it, they carried him down the stairs and out the front door and they didn't stop until they got all the way to the park.

Blue had heard Will come to the kitchen door downstairs and talk to Mrs. O'Day. She could hear most everything that went on in the house. It seemed alive with the movements and activity, and the more she got to know its workings, the easier she could get around and avoid who she wanted to avoid.

She heard footsteps on the stairs, and a, "Hey, Nate," and, "Hey, Will." She heard the fourteen footsteps up her stair and waited for the note. It appeared below her door. She silently picked it up, opened it, and read:

Just want to be friends

She debated a moment and then made up her mind. She went to the door, opened it, and looked right into Will's eyes. Using her eyes, her *vox*, she said, "Okay," and shut the door, but before she did she couldn't help noticing the brightness of his eyes. It has been four and a half years since she had last seen eyes like that. She hesitated—she really wanted to open the door and call after him to . . . to what? Talk to him? Stare at his eyes? Hug him as a long lost brother?

She didn't know what to do. She felt lost, confused. All her emotions started clamoring for her attention. She had to get this under control, but this was so new, she didn't know the right thing to do. She read the note again and leaned back against the door and let herself slide to the floor. A rush of heat started enveloping her like a warm wave. She instinctively started to suppress it. She knew she had to jump on these emotional waves early or they would get out of control. Out of control emotions led to bad things. But this was different. It wasn't panic. It wasn't fear. It wasn't sadness. It was like a warm hug. It was comfortable. It was making her feel . . . hopeful. She decided to let it ride. She sat there for a long time, and the warm feeling sat there with her and kept her company.

7

BLUE FITS IN

Ma Beth walked into the kitchen to start dinner. She loved this part of the day. The rhythm of cooking was something she looked forward to—the challenge of the timing, the lining up of the spices, the coordination of the pots and pans, the precise chopping motions, the gradual, yet inevitable transformation of raw ingredients from individual flavors to a symphony of taste in a grand presentation to the family.

Tonight was chicken casserole and she made two huge pans of it so there was a chance of having leftovers for lunch the next day. She made a big salad and baited it with croutons and bits of real bacon she had saved from breakfast. The boys wouldn't touch a green otherwise, but these magic ingredients seemed to transform the salad into something acceptable to them. Anything to attract them to some vegetables was good enough for her.

Dinnertime was always early, just after Pa Bill got home and changed out of his post office uniform. That made for plenty of time after dinner for family time in the big room off the kitchen. Ma Beth never had to worry about setting the table or clean-up. The kids did it without asking. She didn't know how that had come about—just one day she noticed that she didn't have to ask anyone to do the before or after dinner duties. She went to tell one of the kids to set the table, and it was already set. And after dinner one of the kids just started clearing the table. She asked Pa Bill about it, and he claimed he had no idea what was going on, and he advised her just to enjoy it while it lasted. That was about five years ago, and she hadn't had to say a single thing since—even the new kids seemed to know what to do. She caught Nate signaling and giving stern glances from time to time to the younger kids, but never a complaint.

She loved those kids.

Tonight was no different. Dinnertime came and the table was set. As usual, it was set for everyone, including a place for Blue, even though she had yet to join them at dinner. As usual, when it came time to sit down, Blue's place was empty. Ma Beth sighed. She was a patient woman, but that didn't keep her from worrying and being sad at times. Blue was feeding herself and taking care of herself, she knew, and how she did it without anyone seeing her was impressive, but Ma Beth hoped it wouldn't go on forever like that. Each night she hoped that Blue would show up. Tonight did not look like it was going to be the night. Oh well, she thought, the show must go on.

Pa Bill started serving casserole and passing the plates down the table. Sam took the first plateful from Pa Bill and turned to the right to pass it across Blue's empty place to Ma Beth at the end of the table, and he nearly dropped the plate.

Blue was sitting there.

Sam froze with the plate hanging in mid-air and a look of surprise hanging on his face. The table fell silent. Everyone was staring at Blue as if maybe she wasn't really there, because she hadn't been there a moment ago. Or was she? It was like she materialized out of nowhere.

Blue waited a moment and then took the plate carefully out of Sam's hand and passed it to Ma Beth.

The only one who didn't seem surprised was Ma Beth. She kept her face passive with only the tiniest hint of a smile in the corner of her mouth, and turned and took the plate from Blue and said, "Thank you, Blue." Ma Beth looked around the table with a look that was half disapproving and half amused. She said, "Whatever are you staring at?"

That brought everyone back out of shock, and the table slowly resumed its prior activity until all the food was passed around. Dinner proceeded as it had a thousand nights before, full of talk and laughter and stories. Blue rotated into the family like many before her. She acted like she had been there all along. She still didn't talk except for brief, to-the-point answers to questions, but apparently that was just Blue being Blue.

Ma Beth shook her head as she ate and smiled to herself. Every single foster child had their own unique way of fitting themselves into the daily family routine, but none had made a seemingly miraculous materialization like this one did. Everything about this girl was different. Blue was special. Ma Beth could sense that, and she was looking forward to getting to know this intriguing person.

8

SUMMER JOB

William watched the trembling drips of rain as the wind nudged them sideways across the car window. Behind the window was the blur of familiar houses and streets passing by. It distracted his groggy mind from his anger at having to get up at 7am, struggle into his clothes, cram some cereal into his mouth, and drag himself into the front seat to go to his first day at his summer job, which his dad announced at dinner last night had to start a week earlier than planned. Thanks a lot Dad, he thought. My world is on the verge of colossal change then you go and hit the giant pause button.

He had argued about it, but his protests came off lame and empty. He just didn't want to use his main argument: "Guess what Dad, we're not the last ones! Blue's a vox!" He wasn't ready for that. He knew they would find out at some point, and that maybe he should be the one to tell them, but right now he wanted this secret to himself. Maybe it was selfish, but maybe the rules were a little different for this. Of course, Rose knew about the notes and the remote control incident, but Will had not told her about his *"HEY"* or his visit and Blue's one-word reply *"OKAY."* He was guessing that the secret was safe for now.

He would just have to play it by ear. Maybe he could slip down there after work. If not he would have to wait until his next free day. Fortunately, the job was only three days a week. He would have Friday through Monday off.

He sighed and closed his eyes. Too groggy for this, he thought. The stupid thing was that he had actually been looking forward to the job before Blue came along. He was going to help his dad in the college science labs, cleaning and repairing all the equipment that gets used during the school year. His dad had a grant to do some research, and he used part of the grant to hire Will to help take care of the maintenance he himself usually had to do during the summer. His dad also promised Will that he could help out with some of the research. Will thought that was pretty cool, partly because he loved science and partly because he would actually get to spend some time with his dad.

His dad was great, and Will didn't have any complaints, but he wasn't the totally engaged family guy like some of his friends' dads. He would come to soccer games and basketball games, but he didn't know much about sports and often shouted embarrassing, though well-intentioned, words of encouragement ("Great field throw after that foul on the kickoff, son!"). Where his friends' dads were getting them the best sports equipment and giving them tips on how to play, Will's dad was kind of lost in the sporting goods stores and often had to ask Will to settle for the less-than-best equipment—because of price more than anything else ("Gee, this Joe's Sports glove seems pretty much the same as this Wilson glove, and a heck of a lot cheaper!"). Still, his dad was there for him and never balked at helping him out.

"So tell me about this new girl, Blue," said his dad. "I hear you've managed to have some contact where others have failed."

"Yeah, well you wouldn't call it a lot of contact," said Will, his eyes still closed. "It's been all of a dozen words at most. She keeps it pretty much to the point."

"Ah, well, I hear she's been through a lot," said his dad. "But of course, who in the O'Day household has not?"

Will opened his eyes and looked at his dad. "Do you know any of her background, Dad?" Will knew that his mom was involved with the state Department of Foster Care, the DFC, since she was a counselor at school. He hadn't asked his mom because she couldn't share that information, but his mom talked with his dad, and his dad was not as tight-lipped when it came to sharing information.

"Hmm," said his dad, taking a look at Will. "You know better by now than to ask for information like that." But his voice was wavering. "Let's just say that if you have any kindness in you, you would avoid asking her details about how she became an orphan." He then gave Will a pointed look. "I know Ma Beth has shared that Blue lost her family in a fire. You should leave it at that, because that is traumatic enough." He looked directly at Will. "*Is that clear enough?*"

Great. Now he was more curious than ever. "*Yeah, I suppose. Though not really.*"

His dad was quiet for a moment and then said, "Look, there are things I am doing at the lab that I think you will find very interesting. There are more than enough opportunities there to exercise your curiosity!"

That first day at work was interesting but uneventful. Will spent a lot of time just sorting out the equipment on the lab benches and using a lab notebook to record what was missing or broken, then cleaning and putting away the rest. By the time he got home in the evening he was beat. He wasn't used to getting up that early, and working eight hours straight was a grind; school was a breeze by comparison. He ate dinner and then plunked down on the sofa to watch TV with Rose, and within five minutes he was asleep. His mom had to wake him up so he could brush his teeth and go to bed.

This went on for two more days and got a little easier, but still, by Friday Will was ready for a long weekend. Friday morning was glorious—no work! The only problem was, instead of lounging luxuriously in his bed late into the morning, his eyes popped open at 6 a.m. He tried to go back to sleep but soon gave up. It was pointless, he was wide awake and restless. Finally, he just got up and went down to breakfast.

"*Look who's up early,*" voxed Rose.

"*Mr. Hard Worker can't sleep in anymore!*" added his mom. They were sitting at the kitchen table and eating scrambled eggs and bacon.

"*Don't talk and eat,*" Will replied. This was a favorite joke of theirs because, of course, using vox they *could* talk and eat at the same time. Rose giggled because she laughed at everything.

His mom continued out loud. "So Wu has been like a hungry cat getting in everyone's way over at the O'Days. Apparently, without you around, he can't find anything to do."

As if on cue, there was a knock at the door and without waiting, in bounced Wu. "Hey, Mrs. Woods. Hey, Rose. Hey, Will!" he said in a relieved voice. "How's it feel to have a day off?"

"Nice!" said Will. "Want some breakfast?"

"Great!" said Wu. "I mean thanks! I'd love some." As he was scooping up some eggs and a pile of bacon he went on, "You've really missed some big happenings at our house."

Will wiped his plate down with a last piece of toast. "And you are going to tell us between bites, I'm guessing."

"Yeah," said Wu. "The biggest thing is that on Monday night, Blue actually came down and ate dinner with us—and breakfast, lunch, and dinner on Tuesday! What did you write to her in that note?"

Will was caught by surprise, but replied, "Well, I told her to start eating meals with you guys. She does everything I say now."

"Hah," said Wu, only it came out, "whuh" because his mouth was full of egg.

"You mean to tell us that this is the first time she has eaten with you this whole time?" asked Will's mom.

"Yeah, kind of a first. It turns out she kept dishes in her room so she could just come down, grab something out of the refrigerator, and slip back up to her room." Wu couldn't hide his admiration. "She still doesn't talk much, though. I mean, we ask her questions, and she'll answer, but only with the shortest possible answer. She certainly doesn't encourage conversation."

"But it's a start," said his mom. "And that is encouraging news, Wu."

It was good news to Will, too. If Blue was finally venturing out of her bedroom, there would be more opportunity for him to talk to her face-to-face. He was beginning to regret his cowardice for not talking to her when he had the chance. After all, they had been alone and they could have talked or voxed freely. Now, he wasn't sure what the opportunities would be.

As Will and Wu walked down to the park, Wu filled Will in even more. "So Blue actually said "Hi" to me and asked if you and I were best friends, and before you ask, I said yes. At least you're one of my best friends," and then he thought, "*And then she said not your only friend, but how did she know that?*"

Will caught Wu's *chiss*, but just said, "Well, thanks, Wu, and you know you're one of mine, too."

"Yeah, well, never take anything for granted, as they say," said Wu. "So how is your job going?"

The job is boring work is what it is, thought Will to himself. When his dad suggested it, he thought it would be cool, helping at a lab at the college. He didn't realize how much grunge work there was to do in a science lab even at a small college like Westbury. Fortunately, they were done with most of the cleanup and organization that week.

He told all this to Wu and Wu just said, "Well I guess I've been such a pain at home without you around that Ma Beth signed me up for a basketball camp."

"That's cool, Wu," said Will. "You are going to be a star by the time you are on varsity."

"Yeah, well . . ." said Wu.

Blue watched Wu and Will walking down to the park. She was envious, and she thought maybe the time was right to ask Ma Beth if she could go with them. Hopefully she had shown that she had settled in this week.

As she watched Wu's tall form saunter down the hill, Blue reflected on her encounter with him the night before. She had been downstairs to brush her teeth and was going quietly back up her attic stairs. Just as she reached the top, she could hear Wu walking by in the hallway and then heard him pause. He said, "Hey Blue." She knew he wasn't used to getting a reply from her, and he would just continue down to his room, but this time, before he did, she turned and said, "Hey Wu." Wu looked up at her in surprise. Blue continued, "Just get back from the park?"

Wu smiled. "Yeah, I got in a little after-dinner basketball with some friends."

"With Will," Blue said.

Wu responded, "Yeah, we play a lot." And in his mind, he went on, "*. . . AND USUALLY ONLY WITH WILL.*"

Blue caught it. She said, "Will is a good friend."

"Yeah, the best," said Wu. "*AND ONLY,*" he thought.

"He is not your only friend you know," said Blue.

Wu laughed and said, "Yeah, well my other friends seem to be making themselves scarce then." And then a puzzled look came over his face.

"Well, you have one standing here," she said, and she turned and went the rest of the way up to her landing. She could tell he was still standing at the foot of the stairs, so she stopped just before going in her room and looked back at him. He was looking up at her, the puzzled look still on his face, but when he saw her looking at him, he said, "Hey, thanks. You got one here, too."

That had been last night, and now she smiled as she remembered Wu's reaction. It was nice to make a friend again. As she watched the boys disappear down the hill, she thought that maybe, just maybe, her destiny was not a life of isolation.

9
____

BLUE STEPS OUT

Will stared at the chore sign tacked to the refrigerator door as he munched on his cereal. It was held up by a brightly colored hummingbird magnet.

Will: Mow the lawn
Rose: Water the houseplants

It was a summer Saturday ritual: do your chore before anything else. He didn't mind. He actually liked mowing the lawn. It didn't take long, even with the ancient mower they had. It was a push mower and felt like it was made of lead, but it worked smoothly and quickly, and Will liked the scissor-like sound it made as he pushed it across the grass.

He finished his breakfast and made quick work of the lawn. When he came back in, he crossed off the chore, grabbed an apple and yelled, "Park!" and headed back out the door. He heard a reply from deep in the laundry room, "Be back for dinner!" He yelled back, "Okay!" and was off. He didn't bother to stop by at the O'Days, because he knew Wu would already be at the park. When he got there, however, he was surprised to see a whole pack of O'Days.

Nate had come along, which almost never happened because he tended to hang out with a group of older kids. Will thought it would be interesting having Nate there. To most people Nate was intimidating and a little scary (and probably was if you got on the wrong side of him), but to his family and friends, he was a teddy bear. On the court, he never hogged the ball and gave everyone a chance, shouting encouragement. It was a good thing, because Nate was built like a tank.

Will was also surprised to see Sam. Sam was a good kid, but not very coordinated and a bit of a nerd. He looked awkward on a basketball court, like a lost puppy in a shopping mall.

The big shocker, though, was that Blue was there. He hadn't noticed her at first, but there she was sitting cross-legged on a park bench near the basketball court. On her lap was an open book, which she was reading intently. Next to her on the ground was a backpack. Will set his bike down in the grass near her bench, and she looked up at him briefly, but then went back to her reading without saying anything, as if nothing out of the ordinary was happening.

"Hey Blue, good to see you out and about."

She looked at him again but went right back to her reading.

It didn't feel like she was trying to put him off, so he continued, "What's in your pack?"

"Books," she said.

She didn't smile or elaborate, she just answered the question. Wu was right, she may be communicating, but she wasn't wasting any words. Or vox.

He debated—should he try voxing her now? It didn't seem like the time was right, but when would? There she was, right in front of him with no one else close by. Just as he was about to try, the guys from the court started calling for him to come play. Damn it. He gave her a last look, shrugged, and headed for the court.

The game was a welcome distraction. It was goofy but fun—completely different than when he and Wu were playing one-on-one. They were playing two-on-two with Nate and Sam against Wu and Will. Sam would get the ball and do his best to dribble it, focusing extremely hard on the ball and kind of walking toward where he was trying to go. Nate gave him encouragement, "That-a-boy Sam, you've got it—drive to the basket." Will and Wu gave Sam plenty of room but also made sure it wasn't perfectly easy for him. Sam would then hoist the ball up with both hands and heave it with all his might in the direction of the basket. Most of the time it didn't get anywhere close, but Wu would shout, "Almost, Sam, you're getting closer."

Nate was good but not as good as Wu, so when Nate or Wu got the ball, they really went at it. One time, Nate was driving to the basket, and Sam was just trying to stay out of the way, but Nate, after getting blocked thoroughly by Wu, tossed the ball to Sam and said, "Shoot Sam! You're in the clear!" Sam was so shocked, he just stood there for a second and then saw the basket and heaved the ball. It was a perfect swish. Everyone was silent for a moment, and then went crazy!

Nate shouted, "Sam, that was awesome!" He grabbed Sam and put him on his shoulder and said, "Game over, Sam wins it!"

Wu and Will were pumping their arms and shouting, "Woohoo, way to go Sam!" A nutty, fun game.

Will turned toward the bench and started to say, "Did you see that, Blue?" But she wasn't there. They all looked around and then spotted her on a swing not far away. She saw them looking her way, and she gave a wave of her hand.

Nate said to Will, "We're supposed to keep her close by, but I don't know why. She sure seems fine to me. I don't like being a babysitter."

Wu protested, "We're not babysitting her, we're here to be her family. Ma Beth said we have to stay together. She'll stay close. I think she likes it at our house." He looked down while he dribbled the ball after he'd spoken.

Wu sure is sticking up for her, thought Will. He looked over at Blue. What trouble could she get in at the park? "Well look," he said, "we'll all just check on her from time to time. It'll be fine."

They took another break after about an hour. Blue had wandered back to the bench, but this time, she had a pad and pencil out and looked like she was drawing. The boys grabbed a backpack that Nate had brought and pulled out some juice and granola bars. Will walked over to Blue.

"Snack time, are you hungry?"

As Will got closer she closed her pad purposefully, but not evasively. He caught a glimpse of drawings of faces on the page. They were really good.

He held out a granola bar and juice bottle

Blue took them from him and said, "Thanks."

Will sat down on the bench and said, "Looks like you do a lot of drawing. It's good, what I saw just now."

"Thanks," said Blue again. She looked around the park thoughtfully while she sipped on her juice. It didn't feel like she wanted him to leave, so he sat there and drank his juice too. He wanted to try voxing with her again, but something told him he should wait for her to make the first move. As it turned out, Blue did start a conversation. Out loud.

"See those two guys over there?" asked Blue. Will looked where she was nodding. He saw a couple of young adult guys sitting on a bench smoking cigarettes and talking. "Don't stare," she said. "Just check them out while you're scanning around the park."

Will was bemused by Blue's directness, but he did as she said. He sat back and pretended he was just looking around, but as his eyes passed by the two men, he checked them out quickly before continuing his scan. They weren't old, in fact, one looked familiar— a high-schooler he thought. The other one didn't look familiar and was bearded and older, but not much more than late twenties or early thirties. They looked plain enough.

"Looks like they are a couple of guys taking a smoking break from work," said Will after a minute.

"They've been here at least two hours. They were here before us. They've just been moving around," said Blue. "They've only been on that bench a few minutes. They were down by the parking lot earlier. I could see them from the swing." She looked at him. "You're gaping."

Will snapped his mouth shut and then asked, "So you've been watching them the whole time we've been playing basketball? Were you even reading?"

"Of course I was reading," she said in a slightly put-out tone. "But it's good to look up from time-to-time and rest your eyes."

"Hmm, you sound like my mother."

"Hmm," said Blue, and she grabbed her book in such a way that made it clear she was ready to read again and the conversation had ended.

Will got the message. He wasn't offended. Somehow she communicated in body language in a way that was clear but not impolite. But he also picked up that there was something about those two men that had gotten her attention. "So is there something about these guys that bothers you?" asked Will. "If they are making you uncomfortable, we can go back whenever you want."

She looked at him. Again she had that impenetrable expressionless look, only this time she rolled her eyes. "Go play," she said and she opened her book.

Will grinned. She spoke so rudely, but it didn't come off as rude. He shook his head and got up and ran back to the court. He turned around and said, "It's also good to get up and throw a basketball from time-to-time. Wanna give it a try?"

She looked up and gave him a wry look and replied, "*I think not,*" and went back to reading. As she did, he thought he saw the tiniest hint of a smile in one corner of her mouth.

10

ROUTINE

The next couple of weeks fell into a rhythm of short work weeks and long weekends. Will spent Tuesday, Wednesday, and Thursday at the college lab. After he got used to the schedule, it didn't seem so bad. He actually liked getting up early in the morning, even on his days off. It meant more time before the heat of the day set in. Besides, it wasn't like he was the only one busy. Wu spent mornings Monday thru Thursday at a basketball camp at the college gymnasium. Nate worked all week at a hardware store, so he could only join them on Saturday and Sunday. From Wu's reports, Blue spent the days helping out Ma Beth around the house or hanging out in her room, or when it was too hot, hanging out on the porch drawing or reading. Sam was home all the time, too, but apparently off in his own world of fantasy games and science fiction books. The park became the weekend rendezvous spot for all of them when the weather was good. Blue even started to join in some of the sports—frisbee or basketball or catch, but only for very short periods of time. Most of the time she seemed wrapped up in whatever inner world she was living in. And as for vox . . . nothing but the occasional comment. It was almost like she was avoiding it. It was vexing to Will, but what could he do?

After a couple of more work days fixing lab equipment, Will helped his dad set up some of the research equipment. His dad also started to fill him on what he was doing and why.

"You know when I grew up, I had to learn to fit in the rest of the world just like you are now. Back then, I couldn't find any information on what makes us so different. We didn't have the internet or home computers. We just had encyclopedias, TV, and *National Geographic*. It was *National Geographic* that turned me on to what I'm doing now. They had issues with articles about different light—laser light, ultraviolet, infrared, radio waves, x-rays. I was fascinated and started to get an understanding behind the science of vox."

It was at that moment that Will realized that his father had never really talked to him about vox in this way. Plenty of talk about rules and guidelines, but never the science. In fact, it seemed weird to be talking about it in terms of science. Of course, he had spent plenty of time wondering what it really was, and why they had it and no one else, at least not to his knowledge. When he was young, he would ask his parents, but their explanations had always been superficial—"It's genetics," "We just are what we are," "One of our ancestors a long time ago was born with a mutation." Great, his super smart parents who always had to give him the scientific answer weren't super smart enough to know that they freaked out their kid by saying he was the descendent of a mutant. Thanks, Mom and Dad. He was going to lie to his kids.

But now that he was older, talking about the science of it with his dad was starting to interest him. A lot.

"Dad, why isn't there any information about us, about vox oculis, I mean. I can't even find it on the internet."

Will's dad was concentrating on a fitting for a lens on his optics table. He paused and then said, "Well, first off, just because it's not on the internet doesn't mean the information doesn't exist, don't forget that."

"Don't worry, Dad, you never let us forget that."

"And second of all, consider this. How many people have you known that can vox?"

"Just us. Just you, Mom, Rose, and me. And Grandma and Grandpa Woods." He felt a twinge of guilt that he was leaving out Blue, but he held back from mentioning her.

"Right," said his dad, "And I have only run across half a dozen others, including your mother. Fact is, we are extinction in-process. It's natural selection—thank you, Charles Darwin." His father returned to fiddling with his lens. He looked over toward Will. *"Hand me that Phillips screwdriver there, the small one."*

Will handed him the screwdriver. His father turned back to concentrate on the lens bracket.

"So you think that natural selection is the reason we are so few? You think that vox is a disadvantage to survival now rather than an advantage?" He had learned about Darwin and natural selection just that year.

"Exactly!" said his dad. "Consider how annoying it can be in school or crowds of people without your coated glasses to shut out the cacophony of their thoughts. It's a handicap in a crowded busy world. On the other hand, imagine being in a world where you have a small group of families like ours, living in the woods, where it is much quieter, and every small sound could reveal the location of prey or alert them to your presence and scare them away. In that world, we can communicate in the light or dark without making a sound, just like the games we played when you were younger." He looked over his glasses at Will, *"Find-the-fox, night-tag. You remember."* He returned to focusing on the optics table. "Now think about what an advantage that would be if you were a hunter. You could coordinate a group of hunters without making a sound. You would rule the hunting ground. That's what I'm sure our ancestors were—social hunters. The problem was, agriculture came along, and agriculture worked better than hunting. It made a stronger society and civilization. Now our kind could survive in that kind of world, but since there was no advantage, we didn't seek each other out. Eventually, genetics diluted everything, and there are only a few original pure vox speakers left."

"Yeah, but Dad, we could take advantage of that, couldn't we? I mean, you have made sure we are careful and polite, but wouldn't it be tempting to take advantage of it to steal passwords and combinations and stuff like that? It seems like we could take over the world."

"Yes, people are weak, and they tend to take advantage of situations. However, nature has a way of ridding itself of creatures that are *too* clever. If they are outnumbered, those that stand out are often pecked to death. You know what it is like to get pecked." Will knew. He had several experiences revealing secrets he shouldn't have. Those experiences usually involved fists and kicks.

Will's dad looked at him significantly. "AND THAT IS WHY WE ARE SO STRICT ABOUT HOW AND WHAT YOU DO WITH YOUR ABILITIES. WITH GREAT ABILITY COMES GREAT RESPONSIBILITY. THERE IS NO ACTION WITHOUT REACTION, ET CETERA, ET CETERA . . ." He winked at Will.

Will rolled his eyes. His dad rarely lost an opportunity to drive home platitudes.

"Now imagine growing up without that kind of guidance," his dad continued. "Without someone to carefully protect you, you would quickly stand out and be feared because you can read people's thoughts. 'Remember, the Salem witch trials!' That could be our family motto!"

Will thought of Blue. She acted like she had been pecked a lot, and that is probably where all those defense mechanisms were coming from. He had a sudden urge to tell his dad about her. God, he was bursting to talk about it with someone. He wanted it to be Blue, but he had failed so far. There was that bit of contact while they were in the park, but there was very little opportunity for a private conversation there, even a vox conversation. And when he hung out at their house, she was almost always cloistered in her attic room.

"Right now, we have to focus on the task at hand," said Will's dad, interrupting Will's thoughts. "I think it will help us both to understand more about ourselves if we get this optical bench set up and calibrated. Then we can have some fun!"

They spent the rest of the afternoon working with some very cool optical apparatus and it kept most of Will's mind occupied, but there was a corner of his brain that continued to grind away at his real problem. He had to come up with something other than a chance encounter with Blue at the park or their house. Should he ask her on a date? That was crazy. He didn't know the first thing about dating. And it would be totally weird. She was still a kid. Even though she was fourteen, it was clear she was a late bloomer. The cell phone thing was frustrating. If she had a cell phone he could at least text to her and talk that way, maybe even call her, but it wouldn't be the same if they couldn't vox. And email was out, she didn't even have an email address yet. She seemed totally isolated from any modern means of communication.

By the end of the day, he was no closer to solving his problem, but together, he and his dad were a lot closer to getting his dad's research off the ground. It looked like his time spent in the lab just might satisfy some of Will's curiosity. But not enough. Not by a long shot.

11

HOME

Blue couldn't help herself. She was wary of too much of a good thing but couldn't help letting herself relax just the tiniest bit. For the first time in her life, she felt she was living in a state of stability and safety. At least the first time since before the fire. That had been four and a half years ago. Four and a half years of hell. She was beginning to think that hell was the new normal and she was just going to have to learn how to survive. But now everything had changed. It seemed like that chapter had ended. Her former life seemed just that—a former life. Her former foster families seemed just that—former foster families. They were just stepping stones to a different life.

And now, at this moment, this very real and present moment, she was sitting on the porch in the summer twilight listening to the summer sounds—birds, peepers, crickets, muted music from neighboring houses, and the sounds in the house behind her.

Sam was inside the family room at the computer. He was the geek of the household, completely engrossed in adventure games and science fiction. Nate was more than likely reading sports magazines up in his room, and Wu was watching TV while Pa Bill sat on the couch and read the paper. It was like a scene from a Norman Rockwell painting. And she was a part of it but also still on the outside of it. She felt like she was on the verge of entering the painting, but not quite ready.

Ma Beth was finishing up some things in the kitchen. Blue did her part in the household chores, but Ma Beth always did the final touches. She came out and joined Blue on the porch.

"I like it out here. It is so nice and peaceful in the evening. Do you mind if I join you?" She settled into the porch chair and sat back with her eyes closed.

"Sure," said Blue. "I mean no, that's fine."

Ma Beth never pressured Blue to talk, which made Blue feel at ease when she was close by. It was nice. She tried to savor the moment, at least a little, and she was partly successful, but there was a lot still going on in her mind. Two things in particular. The first was trying to find a way to talk with Will alone. She was desperate to communicate with him now that she finally made contact with one of her own kind and yet she was oddly frightened of what might develop. Would it bring back too many memories too fast? And what about the rest of his family? Was he the only one? She didn't think so. She knew he had a little sister, Rose.

A familiar hot panic surged in her gut. She instinctively closed her eyes and drew in a breath, evenly and slowly. Then just as slowly she let the breath out. Breathe in . . . breathe out. She kept at it until the panic subsided. It had been a while since she'd felt a surge that strong. It caught her by surprise but she was practiced in handling it. Not like in the early days before she'd learned to put that dark episode away in a box and slide it into the back of a closet in her mind and close the door. Since then, she'd learned to avoid the triggers, stop thinking about what might have been, what had been, what was her life before. But there were still times she got caught off guard by some thought, or sound, or picture and that box lid would crack open and she would have to push it shut again.

She shook it off and turned her thoughts to Will's parents. They must be able to vox if Will could. Where else would it come from? On the other hand maybe he was adopted. She hadn't thought of that before. Maybe he was an orphan like her. It didn't matter. What mattered is finding a way to talk to Will alone. It had been weeks since they had first discovered each other, and still, they hadn't exchanged more than a few words and even less through vox. It was strange. She found it difficult and that frustrated her. It had been so long since she had anyone to share with, it was like she had to learn all over again.

Then there was the other thing that was bothering her—those two men in the park. Whenever she went to the park with the boys, it seemed that at least the younger of the two men was there somewhere. The older guy, the bearded one, only showed up once or twice after that first time. The two men didn't seem to take that much notice of her or the boys, and she took advantage of that to keep an eye on them. What she had learned over the past couple of weeks confirmed what she had sensed about those two since that first day in the park, when she had pointed them out to Will. And she was taking notes. In her own way.

She had been drawing pictures of them, along with other people she saw in the park. She liked to make people into anthropomorphized animals (she had loved the word 'anthropomorphize' ever since she'd learned it). She tried to match their personalities with animals. She had drawn Wu as a mink because he was long and lean. Nate was a bear, and Sam was a goat because goats looked awkward but were very smart and clever. Will, she hadn't figured out yet. She tried him as a Collie, but that didn't seem right. She was thinking more along the lines of a Husky and was going to try that next time.

She drew the two men in the park as a pig and a lizard. And she had given them names—Gronk and Greazal.

They were dealing drugs. She was sure of it.

She caught a lot of their *chiss* over the past few weeks. They were easy to pick up, especially Greazal. Gronk was a little less open. It was like that with normal people—some were an open book and others you could only hear the shallower thoughts. Deep thoughts stayed buried almost as if they knew how to hide them, but she knew they didn't. They were all vox-deaf, every one of them.

One of the things she learned the hard way was when to listen to people's *chiss* and when to block them out. If you listen to the wrong ones and give away the fact that you heard them, that's when you get enemies. She had made a lot of enemies when she was a kid, at school, at her foster homes, at institutions. When she finally caught on, she started to learn to ignore the insincere people, the ones that were nice to your face but whose thoughts revealed that they were jealous, or bored, or hateful, or you name it. The list of horrible things people think is long. Of course, she thought bad things about some people, too, but she was not nice to them either. That, at least, is sincerity.

She listened to these two, however. She had a particular visceral hatred of drug dealers. They were the low of the low, the scum of the earth, the sociopaths that didn't have empathy for anyone. All they wanted was easy money, not caring how the drugs they were selling were ruining lives. To her, these two men were already enemies, so eavesdropping on their *chiss* had no downside. Instead, it had an intoxicating potential upside. She could make sure they were caught. She just wasn't sure how.

She felt a gentle hand on her shoulder and looked up. She had been completely lost in her thoughts and forgotten that Ma Beth was there.

"Time to go inside little thinker," said Ma Beth with a smile. She didn't ask what Blue was thinking, and there was no judgment in her voice. She was so kind and gentle that for once Blue felt guilty in thinking dark thoughts about Gronk and Greazal. The last thing she wanted to do was to involve Ma Beth or anyone else in the family in her obsessive trains of thought. She knew it was best to keep these thoughts to herself in the private, controlled part of her brain. She vowed that from then on, she would not spoil these moments with the family by thinking about her obsession. She would reserve that for times when she was alone, or maybe when she finally figured out a way to talk to Will.

12

I THINK THEREFORE IR

"So what we have set up here is a light source." Will's dad pointed to an instrument that looked like a projector. "And here we have a prism, and a spectrometer," he said, pointing to a large metal box with a small video screen with two rows of knobs and switches. On the back of the box was an opening that faced the projector. "The hardest part of the setup is to get all the instruments, lenses, prisms, and mirrors mounted on this table," he patted a large metal table that had slots and holes machined into it in a regular pattern. "And last, but not least, we need to calibrate the whole she-bang. We do that with these." He held up a box that had a bunch of slides in it. "These are super-accurate filters. Each slide only passes a narrow spectrum of light. This is how we know our spectrometer is reading things correctly."

He turned on the projector and a beam of white light came out. The light went through a prism mounted on the table and some of the light split out onto a small screen that had been mounted at a right angle to the prism, and a rainbow appeared on the screen. Another beam of light came straight out of the other side of the prism and went into the hole on the side of the spectrometer.

"So look carefully at what happens when I put this filter over the lens." His dad slid a piece of dark glass into a slot in the projector. The white beam went away.

Will said, "You blocked the light."

His dad smiled and said, "No! Take a look at the screen!" And there on the screen was a single line of bright red light. All the other colors of the rainbow were gone. "You see, this filter blocks all colors of light except red! In fact, this filter passes only a very specific wavelength of light and we will use it to calibrate the spectrometer and make sure it is reading correctly."

His dad busied himself with checking the readings on the spectrometer and fiddling with the switches and knobs to adjust the readings so they matched the filter. Will looked at the box of little glass slides. They all had labels like "810 nanometers."

"So what do all these numbers mean?"

"Those," said his dad, "Are the wavelengths of the light that the filter lets through. They are measured in nanometers—one billionth of a meter."

"So light is a wave? Like a water wave?" asked Will.

"Mmmm, sort of. Definitely a wave but a little more complicated than that. I will explain it to you sometime. But a wavelength relates directly to color! And color is what we are interested in, or rather the color of a color that we cannot see . . . but we can see!" said his dad, cryptically.

"You're talking about vox, right?" asked Will.

"That's right. The light that you and I can 'see', or rather 'hear through our eyes' is what vox oculis is. Our eyes are sensitive to light that other people are not sensitive to. Specifically, infrared light. Now, you know this already because of our sensitivity to remote controls on TVs and radios and such. That annoying high pitch sound is caused by the infrared emitters on the remote controls. That is one of the reasons we gave you the glasses that you and Rose wear at school."

Will and his sister each had glasses with a special clear coating on the lenses. When they were at school, putting on the glasses made it possible for them to concentrate. Without them, the crowded classrooms and hallways were distracting with all the *chiss* everywhere. And some rooms had fluorescent lamps that buzzed in their head like crazy if they didn't wear the glasses. Wearing glasses was not unusual at school, and these glasses looked just like everyone else's so they weren't out of place, and they sure helped Will and Rose a lot in school. It made them feel normal, so much so that they took the glasses for granted.

"Dad, did you have glasses when you were in school?"

"Yes, we did," said his dad. "Your mother and me both had regular glasses, and they helped, but they weren't nearly as good as the ones you have now. You know how you can 'hear' through a window, but how it is quieter?"

Will knew of course. Sometimes it felt like a superpower—being able to "*hear*" vox through glass.

"Well, that's about all the glasses did, make it a little quieter—except correct my nearsightedness, of course. The worst thing about it for your mother and I in those days was the fluorescent lights. The ones they have now are much better. I would just spend a lot of time with my eyes closed or squinting a lot when I was in the classroom. Kids thought I was a squinty-eyed nerd."

"Wow. I just kind of assumed that you would have had glasses like ours. So where did our glasses come from?" asked Will.

"I invented the coating on them! Now do you have an idea of why I became a scientist? And do you ever wonder why your mother became a psychiatrist?"

Will stopped to think. Of course—his dad became a scientist because he wanted to find out how vox works. "So mom became a psychiatrist because . . . she wanted to know why people reacted funny to her?"

"Not exactly funny—harassed and bullied her is more like it," his dad said.

Will had a hard time picturing anyone bullying his mother. It seemed like everyone was her friend, and she was so calm and poised all the time.

"I know. Hard to imagine your mom being bullied, eh?" He looked sidelong at Will.

"*Did I leak just now?*" asked Will.

"*No, but your face gave you away. You can read people by more than chiss, you know.*" His father turned back to what he was working on.

So his mother was the same way, as abnormal as he felt, only she tried to find out why it made her so different from other people and why people reacted to her the way they did by studying psychiatry.

He thought about Blue and her world. She did not have glasses of any kind. For her vox is 'on' all the time unless she closes her eyes. She didn't have a scientist father to make special glasses or a psychiatrist mother to explain people's behavior. All she had was the ability to close her eyes or hole up in her room, and act distant and aloof, and answer in short sentences.

"You see, son, there isn't a lot of science about our family trait. I decided there should be some, even if it is only for our benefit. Along the way I discovered that there is a lot of neat science that has nothing to do with vox, so it was a win-win decision for me."

"So what have you discovered so far? I mean besides the coating on the glasses?" asked Will.

"Ah!" said his dad. "A very great deal," "*And yet not very much!*" "So let's start with what you know. You do know that the coating on the glasses helps, but do you know why it helps?"

"Well, you said we are sensitive to light that isn't visible, right?" said Will.

"Go on," said his dad, nodding.

"So is it a filter, like the filters you are putting in the projector, here?"

"Exactly!"

"And so this setup you have here, you are using that to test different filters?" asked Will.

"Yes! And no. Yes, because I do use this setup for that, but no, because I am using it for a different test today. Today and for the next few weeks, I want to test light sources! I told you that our eyes are sensitive to certain wavelengths of light that others are not, BUT, where does that light come from?"

Will thought it was a stupid question because his dad knew very well that somehow their eyes were the source. "Well," said Will, "It comes from our eyes somehow—I always thought it was reflections like with dogs and cats."

"Ah, no, it can't be reflections. We can vox in complete darkness, even infrared darkness. Now with dogs and cats and other nocturnal animals, that actually *is* reflection—animals have a lining in their eye that reflects light back through their retina. That's what allows them to see in low light. But even animals can't see in complete darkness. The reflective lining is called 'tapetum lucidum.' It literally means 'bright tapestry.'"

"But we don't have that tap . . . tapetum . . ."

"Tapetum lucidum. That's right," said his dad. "But what I am quite sure of is that we have a lining in our eyes *like* tapetum lucidum. Only instead of reflecting light, our lining *glows*!"

"Glows!" said Will. "Like a firefly . . . only in infrared?"

"Well, that was my first guess, but I eliminated that right away. There *are* some deep-sea fishes that can glow in infrared and ultra-violet colors, but that's a chemical reaction and not fast enough to vox. There *are* however other ways of generating infrared light and evolution has always proven to be more clever than we are. Science, in fact, is a very humbling discipline in which we are constantly amazed at the genius of nature and evolution."

"So just how *do* we generate this light?" asked Will. He was starting to get interested and impatient for the answer. He also was getting exasperated by his dad's drawn-out explanations. But his dad finally got to the point.

"I don't know!" He smiled broadly.

"You don't know? Doesn't anyone know?"

"No, that's what is so exciting—that's what we are setting up to work on now. We can be the first ones to discover it. That's what makes science so cool!" He clapped his hands and danced around as if he had just won the lottery.

Will's dad often got a little over-excited when talking about science. When he got this animated, Will worried that his dad might be just a little bit insane. Problem was, Will was starting to get a little excited about it, too.

13

DINNER AT THE O'DAYS

After a few weeks in the lab, the initial excitement had subsided, gradually replaced by the monotony of what, according to his dad, was the heart of serious research: tedious, detailed, repetitious experiments. Will had no idea how much information he would have to record and how carefully all the experiments had to be done, and then repeated, and then verified. If this was the heart of research, Will wasn't sure he wanted to see what the soul was like.

There had been one thing that broke the monotony, at least for a couple of days. They tried something called luciferin—the bioluminescent chemical in fireflies. They modified it with some chemicals and, amazingly, got it to glow in the near-infrared—the same frequency as vox. Looking through the infrared camera they could see it glow, a lot like their eyes glowed, and that was pretty cool. "We could make infrared fireflies!" said his dad. But there was no *chiss,* no *vox,* no *klax.* They even tried stimulating it with electrodes hooked to an audio amplifier but there was nothing vox-like coming out of it, just smoke. "Well, at least we're making smoke signals," his dad had joked.

They had also tried some electronic circuits they got off the web that were like the ones in remote controls. They managed to get them to make irritating sounds in their heads, like the remote controls. But no matter what they tried—even playing voice and music through the circuits—all they managed to create was a very large variety of screech, squawk, hiss, shhh, and eeeeee *klax* noises in their head.

"Our brains must be doing some sort of encoding and compressing into something that our tapetum can convert to light. Then our receiving brain decodes it and turns it back into something we can understand," said his dad. "I think we should record some of our own *vox* in this receiver. Then there may be some way to decode it. The problem is, I don't know how, and I don't know who I could trust to decode it without giving up our secret." He was thoughtful for a moment. He shook his head, "It's still a mystery, but at least we're eliminating things."

Eliminating things. That isn't exactly what Will had been hoping for. Where was that "Eureka!" moment? Was that only in the movies? His dad said no, that he just had to be patient. Life wasn't a two-hour movie. "*THANKS, DAD,*" he had voxed. "*PATIENCE IS YOUR GO-TO ANSWER FOR EVERYTHING.*" Still, the luciferin experiment, *had* been a bright spot, and there were other interesting things they hadn't tried, and that was enough to keep him going.

Outside the lab, the other research wasn't going well, either. It was starting to get ridiculous—it had been weeks and he had yet to find an opportunity to sit down with Blue and just talk without having to look over their shoulders. Their exchanges so far had fallen into a perfunctory norm, just snippets of normal conversation and an occasional joke. She did have a sense of humor, but it was very dry and hard to read, which made her even more intriguing. He did manage to get smiles out of her from time to time. They were odd, half-smiles. Not sarcastic, but more like a battle between one-half of her face and the other—like half of her wanted to smile, but the other half was being more cautious, more reserved. He had also noticed that their interactions, especially the vox, seemed to relax her a little, making her a little more civil.

But it wasn't conversation. It wasn't sharing experiences. It wasn't discussing stuff. That's what he was looking for. And so far it was going nowhere. *"You just have to be patient, life isn't a two-hour movie,"* said the Dad-voice in his head. *"Just shut-up, Dad-voice,"* he said back.

So between the work frustrations and Blue frustrations, it was starting to look like this whole summer was going to fall into a giant rut. That's the way it seemed, at least, until his parents announced they had to go to the city for a conference and were going to be gone overnight. He and Rose would have a day and night without their parents around. No work and no parents—it was almost too good to be true. To make it perfect, he tried to convince his parents that he and Rose were capable of staying at home by themselves.

This is how the discussion went:

Mom: "I'm sorry kids, you can't stay home by yourselves, you are going to have to go over to a friend's house." *"SORRY."*

Will: "Mom, really, what could go wrong? What is there that you don't think I could handle? I'm almost sixteen—in some countries that's manhood and people get married and start having kids." *"DON'T YOU TRUST US?"*

Rose: "Yeah Mom, Will is a great babysitter and I don't cause any trouble . . . well I mean, I won't cause any trouble, I prommii-isse! Please, please, please, can't we stay here by ourselves?" *"REALLY, NOTHING IS GOING TO HAPPEN, I PROMISE!"*

Mom: "It's not that we don't trust you or feel that you are capable of staying home by yourselves, but you have to realize that until Will is eighteen, he is not considered an adult by law. You wouldn't want to see us thrown in jail, would you?" *"IT'S NOT WHAT YOU DO I'M WORRIED ABOUT, IT'S WHAT COULD HAPPEN THAT'S NOT UNDER YOUR CONTROL."*

Will: "Would it mean we could stay at home by ourselves while you were in jail?" *"JUST KIDDING!"*

Rose: (Laughter) *(LAUGHTER)*

Mom: *"HAHA MR. FUNNY GUY!"* "We talked to the O'Days and you can both stay with them while we're gone, so it's no different than spending the night there, like you do with your friends, Rose, and like you used to do, Will."

Rose: "Moth-er, I have to stay *there*? That means I have to play with Sam. Can't I stay at Emily's or Sarah's?" *"SAM IS A GEEK."*

Mom: "They're both out of town. You can be sure I called them first, but you like Sam, don't you?" *"HE'S NOT A GEEK, HE IS AN INTROVERT WHICH IS NOT A BAD THING. AND HE'S A VERY NICE BOY."*

Rose: "I like him well enough in small doses, but a whole two days!" *"ALL HE LIKES TO DO IS THOSE COMPUTER RPGS."*

Mom: "It won't be a whole two days, we'll be leaving on Tuesday morning and be returning on Wednesday by dinnertime." *"RPG, WHAT IS AN RPG?"*

Will: "Hey, Rosie, it's not like he is allowed to spend all his time on the computer. He only gets, like two hours a day and some days none." *"RPG MEANS ROLE PLAYING GAME, MOM."* "Besides, he likes to play board games—you like to play board games—and you're good at it." *"REALLY GOOD. YOU COULD PROBABLY CREAM HIM AT RUMMIKUB."*

Rose: (sullenly): *"OKAY . . ."*

Mom: (stern look): *"IT'S SETTLED THEN! NO MORE DISCUSSION!"*

Not quite what he was looking for, but after some thought, he realized staying over at the O'Day's might even be better. He would be spending over 30 hours with the O'Days and Blue. There *had* to be an opportunity during that time to get her alone.

The day of his parent's trip came quickly. It was a Tuesday, and instead of going to work with his dad, Will packed an overnight bag. They hung around home, had breakfast, and then his parents made ready to leave.

"THE USUAL LITANY OF CAUTIONS," advised his dad, winking.

His mother frowned and rolled her eyes. "We'll be back tomorrow around 2pm. We'll drop by the O'Days and let them know we're back and then you make sure you are home by dinner-time." "*Best behavior please, okay?*"

Their mom and dad dropped them off at the O'Days and had a few words with Ma Beth before giving a wave and driving off. As usual, the gang of kids headed for the park almost immediately. It wasn't the usual crowd, however. This time it was Wu, Will, Sam, Blue, and Rose. Nate was working.

Blue went immediately to her bench to read or draw or spy or all of the above, and Sam and Rose started playing basketball with Wu and Will. Sam started out with enthusiasm, but without Nate there as his cheerleader, he quickly lost momentum. Rose was impossible—she clearly did not want to be doing this and she showed no effort at all. Wu and Will were exchanging glances of exasperation and Will was beginning to think this was going to turn into a long afternoon. Then all of a sudden he heard a vox. "*Rosie! Rosie, I'm open, throw the ball to me!*" And there was Blue, on the court, behind Wu.

Will was shocked, and so was Rose, but a big smile appeared on Rose's face, and she chucked the ball as best she could towards Blue. Blue was lightning quick and dashed around Wu, who was caught completely off guard. She snapped up the ball, dribbled, and then passed it to a grinning Sam, who gave it one of his patented best-effort shots at the basket. It totally missed, but the game had turned around. It was now three on two, and Rose finally showed some interest in the game. It turned into another crazy but fun game which wound up with new rules—if any of the little kids even touched the basket or net with the ball, they got two points. The big boys had to shoot outside the line and it only counted two points. In the end, the big boys still won with 22 points but the little kids had 20 points and were ecstatic. It was clear, however, that the little guys only had one game in them. Blue, characteristically, was done when she was done, and Rose and Sam lost interest, but on their way to the swings chattered excitedly about each of their baskets.

Blue went to the swings also but was lost in her own world. Will and Wu found a couple of other boys and started a new game. They stopped from time to time to check on Sam, Rose, and Blue. Rose went over to some girls she knew from school. Pretty soon it was time to head back, so Wu and Will went to collect their "charges." Blue was back at her bench bent over her drawing pad, and Sam and Rose were with her watching her intently. Wu and Will looked over their shoulders.

Blue was making a drawing of two creatures that were clearly caricatures of Sam and Rose. The two creatures were on a basketball court, and the Sam-creature was throwing a pumpkin toward the basket.

"Whoa, Blue, that is really cool!" said Wu. "I had no idea your drawings were that good. That really looks like Sam and Rose!"

Blue kept on drawing intently but said, "Thanks, Wu." Will was surprised because he thought that Wu would have seen some of Blue's drawings by now since they lived in the same house.

Sam was very excited. "Yeah, and look how realistic the pumpkin looks. And the fur! It looks a lot like the characters from 'Realms of Zokar!' Blue, do you think you could draw my avatar sometime? That would be sooo cool! Please?" begged Sam.

Blue smiled her very slight and crooked smile and said, "Maybe." Will thought he caught a tiny sparkle in her eyes.

"*SAM WOULD REALLY LIKE THAT. ME TOO,*" voxed Rose to Blue. Blue looked at Rose and her face became very hard to read. She didn't reply to Rose, instead, she appeared to take in a long slow breath and then let it out just as slowly.

The moment was interrupted, as Wu spoke up. "Well, that will have to wait 'cuz we have to get home and help with dinner prep, so pack up your stuff." And then he leaned over to Blue and said in a low voice, "Very cool."

Dinner at the O'Days was a fairly raucous affair. Pa Bill encouraged conversation during the meal and could keep things going with interesting stories of his own. Ma Beth was the quiet one at dinner. The kids were more than willing to share their adventures.

Sam was enthusiastic describing the basketball game with its own special rules. Pa Bill exclaimed "Ingenious! Adaptability is a very fine quality!" And he gave an appreciative nod toward Will and Wu.

Wu responded, "Well it all started because Blue jumped in and got things going the right direction."

Blue didn't look up from her plate but put on her half smile.

Rose spoke up and said, "Yeah, she snuck in behind Wu and then . . ."

"*Rose! Be careful! Don't say vox!*" Will gave Rose an intent look of warning. Blue froze, her fork halfway to her mouth.

". . . And then she . . . signaled to me . . . to throw her the ball! So I threw it to her . . ." "*I wasn't going to say 'vox'!*"

"Passed it to her . . ." interrupted Will. "*And now we'll never know . . .*"

Rose stuck her tongue out at Will.". . . passed it to her, and then she went right around Wu and passed it to Sam and Sam took a shot!" "*Stop voxing!*"

"Well done, then, Blue!" Pa Bill responded. "Did Sam get a basket?"

"*You stop voxing!*"

"Not that time," said Sam, "but then we changed the rules so it was easier for us to get baskets. It worked out really well!"

"*No, YOU stop voxing!*"

"*Children!*" Rose and Will glanced carefully at Blue in shock. She had a motherly scowl on her face.

"Well that sounds like fun," said Pa Bill. "I wish I could still move well enough to play basketball again."

Wu said, "You should come play sometime. We could make up some new rules."

"Thank you, Wu. You know I might just do that sometime," replied Pa Bill.

Will breathed a sigh of relief. They got through that without revealing anything. He was going to have to have a little talk with Rosie about being extra careful now that Blue was in the equation. It was easy enough between themselves to conceal their vox because they had years of practice, but they didn't have much experience with an outsider.

After dinner, Will and Rose were incorporated into the O'Day family drill. Rose and Sam cleared the table, Nate washed dishes, Will rinsed, and Wu dried and put them away since he knew where everything went. Ma Beth took care of all the other clean-up details. Blue had the night off. Apparently, Pa Bill never did dishes. "My job is to put food on the table," he said. "Not clean it off."

"Hmph," was Ma Beth's reply to that.

Nate was putting washed dishes in one basin of the sink. Will picked up a dish, rinsed it under clear hot water, and put it in the dish rack next to the sink where Wu would pick up a dish, dry it, and put it away. The three quietly went about their work, but after a few minutes, Wu said, "Guys, check this out." He nodded his head through the broad entrance to the family room. In the corner, Blue was sitting in front of the computer that Sam used to play his RPG games. She was intently working on a drawing while glancing up at the screen, and Sam was jumping up and down. Sam was a very excitable guy, and he twitched and giggled, and then every now and then would point to something on the screen. Rose was excited, too, but much more reserved—at least outwardly. Inside she would make this interesting little chant that went something like this: "*EEE EEE EEE AH EEE AH EEE AH, OOH AAH AAH EEE EEE AH OOOH AH*" which of course only Will, his family, and now Blue could enjoy.

Blue had her crooked grin on, which meant that she was enjoying the appreciative audience of Rose and Sam.

When they were finally finished with dishes, they went over to where Sam and Rose were admiring the finished work, which Blue had pulled out of her sketchbook. Sam was ecstatic. "This is soooo ridiculously cool, I can't believe how cool this is, I can't wait to show it to Chip and Merv and Tucker. Blue, you are a genius, you could make jillions doing this stuff!" He was on his back rocking back and forth with the drawing at arm's length above him.

"Well c'mon, Samster, let us look," said Nate. Sam jumped up and held the drawing up to them. "Look at how she got everything —the Sword of Gilfarunda, the Crystal Pouch, the Fleet Boots, and the Star of Elikar!"

"Whoa, look at that," said Will, who didn't know what the heck Sam was talking about but could clearly identify the items that he was referring to in the drawing. The drawing was skillfully done, with beautiful shading and shadows, and very realistic folds and texture in the clothing. There was even a sparkle in the eyes of Sam's avatar.

Nate said, "You are going to blow everyone away in art class at school."

"Thanks," said Blue with a little more emotion than she usually did.

"Congrats, Sam, you should pin that up above your computer," said Will.

"I'm going to scan it and post it in my game. When I do, I bet everyone will want you to do their avatar, Blue," said Sam.

"Hmmm," said Blue, and her face fell a little. "I only do this for family." She gathered up her things and headed for the back stairway.

"You could charge for them, I know lots of kids that would pay you. Really, you could get rich!" said Sam, but Blue was already heading up the stairway.

Ma Beth said, "Money isn't always what motivates people, sometimes it is just for the love of being creative."

Will watched Blue, thinking this was finally the opportunity to talk to her, but as he watched her go up the stairs, something told him he should not follow.

Blue went up the stairs slowly, clutching her sketchbook to her chest. She was savoring a rare moment where it seemed like everything was in balance and she felt comfortable, safe, and relaxed. She was happy. Part of it was Sam's reaction. It was so genuine and effusive, it was hard not to feel his joy. Part of it was the game in the park. It was the first time she felt like she had used her *vox,* for fun. At least the first time in a long, long time. And then there was dinner. Will and Rose bickered with their *vox* just like she and her sister had done long ago, and Blue bantered back—and she didn't feel the dreaded panicky fear and anxiety swelling up.

Since the moment she first had contact with Will, she had been tentative about voxing with him, but now she could tell, that page had turned. Instead of feeling tentative, she now suddenly felt like she couldn't wait for an opportunity to talk to him. She stopped and turned around. Why not now?

She stood there for a moment, about to step back down, but instead she sat down on the stairs and just listened to the sounds flowing through the hallways and rooms of the house—the chatter and laughter, the thumps and creaks and groans of the floors as feet moved across them, the night sounds outside the open windows. It was a healthy, living, and breathing home.

"Hey Blue, c'mon down, we're going to play Settlers of Catan," came Sam's voice.

And at that moment, she knew what her next step was.

14

NOT ALONE

It was a hot, humid night, and Will's only window was as wide open as he could get it. He had stripped down to his boxers to get some relief from the heat, but sweat beaded up on his forehead anyway. He laid on top of his covers trying to find a comfortable position, but nothing worked. He was as restless as the warm breeze that was rustling through the bushes outside his window. It wasn't the heat making him restless so much as what was bouncing around in his head. It was buzzing with what happened the night before at the O'Days. Blue's drawings were amazing. Not just good. Amazing. Sam's reaction was priceless. Sam loved stuff like that—people with animal traits, all that mythology and fantasy stuff. Will had to admit, it was pretty cool. But what he was really thinking about were the sketches she had shown only to him.

After their game of Settlers of Catan (which Nate won, much to Rosie's disappointment) Blue had taken Will aside into the front hallway and shown him drawings she had done of the two men in the park. She had made them into animals, but she had done more; she had drawn a sequence, like a page from a manga novel, showing what they were doing.

She didn't say anything, just showed the drawings to him. He looked at them admiringly, but then as soon as he figured out what they were doing, his jaw dropped.

"*You're gaping.*"

He snapped his mouth shut and looked at her with a creased brow. "*Are these pictures supposed to mean . . .*"

"*. . . that they're dealing drugs. Yes.*" That was all she said, and then she had to snap her book shut because the boys were coming out of the family room. She flashed one last vox, "*We have to talk.*"

Will managed to reply, "*Yeah, but when?*" And that was it. The boys were in the room, and it was bedtime, and bedtime at the O'Day's meant you went to your room. You could stay up late and read or write, but no TV or internet after 11 p.m. and no more social time—it was quiet time. Will hadn't talked to her since. But at least she said what he felt: "We have to talk!"

He couldn't stop thinking about her drawings. If they really were doing drug deals in the park, he wondered how he had missed it. Of course, Blue was more or less on her own while they were playing basketball or frisbee or catch, even though she did continue to join in from time to time. When she did, she was pretty good, too, surprisingly good. She moved like lightning and was aggressive. But they could never get her to play for very long. When she was done, she was done. And then she would wander off on her own, and now Will knew where and why.

Will thought it over. Drug dealers in Westbury? It didn't seem possible, but maybe this is just how it starts; two innocent looking people just hanging out in the park. He knew kids at school that smoked pot and drank alcohol, but he couldn't picture that together with "drug dealer." He never thought very much about how they got their pot and booze. He had always figured "a friend of a friend of a friend." Maybe that's who those guys were, friends of friends. He knew he recognized the younger guy from school. A guy named Jack.

Drug dealers. In the park. He just didn't want to believe it. He sighed and stared at the shadowy blankness of his ceiling. The blades of the ceiling fan flitted across his vision, doing their best to push warm air down and around his exposed skin, cooling the spots where his sweat had dripped down and on to the bedspread. His eyes followed the blades as they went around and around and his eyelids grew heavier and heavier. Drugs, drawings, pigs, lizards – they all started dancing around in his head in a swirl, and they would have lulled him down into an uneasy dreamland except a gust of warm air from his window swept his hair across his face and tickled him back alert. God, he thought, I'm never going to get to sleep. He stared back up at the ceiling and tried to empty his mind. He listened to the night noises. The wind had picked up and made a rushing sound in the trees and there was a tapping on his windowsill. It could've been a branch from the bushes outside, but there was something oddly rhythmic about it. And it was accompanied by a *chiss*-like sound. It was like a squirrel was sitting on his windowsill tapping his claws and voxing, "CHT, CHT, CHT . . ." He sat bolt upright. Squirrels didn't vox. He looked at his window. It was a dark night, but something materialized while he stared and when he recognized what it was, he nearly jumped out of his skin. It was a face pressed against the screen.

"ARE YOU GOING TO LET ME IN?" came a wry vox from the window. "OR ARE YOU JUST GOING TO SIT THERE WITH YOUR MOUTH OPEN?"

"Jesus, Blue!" Will hissed in a loud whisper. "What in *hell* are you doing here?" He realized he was sitting there half-naked and started frantically searching for his t-shirt.

The dark head-shaped shadow in the screen tilted in disapproval. "REALLY? YOU WANT TO LET THE WHOLE WORLD KNOW I'M OUT HERE?"

"NO! WELL, MAYBE! JESUS! WHAT WERE YOU EXPECTING? YOU SURPRISED THE HELL OUT OF ME!" His hand landed on his crumpled shirt and he seized it. "YOU SHOULDN'T BE HERE! YOU COULD GET US BOTH IN SO MUCH TROUBLE!" He thrust his arms up through the shirt and heard a rip as he yanked it down over his head.

"*Yeah, tell me about it,*" and she nodded at the window sill. "*Are you going to let me in or not?*"

He hesitated. Letting a girl in his room at night through the window? A little voice in his head was saying "*bad idea, Will!*" but the voice seemed tiny against the regular rock band of other stuff going on inside him. His heart was beating hard, his eyes were still trying to make sense of the film noir scene in front of them, his brain was still making the transition from imaginary little animals dancing in his brain to a very real human standing outside his window.

"*Well, should I leave?*" Blue asked impatiently.

The little voice inside his head reacted in panic, "*Don't you dare! nothing good will come of it!*" Will hesitated, and then stepped over to the window.

"*No, no! I'll let you in. Let's just be careful and quiet.*" He pulled at the catches on the screen and it popped out suddenly causing him to fall back onto his bed still holding the screen. Blue slipped lithely through the open window.

"*So this is your idea of being careful and quiet?*"

He gave her a dirty look and hoped she could see it through the dark. "*You might find this shocking, but I am not used people showing up in my window in the middle of the night!*"

"*Okay, okay. I'm sorry I surprised you,*" voxed Blue. "*Sorta. Kinda. Well, let's face it, I'm having a hard time not laughing.*"

"*Ha. Ha.*" Will set down the screen and tiptoed to his door. He listened carefully. It didn't sound like anyone was stirring. All he could hear was the pounding of his heart. He looked over at Blue. She was sitting cross-legged on the floor below the window as if this was the most normal thing in the world. There was just enough light that he could make out her familiar form. She was wearing black jeans and a dark shirt and her loose dark hair flowed down around a face that had a faint look of amusement on it. He sat down on the bed and let out a long sigh. He wondered if he had breathed at all until that moment.

"*Really, what are you doing here?*" he asked her.

"*I got tired of waiting.*"

"*Waiting for what?*"

She didn't answer. She didn't have to. He didn't even know why he asked it. Here they were. Alone. Finally. Able to converse without looking over their shoulders or hiding anything. All this time trying to find a way to interact, and here it was. So simple, so risky. It was brilliant. They sat without moving for a moment as the warm breeze gusted through the screen-less window carrying the sounds of rustling leaves and the hiss and chirps of the night critters.

Will looked at Blue. "*So how is it going with the O'Days and everything,*" he asked her. His vox voice didn't disturb the night sounds in the least.

Blue didn't reply right away. It seemed like she was choosing what she wanted to say very carefully. "*It is the best situation I have had since . . . in a long time.*" She looked down as if she was embarrassed to confessing a tiny bit of happiness.

"*That's awesome,*" he voxed. "*I guess I'm not surprised. The O'Days have been practically like our extended family—well, for Rose and me, but really mostly for me. Wu is the best friend I've ever had.*"

"*I like Wu,*" voxed Blue. Then she blurted out, "*My other foster brothers were jackasses!*"

Will got caught off guard by Blue's burst of profane honesty, but he also found it refreshing. It was like the ice was melting off of her and a bit of color was shining through.

"*So, not so great at your other foster homes then,*" asked Will.

"*No, not so great,*" she answered. "*And let's leave it at that.*"

"*Fair enough,*" replied Will.

Another pause. This time it was Blue that broke it.

"*What about you, and your family? Can all of them 'hear' like this? Are there others like us? How do you manage to keep it*

SECRET? HOW DO YOU KEEP PEOPLE FROM . . . FROM HATING YOU?" Her questions came out like a dam breaking.

"Wow. Where to start?" voxed Will. "Yeah, my Mom, Dad, and Rose can vox, and so can my grandma and grandpa." Will thought over her questions again and asked "You said 'hear'? Do you mean vox?"

"Yeah. Vox. That's what we . . . what I . . ." she paused. "I mean I wasn't sure if you would call it the same thing. I never knew anyone outside my family."

"Yeah, vox. Vox oculis—you know, 'voice of the eyes'," said Will.

"Vox oculis?"

She sat there quietly.

"You didn't know?" asked Will.

"No. I mean, we just called it vox. My m . . ." she paused again. ". . . We called it the 'voice from your eyes'."

Will thought for a moment. He hadn't really considered that. It seemed so normal to say 'voice of the eyes' but he guessed it could be *from* the eyes. "That would be 'vox oculos', I think. Oculis is accusative, and oculos is ablative, so I guess it could be vox oculos, 'voice from the eyes'."

"What are you talking about? Accusative, ablata . . . blatism, whatever?"

"It's Latin," voxed Will, "I am taking it in school."

Blue was silent. Her shadowed face was deep in thought. Will tried to wait patiently to let her speak next, but he had questions of his own that had been building up all summer. Where was she from? Did she have relatives? How did she wind up here? These questions had been pounding away at him for weeks, but with what had happened recently, he had a more pressing question.

"Blue, these two guys in the park . . . are you sure you aren't imagining it?"

Blue's form instantly became rigid. Her vox shot from the shadows and burst into his brain like a firecracker. "Imagine it?

Jesus! I thought i'd finally found someone that would actually take what I said seriously and not assume I lived in a dream world!"

"*Whoa . . . I didn't mean it that way!"* Will wasn't quite sure what just happened.

She stood up. "*If you didn't mean it that way, why did you say it?"*

"*Jesus Blue! What the hell?"* He felt like he had just been sucker punched. It made him angry. "*Well, maybe I did mean it that way! You hole up in your room for weeks, barely say a word edgewise, and then show up at my window at night, scaring the crap out of me, and then you go nuts when I ask you a reasonable question? If it's not a dream world, exactly what kind of world do you live in?"* His room suddenly felt unbearably hot.

The fierce look that had taken over Blue's face vanished. It looked now like she was fighting an internal battle. It ended with a sigh, "*Okay, I'm sorry. I'm sorry. Just don't . . . don't . . ."* She stopped, as if she'd run out of words. The branches of the trees outside the window clicked and creaked, filling the silence until she said, "*Just listen . . . please."* She sat back down.

Will didn't answer right away. Blue waited patiently, like this was familiar territory to her. He finally said. "*Okay. I'm listening."*

She began, "*It started the first day I went to the park. Do you remember? I pointed those two guys out to you?"*

"*Yeah, I remember that. That was only the second time you voxed to me. You said 'I think not.'"*

In the shadows, Will could see one of Blue's eyebrows rise quizzically. She went on. "*Just before we left I saw Greazal talking to a kid. While they were talking, they swapped a plastic bag for some cash. It was so quick that if I wasn't looking right at them at the exact right time, I wouldn't have seen it. Since then I've been watching them—mostly Greazal. Gronk only comes around every now and then, and I haven't seen him now for a while."*

"GRONK? GREAZEL?"

"DON'T LOOK AT ME LIKE THAT! THEY AREN'T IMAGINARY! IT'S JUST WHAT I CALL THEM. GRONK IS THE OLDER GUY. I DON'T KNOW HIS REAL NAME YET, BUT GREAZAL'S REAL NAME IS JACK. I CALL HIM GREAZEL BECAUSE IT SOUNDS LIKE 'WEASEL.'"

"HOW DO YOU KNOW THAT GRONK IS A DEALER? MAYBE HE'S A CUSTOMER."

"I CAUGHT THEIR CHISS AND THEN JUST PIECED IT TOGETHER . . ." She stopped. "YOU KNOW WHAT I MEAN BY CHISS?"

"YEAH, CHISS, OTHER PEOPLE'S LEAKED THOUGHTS, RIGHT?"

"YEAH." Blue paused, "DON'T YOU THINK IT IS STRANGE THAT WE KNOW THE SAME WORDS? WHY WOULD WE KNOW THAT? DO YOU THINK OUR PARENTS KNEW EACH OTHER? OR OUR GRANDPARENTS?"

Will didn't say anything. The same thought had gone through his mind. His parents had always been kind of vague about their origins. Whenever he asked them about it, they hemmed and hawed and changed the subject so he had given up asking them long ago. But now it was different. They couldn't dodge around this one. Then again, he wasn't sure he wanted to ask it just yet. Blue's vox ability was still a secret, so far.

Blue didn't dwell on it. She went back to her story, "GRONK BASICALLY RECRUITED GREAZAL, BECAUSE HE'S STILL IN HIGH SCHOOL, SO HE CAN SELL THERE EASILY. AND HE'S NOT EIGHTEEN YET, SO EVEN IF HE'S CAUGHT HE'S NOT GOING TO GET IN THAT MUCH TROUBLE. AND HE IS STUPID AND EASY TO MANIPULATE." She added the last bit with contempt. "I DON'T KNOW WHY I STARTED MAKING SKETCHES OF THEM, IT JUST SORT OF HAPPENED."

Will sat there shaking his head. "IT'S CRAZY FOR YOU TO BE SPYING ON THEM. IF THEY ARE DEALERS . . ."

Blue glared at him from the shadows.

"ALL RIGHT, SINCE THEY *ARE* DEALERS," Will continued, "THEY COULD BE DANGEROUS. WHAT IF THEY CAUGHT ON TO YOU? IF YOU'VE BEEN WATCHING THEM THIS LONG, HOW DO YOU KNOW THEY HAVEN'T

NOTICED YOU? HOW COULD YOU GET ALL THIS INFORMATION WITHOUT THEM NOTICING?"

Blue gave Will another unbelieving look. *"YOU'RE KIDDING ME, RIGHT? THESE IDIOTS ARE PRACTICALLY SHOUTING THEIR CHISS. I'D HAVE TO GO OVER AND ASK THEM TO SHUT UP TO NOT EAVESDROP ON THEM, AND THEN THEY'D THINK I WAS A NUTCASE, JUST LIKE EVERYONE ELSE. ARE YOU TELLING ME YOU DON'T EAVESDROP?"*

"WELL, YEAH, BUT WE HAVE SOME PRETTY STRICT RULES IN OUR FAMILY ABOUT EAVESDROPPING ON PEOPLE'S CHISS. I'VE LEARNED TO BLOCK MOST OF THEM," voxed Will. *"WELL, MANY OF THEM,"* he added. He saw her glaring at him. Again. She sure could penetrate the dark with her glares. *"OKAY, I HAVE EAVESDROPPED ON PEOPLE ON PURPOSE, BUT THEY WEREN'T FRIGGING DRUG DEALERS!"*

She stared at him for a moment. *"YEAH, WELL, I DON'T THINK IT'S EAVESDROPPING WHEN YOU'RE TRYING TO KEEP PEOPLE FROM DOING BAD THINGS."*

"WELL, I GUESS THERE'S SOMETHING TO BE SAID FOR THAT," Will admitted. *"SO GRONK DOESN'T SELL ANYTHING? HE JUST GETS GREAZAL TO SELL IT?"*

"GRONK IS THE LEADER, AND HE DEALS HARD STUFF SOMEWHERE ELSE. I HAVEN'T FIGURED OUT WHERE OR HOW YET. GRONK IS TEACHING GREAZAL HOW TO DEAL POT, BUT ONLY POT. NOTHING ELSE. GRONK DOES ALL THE HARD STUFF, AND HE DOESN'T TELL GREAZAL ANYTHING ABOUT IT. HE DOESN'T TRUST GREAZAL YET," voxed Blue.

Will realized he was starting to buy into this story. As Blue was describing it, he started putting some of the pieces together, and it was beginning to make some sense.

"I GUESS THAT WOULD EXPLAIN WHY GRONK HAS BEEN AROUND LESS AND LESS. HE IS LETTING GREAZAL TAKE OVER THE POT-DEALING PART. OR MAYBE JUST THE POT DEALING IN THE PARK. MAYBE HE HAS OTHER 'GREAZALS' DEALING POT OTHER PLACES," Will ventured.

"YEAH, THAT'S POSSIBLE," replied Blue. *"YOU NOTICED THAT GRONK HASN'T BEEN HANGING AROUND AS MUCH? I THOUGHT YOU WEREN'T PAYING ATTENTION."*

"*Yeah, well,*" voxed Will. "*So now what do we do?*"

"*We?*"

"*Yeah, we.*"

There was a long pause before Blue voxed, "*You said you had rules?*" Her tone had softened noticeably.

"*Yeah, pretty simple rules. Rule one is not abusing our ability. Rule two is to keep it a family secret. Talk to no one outside the family about it. Except I am talking to you about it. I don't think rule two applies with you. I don't think Mom and Dad were expecting us to find any other vox outside the family. To tell you the truth, it's pretty weird voxing with someone new. Just voxing with Mom and Dad and Rosie and gram and gramps gets pretty monotonous . . .*" He trailed off. "*Shit, I'm sorry, I guess you . . . I mean . . . has there been anyone?*"

It was as if a dam collapsed when the reply tumbled out of Blue's eyes. "*Nope. Just me. Talking to myself. For four and a half fucking years!*" She looked away from Will as she said it, as if she were directing the bitterness away so it wouldn't hit him. The hot night breeze paused and all the night sounds came to a stop as if hushed by some unseen cue.

You idiot, thought Will. He reached out and gently touched her shoulder. She turned towards him. Her face was still in shadow but he knew she was looking at him. He looked steadily back. "*Hey. You're not alone anymore.*"

Blue really was taking a risk, and she knew it. She used to sneak out at night at her other foster homes and that was one of the reasons she kept getting booted from them. Breaking the rules. But Jesus, she only started doing it because it was the only way she felt like she was free and in control. And some of the situations were really bad, so it wasn't like she had a choice. It was 'stay in and get beat up' or 'get out and get booted'.

But she did not want to risk getting caught when she was staying with the O'Days. She didn't want to lose this family. She had thought long and hard before sneaking out to visit Will.

She got back to her room without incident. No one had locked the door after she had slipped out earlier. A light was on in Wu and Sam's room, but their door was closed. Everyone else was asleep. It was 2 a.m. after all. She sighed in relief of getting back undetected. It was worth it. So worth it. She couldn't believe it took so long for this to happen.

She kept going over and over how fantastic it was to feel normal again. First the basketball game, then the dinner, and then tonight. Will and she had voxed back and forth for over an hour and her head was aching with the effort. She hadn't voxed like that to anyone in . . . in . . . well, ever! She was little when her family was alive and she just voxed childish things. But she hadn't forgotten how—it was just a matter of having someone to listen at last.

And that name! All her life, it was just "vox", but all along, it had been an abbreviation for something more—a scientific name, in Latin. Vox oculis. It sounded so much more . . . real, like it was normal instead of . . . a deformity. A deformity would have been 'vox oculitarianism' or something like that.

Vox oculis. Somehow, having that Latin name gave it legitimacy. Gave *her* legitimacy. And Will knew the same words she did: "*chiss, vox.*" That meant they had to have a common background some-where—common ancestors or community. But when? Where? She knew nothing of her ancestry—did Will know his?

These questions and so many more were buzzing around in her brain—she thought she was never going to fall asleep, but the next thing she knew, the sun was shining, and she opened her eyes and felt that she had slept better than she had in a lifetime.

Will couldn't sleep. He sat at his window and listened to the soft warm breeze as it rustled its way through the leaves and branches and fences and rooftops. He was still electrified with what had just happened. The long anticipation of what it would be like to vox to someone new, someone outside his family, someone with such a different background. It was unlike anything he had expected. Blue had been so tight up until now—stiff, controlled. But tonight, it was like there was an entirely different person living underneath. It was like he had met "Blue Two." She was emotional, intelligent, explosive, expressive, and a little foul-mouthed. She didn't act like she was only fourteen. She seemed to have the poise of a . . . what, sixteen-year-old? twenty-year-old? Age didn't seem to be the right measure. It was more like she had the poise of a veteran soldier. Was there an age for that?

It was a little intimidating. Next to Blue, he felt naive and overprotected. It seemed like his life could have been a little harder and made him a little stronger, like she seemed to be. She even had the guts to sneak out in the middle of the night and slip into his house. There was no way he would've done anything like that.

He asked her how she had managed to get in and out of the O'Day's house undetected. She didn't brag or explain, she just said matter-of-factly, *"I'LL TEACH YOU."* Will was more than willing. It seemed risky, but that is exactly what he felt his life needed right now. They had agreed to meet again in a couple of nights. She would come to his window again, but this time, he would slip outside with her, and she would start teaching him. She told him to wear dark clothes that covered all of his skin. They didn't need to be black, just dark enough that they wouldn't stand out if a light shined on them.

The wind picked up and made a swirling sound in his screen. His brain was swirling, too. He looked at his clock. 3 a.m. and it felt like 3 p.m. He finally got up and started going through his drawers and looking for the best clothes for camouflage. He didn't even turn on his light—he just used the faint illumination from the lone distant streetlight to rummage through his clothes. He picked out some black pants and shirt and tried them on. He tilted his mirror, so he could see himself against the background of his room. He went back and forth into the shadows—out of them, and back again. The black was best in the darkest shadows, but it actually stood out a little against a lighter background. He pulled out some lighter clothes and tried them on. He kept going until almost every item in his dresser and closet were scattered through his room. He noticed that it was getting brighter in his room and when he looked out of his window, he was surprised to see the early pink of dawn. The sight of it triggered a yawn so immense, he thought for a moment that his face would split. He leaned back and collapsed onto the pile of clothes lying on his bed. It felt like a cozy nest. He turned on his side, tucked his legs up and snuggled into the pile. It was so comfortable he decided he was going to make his bed that way every night. That was the last thought that went through his head as his eyelids slid down and dimmed out the brightening dawn as it swelled into the eastern sky.

15

NIGHT STALKERS

Will sat in the grass, one hand rubbing his forehead on a spot where he was sure he was going to have a nice bruise by morning. He leaned back against the tree that had just whacked him in the head with a gnarly branch, though he supposed it was really the other way around.

"*I don't know if I am going to survive this,*" he voxed into the darkness.

"*Yeah, I agree,*" came the reply. "*You move like a sack of rocks.*"

"*Thanks for the encouragement,*" he voxed. This was the third time they had met since the first night Blue had shown up in his window a couple of weeks earlier. It had been exhilarating, being out at night, without permission, picking their way around the neighborhood without being seen, exploring the dark. Blue moved with stunning skill. Her footsteps were completely silent and the way she flicked from shadow to shadow, he began to wonder if she wasn't a ghost. She tried to teach him to move the same way and Will had picked up some things, but he discovered a baffling problem. In the dark, he had the balance of a dog on a hockey rink. It was ridiculous because he had some really deft moves on the basketball court. It was like the darkness had sucked away all his balance.

"IT'S BECAUSE YOUR VISUAL REFERENCE IS TAKEN AWAY."

Will stared at the dark silhouette that Blue's head created, like a hole in the night. If he didn't know better, he'd swear she just read his mind, for real. There was no way he leaked those thoughts out of his eyes.

"SO WHAT DO I DO?" he asked.

She didn't answer right away, she just stared at him, or at least it seemed that way—it was hard to tell with her face so deep in the shadows. After a moment she voxed, "MOVE LIKE A CAT."

"WHAT?"

"I SAID, MOVE LIKE A CAT."

"A CAT HAS FOUR LEGS!" he voxed back.

"USE YOUR IMAGINATION! THINK LIKE A CAT—BE A CAT. AND THEN MOVE LIKE ONE!"

"IMAGINE A CAT STANDING ON TWO LEGS? THAT DOESN'T MAKE ANY SENSE." He tried to imagine a cat standing on two legs. It kept falling over.

"YOU'RE THINKING TOO HARD ABOUT IT. JUST PRETEND . . . YOU'RE A CAT! DON'T THINK ABOUT IT! HONESTLY, YOU OVER ANALYZE EVERY-THING." She sounded exasperated.

He didn't say anything. He realized that he suddenly felt tired and irritated.

Blue continued, "THAT'S ANOTHER THING, YOUR LIGHT HAIR SHOWS UP TOO MUCH. YOU SHOULD WEAR A CAP. A DARK CAP."

"ANYTHING ELSE I'M MISSING AS LONG AS WE ARE LISTING ALL MY FAULTS?" he asked, half sarcastically.

"YOU NEED SOMETHING TO HIDE YOUR FACE, TOO. YOUR PALE CHEEKS SHOW UP TOO MUCH."

He rolled his eyes and wondered if she could see it. She didn't seem to be getting the hint. "IT'S NOT LIKE YOU AREN'T MISS PALE-FACE."

"I'VE GOT LONG DARK HAIR TO COVER MY FACE."

"*So, what are you suggesting, that I wear a cat mask?*" This time he didn't hold back on the sarcasm.

Blue ignored him. Her shadow shrunk low as she leaned down, apparently reaching for something on the ground. He heard her spit and the next thing he knew he felt something slimy being smeared on his cheeks.

He jerked back. "*Jesus! What the hell are you doing?*"

"*Don't be a wuss,*" she said. "*I'm just putting some dirt on your face.*"

"*With your spit!?*"

"*Hold still!*"

He felt her fingers slime more dirt on. He pulled away again. This time she let him. Her silhouette head tilted back and forth, considering her work. He rubbed some of the dirt off. It felt gooey. "*God that's gross.*"

"*Not bad,*" she voxed. "*But ashes would be better.*"

"*Ashes? And spit? This just keeps getting better and better.*"

"*Don't be stupid. You don't need spit when you use ashes.*"

He wiped away as much as he could but as the remaining dirt dried, it made a crusty coating on his cheeks that crackled if he moved. "*I'm not sure I'm up for this anymore. I mean, what's the point anyway if I can't balance in the dark?*"

Blue put her hand up to her mouth and stared at him. Her finger tapped her cheek thoughtfully.

"*Try this. Every time you are standing around, lift one foot, close your eyes and balance,*" she voxed. "*And walk around with your eyes closed. I practice walking around the house with my eyes closed all the time. And I don't just walk around, I do other things, like getting out my toothbrush and toothpaste, and brushing my teeth all with my eyes closed. It makes you work to remember where everything is.*"

"*Doesn't everyone give you strange looks when you're doing that?*" asked Will.

She looked down. "Strange looks are about all I get any time."

She picked up a small stick and started poking at the ground absent-mindedly. "I don't much care what anyone thinks about what I do anymore," she said.

Will didn't say anything for a moment. He couldn't stay irritated with her. She was well-meaning in her own way. And he was actually having probably one of the best times of his life sneaking out at night with her. "Well, I care," he said at last. "I think it's cool, you trying to teach me, and all."

Blue just kept poking away at the ground.

"Why did you to learn this stuff in the first place?" he asked.

"I had to," she said, still not looking up.

"You had to?"

There was a short silence before Blue's reply. "I don't want to talk about it." She stood up abruptly and started walking away.

"Hey! Wait up!" He jumped up after her.

Blue didn't look back, she just kept moving, but she slowed down. Will kept pace with her but gave her space. She wasn't trying to stay concealed anymore. She just walked like she didn't care. They reached the O'Day hedge. She stopped but didn't look at Will.

It was making him uncomfortable that they were just standing there out in the open. It wasn't likely that anyone in the house would see them, but if they did, these little excursions really would be over. And who knows what would happen to Blue.

"Blue, we should at least get out of the light," he whispered.

She turned to him, the slanting shadows highlighting a face with a complete lack of emotion, as if her brain was too busy to bother updating her expression.

"Hey. You okay?"

Her face woke up just a little and looked at him as if it just remembered he was there.

"I'm fine! Just go home," she voxed in a flat tone. She turned away again as if to go and then abruptly turned back. She glanced up at him, the stony look on her face gone and replaced with something that looked more alive. She started to say something, then stopped, paused and put her hand on his chest. "*JUST PRACTICE,*" she voxed softly. It was less than what she was going to say, he could tell, but exactly what she was going to say was still too much for him to guess.

Without another word she turned and slipped through the bushes and across the yard. Whatever had been going on inside her, she had shaken it off because she moved exactly like a cat over to the trellis on the end of the O'Day house. She climbed the trellis like a squirrel and slipped into the half-open window on the second floor.

He shook his head half in exasperation and half in admiration. He wasn't quite sure what to make of her. Sneaking out with her had been fun and exciting, but it was like walking on eggshells around her sometimes. Some things just set her off. Especially when he asked her about her past. But her past is what he wanted to know, for God's sake. He'd been like an open book to her about his. The only thing he knew for certain about her past was that a lot of demons seemed to be lurking there.

Blue stared at the ceiling above her bed trying to get a grasp on the jumble of thoughts in her head, but each time she focused on one, another would nudge it out of the way like a room full of noisy puppy dogs nosing for attention. She sighed and rolled onto her side and stared at the shadows dancing on her dresser from the dim cast of the waxing moon shining through the trees outside her window. They were fuzzy and complex, just like her thoughts. She had shut Will down when he asked her about why she started sneaking out. And she felt bad about it and that confused her. Why should she care about how he felt? These damn caring feelings were happening an awful lot lately.

She tried to think about something less confusing She thought about how clumsy Will was and how hard he was trying. He had run straight into that branch and plopped right onto his butt. And she had giggled. Actually giggled. It felt so strange. She tried to remember the last time a giggle had escaped her lips. It sounded so girly yet she didn't mind. Maybe it was because it was the first time she was with someone who wouldn't judge. Will accepted her for who she was. A really decent guy. When she had shut him down, he had even asked her if she was okay. He acted as if he cared. God, there it was again, caring feelings!

The problem was they felt good. They comforted her. Comfort, care, care, comfort. It was like a soft chant that drowned out the other crazy thoughts. She realized these thoughts were relaxing her. Sleepiness started to creep up on her. She welcomed it, pushing off her instinctive built-in wariness that she should never relax. Relaxing meant letting her guard down. Letting her guard down always led to bad things. The problem was, it hadn't lately. And relaxing felt so good. Yet the wariness remained there, like a tired old guard that was starting to feel like his usefulness was outgrown but still had a duty to stand his station. "Just sleep tonight, Mr. Wariness," thought Blue as she settled her head in her pillow and pulled the covers up around her like a soft cocoon. "Just sleep." And he did, and she did—a sweet peaceful sleep.

And that's when it returned—her night demon. She thought she had seen the last of it years ago, but here it was creeping up on her in a way that was far too familiar. She was asleep, but aware she was asleep and dreaming. It was always vivid, one of those dreams you swear was real, but this one was terrifying and the terror always seized her in a suffocating grip and never allowed her to wake up until the entire dream had played itself out, leaving her feeling shipwrecked. Shipwrecked on the shores of morning. It was like living through death.

In the early days after the fire, when she was out of control and when she suffered the first visits of this night demon, she was glad of the sedatives they had given her. Those were the only thing that seemed to quell the nightmare. But it wasn't long before the sedatives themselves started wreaking their own havoc on her sanity. She was sleepy and dizzy all the time, and she started seeing things, dreaming during the daytime. They very soon had to take her off the sedatives. However, to her relief, the dream had stopped, at least for a while. It stayed away until, in her first foster home, it came back. That time she hid it from everyone, because she didn't want to go back on the horrible sedatives.

At first she tried to change something in the dream in order to change the outcome. Instead of changing the outcome, however, something new and horrible would happen, but the ending was always the same. Then, for a while, she tried to hide *in* the dream, so she wouldn't see what happened. It didn't matter. No matter what she did, she knew that the story was going to end the same. She knew it was a dream, but it was a memory, too, and she couldn't change what was real. It had to play itself out with the same ending every time.

This time, however, she was ready. She had changed a lot since the last time it came. Her world was finally stable. This time she was going to accept it for what it was—a very bad memory. She had grown out of it now, she was confident. She had to accept the past. Still, once the dream had started, she knew she had to let it play out to the end.

It started the same way every time. She and her father, outside after dinner playing night-tag. It was the week of her tenth birthday. Her mother and little sister were inside washing dishes—it was Heather's turn to help and Blue's turn to play. She heard a soft, "*Coo coo! Coo coo!*" It was her father's call. The game was that one person would hide, but they would call with their voice—their *vox* —and the other person would try to find them. Because of how their vox reflected off of so many things, it was a game of ventriloquism—make your vox come from a tree, or the greenhouse, or the pond. It was great fun. He called again, "*Coo coo! Coo coo! Come fiiiind meeee!*" It seemed like it was from the greenhouse, but Blue had been fooled by that too many times. She knew it was reflecting from someplace opposite the greenhouse. She started tip-toeing toward the bushes across from the greenhouse.

Just as she started to move, she heard a car and she turned to look down their long twisting driveway. She could see headlights weaving slowly through the trees. Her Dad came out of the darkness and stood quietly beside her, just like he had done in the dream a dozen times before.

Her conscious mind tried to be indifferent to the dream, knowing that it didn't matter. She knew who was in the car coming up the driveway and she knew what her father was going to say. She would try to run away before he said it, but that changed nothing, and then she tried warning him, but he didn't listen. This time she just waited for him to say the words.

He turned to her and started to speak. She looked up at him, waiting for the words. But for the first time, the dream had changed. It wasn't her father looking down at her.

It was Will.

A searing hot wave of panic surged through her. She screamed —that is, she opened her mouth, but nothing came out. She tried to vox, but it was silent. She did everything to keep the words from coming, but they came anyway. They were her father's words, only in Will's *voice*. "YOU STAY PUT HERE, LITTLE BLUEBELL. BE QUIET AS A MOUSE, AND STAY HIDDEN! YOU KNOW HOW! I'LL COME GET YOU AS SOON AS THESE PEOPLE ARE GONE. NOW LOOK AT ME." He held her chin in his hand—she tried not to look but it was part of the script, she had to look. She always looked. She needed to—to get that last glimpse of her father. It was the last time she would see his face. Only this time it was Will's face. "YOU HAVE TO STAY HIDDEN NO MATTER WHAT! PROMISE ME THIS. PROMISE!" He looked her straight in the eyes with the eyes that only those who can vox have, and she nodded as she knew she had to. And he went to meet the car.

She could feel she was drenched with sweat and she tried to wake up, but she couldn't. She knew what came next and she was afraid of what she would see, because she knew this dream was different, so much different than before. But her role didn't change, she was powerless to prevent herself from going through the same motions. She looked toward the door of their house and she saw her mother and sister standing there, as she knew they would be, looking out the door and, curious to see who was coming. But father—Will—shooed them back inside. She saw their faces as they turned into the light to go back inside, but the faces didn't belong to her mother and her sister this time.

This time, the shock was so absolute, she couldn't stay asleep. Even though the dream had not played out to the end, it had already surpassed itself in its devilishness, and it willingly released her. She woke up with a gasp, unable to take a breath, her arms pushing her away from her bed and her back arched in a spasm of shock. Her pajamas were soaked, her sheets were soaked, and her head was dripping with sweat. She felt the scream welling up from the deepest darkest part of her, and she plunged her face into her pillow before it could escape. The scream slammed into the pillow as she clutched it to her face desperately. She was terrified that someone would hear her. She nearly suffocated herself to keep from being heard but she couldn't stop. She rocked back and forth shouting, "NO! NO! NO! NO!" into the pillow, demanding that the vision leave her head. But the faces wouldn't leave.

They were the faces of Ma Beth and Rose.

16

———

LAB DISCOVERY

Will had trouble dragging himself out of bed the next morning. He and Blue must have been out until about 2 a.m. so he'd gotten five hours of sleep, max. And this morning was a work morning. His mom kept having to nudge him to wake him up.

"Come on kid, time to get up and at 'em," she said, giving him a push with her foot, for the third time.

"Uh . . . did I fall asleep again? I'm coming, I'm coming. Just five more minutes . . ." replied Will in a groggy voice.

"Not this time, Mister. You've had your five minutes. Twice. Now get up! Honestly what has gotten into you the past week? You've been oversleeping almost every morning!" His mom felt his forehead. "*No fever, so no skipping work. C'mon, your father's waiting.*"

Will managed to pull his clothes on, drag himself to the bathroom, stuff some breakfast down, and flop into the passenger seat of his dad's car.

His dad didn't seem to notice Will's lethargy, and he launched excitedly into talking about what they were going to do today. "Will, I think you're going to find this incredibly interesting. I've been waiting for an opportunity to experiment with this for a long time but never had the funding to do it. That and the technology has gotten more affordable and with my grant money, I'm finally able to do it. I've just received an infrared night vision camera for my research and, well . . . you'll just have to see for yourself. It's one of those things that you can explain and theorize about, and then one day you think of a way to visualize it and *boom*, there you go. It is so obvious! They say a picture can paint a thousand words, and it is true . . ." He trailed off as he appeared to slip deep into thought.

This outburst of speech brought Will out of his stupor, "Whoa, whoa Dad, slow down. What are you talking about? Night vision camera? But we don't have night vision—not really, just infrared voice . . . eyes . . . vox oculis. What is it you are talking about?"

"Well, my 'official' research actually *is* about night vision and other types of vision, but for us, for vox, well you'll just have to see!" said his dad.

<hr>

The night vision camera *was* very cool. It had an infrared illuminator—like a night vision flashlight—on top of what looked like a small telescope, only with buttons and switches like a camera.

"Is this a telescope or camera or a flashlight?" asked Will.

"All of the above," said his dad. "It has lenses like a telescope, but instead of the light going to your eye, it goes to a video sensor that then turns the light into an image and displays it on a tiny screen inside the eyepiece, which you look through like a camera. The sensors can detect not only visible light but short infrared, too. . . the same sort of light that our eyes use for vox oculis."

"You mean you can see the light in our eyes?" said Will.

His dad smiled. "See for yourself. Just flick the red switch on the side, and look through the camera and focus on me, but don't turn on the flashlight part." Then his dad moved to stand opposite him.

Will turned the switch on. A slight glow came from the eyepiece as the internal screen lit up. He looked through the eyepiece at the screen and then pointed the camera at his dad.

At first, he didn't notice anything except that the image in the screen was sort of off-color—more like a black and white image than a regular color image. He pointed it at his dad's face and focused on his eyes. They looked normal but then suddenly they flashed bright and Will heard in his head a strange chopped up vox "*C..A..R..P..E..D..I..E..M.*" He nearly dropped the camera.

"Holy crap! Dad!"

His dad started chuckling. "Cool, eh?"

"Oh my God! Do it again!" He held up the night vision camera once again. This time, when the flash came he heard "*T..E..M..P..U..S..F..U..G..I..T.*" He put the camera down. "Dad, this is incredible! No one has ever tried this before?"

"Well, no one that I know of," said his dad, "And I think I know every one of our kind that has studied this."

"So why does your vox sound all chopped up? How did you do that?" asked Will.

"Well, it's because this camera wasn't designed for sound, it was designed for images," said his dad.

"I don't get it. Why would that make a difference? Isn't sound simpler to capture than images?" asked Will.

"That is a very keen observation, and that is indeed true. But an interesting thing about our vision is that it responds slower than our ears. Our brain can only process images at about 40 images per second, but it can process sounds coming to our ears at up to 20,000 cycles per second! You see, this camera only captures light at 40 frames per second, but our eyes vox sound signals at much higher frequencies. You can only hear very low-frequency vox through the camera, which is why I said 'carpe diem' very low and slow."

"So you're saying that we can only hear really low vox tones through this, but it can still capture the infrared light?"

"I know it seems complicated, but basically, yes that is correct.

Our eyes glow, but they change brightness like your vocal cords change sound pressure to make sound. That's what our eyes can detect—the very subtle high-frequency changes in light. That is what was lost in almost everyone else around us—the ability to detect and process those subtle changes."

"But why would people keep the ability to *chiss* but not hear it?" asked Will.

"That's a very good question, and I don't know the answer, just like I don't know the answer to a lot of things. But I do know this: it is very easy to make sounds, however, hearing is a much more difficult proposition. Vocal cords are very simple organs, but ears are enormously more complex and delicate. I think the same goes for vox. It is easy to create light—just like a firefly or deep-sea fishes, but detecting light and processing it into images or sound is a very complex process. Your eyes are probably the most amazing part of your body, in terms of advanced sensing biotechnology. If you did not use your eyes, then your body would probably put its energy into better things rather than maintain a complex organ that is useless, just as deep-sea fishes still have eyes, but have lost the ability to see. They don't need their eyes in the pitch blackness of the ocean floor."

"So you are saying that people still need their eyes for vision, but they don't need them for vox anymore, so their eyes have evolved to be just vision, and the vox part has just atrophied into glowing, but not listening? Sort of like an appendix?" asked Will.

His dad just stared at him. "Wow, son, that was amazing. You hit the nail on the head. I couldn't have put it better myself."

Will felt himself blush. The technology was starting to make sense to him now, though. "Dad, can non-vox discover us with this camera? Don't they use night vision cameras for surveillance?"

"I thought about that. I imagine they could, but I think they would mistake it for something else. You know what 'red-eye' is in photography, right? It's when the camera's flash illuminates your retina because of its close proximity to the camera lens."

"Sure, but red-eye happens to everyone, not just us, right?"

"True. The flash illuminates the retina of the eye, and the eye is focused on the camera, so the camera receives a magnified image of the retina of your eye. I think if anyone does see us in a surveillance camera, they would just assume it was some sort of red-eye effect. Fortunately, there is no camera that I know of that is designed to pick up modulated infrared light and amplify it into sound. Just like this camera, there wouldn't be enough information there for them to decode it into anything."

His dad went into deep thought again, which was fine with Will. He was starting to find it hard to follow what his dad was saying. But he was starting to go into deep thought, too, and he had an idea.

"Dad, can I borrow this camera sometime, just to see what it can do? It would be cool to just see what infrared light there is around us." Will wasn't very hopeful. The camera looked expensive, and his dad had just gotten it and was probably anxious to start experimenting with it himself. So he was surprised when his dad was actually agreeable.

"Why not? Sharing a discovery is part of the fun. But take pictures of interesting things you see with it. That is part of research, collecting interesting things you might want to study later. Remember, we are still looking for sources of infrared light. And I don't have to tell you to take good care of it. Just make sure it comes back to the lab in the morning in good condition." "*Use, don't abuse the privilege!*"

Platitudes, platitudes. That was a Latin word Will was overly familiar with, but he was ecstatic about being able to borrow the night vision camera. And he was even more excited to see what Blue's reaction would be.

17

FIELD DISCOVERIES

As soon as he and his dad got back from work, Will slipped down the block and put up his signal. He and Blue had worked out a system so they didn't have to pass notes or call and risk giving away their secret meetings. Will would jam an old plastic Smurf doll in the crotch of a tree across the street from the O'Days where it couldn't be seen from the street but could be seen from Blue's window. Blue would pick it up and bring it back to him at their rendezvous. Blue's signal was a little plaster garden gnome in the yard. She would turn it so it was facing sideways when viewed from the sidewalk whenever she wanted to meet. She would turn it back after their rendezvous.

He reached their rendezvous tree a little early and hoped she showed up, given the short notice. They didn't usually do back-to-back nights but tired as he was, he was amped up about the IR camera and figured she would get amped up about it, too. He didn't have to wait for more than a minute before a Smurf flew out of the dark and plopped on the ground at his feet. Blue materialized out of the dark like she usually did but there was something wrong about it. She didn't glide in and vox *"Hey"* like she usually did. Instead, she crept up to him slowly, staring at him warily, and then sat down a good two arm lengths away. She didn't say or vox a single thing. It was exactly as if she were approaching a wild animal she wasn't sure would bite or not. Will wasn't quite sure what to say, so he just said what he usually said.

"*Hey.*"

She didn't reply. She just kept staring at him. He felt off balance. Then he remembered why they were here. "*Uh . . . Hey,*" he began again. "*Uh, I wasn't sure you would get the Smurf.*" He paused to see her reaction. It was kind of a joke between them and she would usually reply with a sardonic grin and, "*ba-dum-dum-dah,*" but tonight her face remained motionless in stony silence. There wasn't much else he could do except keep going. "*I know it's risky to meet again so soon, but my dad got this infrared camera for his lab. I really thought you'd like to check it out. You won't believe what you can see with this thing.*" He held up the camera for her to see. He felt like he was coaxing a stray dog to befriend him by holding out a treat. She cautiously scooted close enough so she could take it from him, but then she scooted right back.

"*The controls are on the side.*" He stepped over to her and reached out to the camera. "*I'll turn it on and then you can look through the eyepiece. The focus is right here.*" She stiffened as he reached out, but she let him work the switch on the side of the camera. Her movements, her attitude, everything was screaming that something had happened and he had no clue to what it was. Was it him? Was it that tension from last night?

Blue examined the camera. She was still dead quiet, but appeared to relax as she turned the camera all around, studying its features with interest. She put the camera up to her face and started looking around her. Then she turned it towards Will's face. She started fiddling with the focus and leaned forward and back. He felt like he was on an examining table. Then she spoke for the first time that night. Her voice was flat and expressionless, but edged with a tinge of curiosity.

"Have you actually looked at vox eyes with this?" Blue asked out loud. With the camera held up to her face, she looked like a cyborg.

"Yeah, I looked at my dad's eyes while he voxed," replied Will. "Are you ready? I'll vox something . . ."

"No, wait! That's not what I meant. I meant your iris. Just keep looking at me with your eyes as wide as you can." There was a little excitement of discovery in her voice.

"What is it you see?" asked Will.

Blue didn't answer right away. She was concentrating on something. Finally, she voxed, *"HERE, SEE FOR YOURSELF,"* and she handed him the camera. *"ONLY DON'T TOUCH THE CONTROLS AND STAY ABOUT AS FAR AWAY AS WE ARE NOW. I HAVE IT ZOOMED IN AND FOCUSED AS CLOSE AS IT WILL GO."* Blue opened her eyes wide and looked at Will as he put the camera up to his eye.

For a second he fiddled with getting her eyes in view. Then he took a good look. What he saw caused him to take in a sharp breath. Her iris was highlighted by a very thin ring that surrounded it with a very faint luminescence. The iris itself had a deep, fibrous texture to it, and the luminous ring provided just enough illumination to give it a startling three-dimensional look.

"Whoa." That was all his brain came up with. Whoa. He lowered the camera. *"DO YOU THINK EVERYONE'S EYES LOOK LIKE THAT OR JUST OURS?"* he asked.

"I DON'T KNOW. I'VE NEVER USED A CAMERA LIKE THIS BEFORE." She looked thoughtful for a moment. *"LET ME SEE YOUR EYES WHEN YOU VOX."*

Will handed the camera back. She took it and held it up to her eye and Will looked straight at the lens and voxed low and slow, *"TEMPUS FUGIT."* She gasped. Will laughed.

"Again!" she said emphatically.

"CARPE DIEM! WASTE NOT A MOMENT! USE DON'T ABUSE! WHEN THE GOING GETS WEIRD, THE WEIRD GET GOING!" Will stopped and said, "Should I go on?"

Blue lowered the camera, her mouth open in amazement. *"I*

CAN'T BELIEVE IT . . ." She sat there in silence looking not at him, but at something far far away.

Will broke the silence, "IT'S AMAZING, ISN'T IT? I MEAN YOU CAN SEE IT—WHAT OUR EYES ARE DOING."

"IT'S REAL," voxed Blue. "I MEAN IT'S NOT MAGIC OR TELEPATHY OR MENTAL ILLNESS. IT'S A REAL THING, JUST LIKE HAVING BLUE EYES INSTEAD OF BROWN EYES, OR DARK HAIR INSTEAD OF BLONDE."

"OR HAVING A TAIL OR WINGS OR GILLS. YOU JUST CAN'T SEE IT," voxed Will. "AT LEAST NOT WITHOUT THIS CAMERA. THERE MIGHT BE ANIMALS THAT CAN, THOUGH. MY DAD SAID THERE ARE LOTS OF DIFFERENT EYES, LIKE A FLY'S EYES OR A BIRD'S EYES OR FOX EYES. THEY ALL HAVE DIFFERENT TYPES OF RODS AND CONES AND TAPETUM."

"WHAT'S TAPETUM?" asked Blue.

"IT'S, LIKE, A SPECIAL LINING IN THE EYE. THAT'S WHAT WE'RE STUDYING NOW IN DAD'S LAB. HE THINKS WE HAVE A TAPETUM THAT LETS US VOX. THAT'S WHAT YOU SEE . . . OUR TAPETUM GLOWING. HE CALLS IT LUCET A RETINA WHICH MEANS 'LIGHT FROM THE RETINA.'" replied Will.

"BUT NORMAL PEOPLE CHISS, SO THEY MUST HAVE THIS . . . TAPETUM . . . OR WHATEVER . . . LIKE OURS. SO WHY CAN'T THEY HEAR VOX?"

"THAT'S THE RODS AND CONES. THE RODS AND CONES ARE CELLS IN YOUR RETINA THAT CAN DETECT COLOR AND LIGHT. HE'S PRETTY SURE THAT WE HAVE DIFFERENT CONES THAT LETS US DETECT THE GLOWING OF OUR TAPETUM."

Blue had moved closer to Will, his wild animal aura apparently wearing off. She was acting more like she had the past few weeks, as if the weird start to the evening had never happened.

"WHAT ABOUT WHEN WE'RE NOT LOOKING RIGHT AT EACH OTHER?" voxed Blue.

"YOU MEAN CAN THE CAMERA SEE US AT AN ANGLE?"

She nodded, then stood up and pointed the camera at him. "STAND UP AND TURN AROUND SLOWLY WHILE YOU'RE VOXING."

They discovered that they didn't have to be looking directly at the camera in order for it to detect the glow of their eyes. They could still see it even when they looked to either side of the camera, though it was fainter.

"*So that must be why we don't have to be looking right at each other in order to pick up vox. It's like our whole retina is glowing,*" voxed Will

"*Yeah, but what about when we're not looking at each other at all?*" voxed Blue.

"*You mean reflections?*"

"*Yeah. If we can hear reflected vox, this camera should be able to see it.*" Blue looked around searching for something and then said, "*There.*" She pointed to a park trash can about ten feet away.

Will looked where she was pointing and then heard, "*Can you hear me?*"

He voxed back, looking at the trash can, "*Yeah. Can you hear me?*"

She didn't answer. She just held the night vision camera up to her face and said, "*Okay, now do it again.*"

He did his signature "*click, click, click.*"

"*I could see that!*" she said, without lowering the camera. "*Do it again but say something different.*"

Will recited, "*On the shores of Gitche Gumee, Of the shining Big-Sea-Water . . .*"

Blue lowered the camera and looked at Will. "*So why is it garbled? It sounds like you are underwater.*"

"*My dad says it's the camera — it chops vox all up*" He held out his hand for the camera. She gave it to him and he pointed it at the trash can. "*My turn.*"

He looked through the camera and then heard the strangest thing in his head. It was like folk music coming from a bad radio connection, like some sort of static-y techno-pop. "What the . . . are you singing?" He lowered the camera and stared at her. The static caused by the camera was gone, and what played in his head was clear and amazing, "*. . . So, we'll go no more a roving, so late into*

THE NIGHT . . ." It was an almost perfect imitation of a famous old folk singer. Of all the things that had happened over the last 24 hours, this had to be about the most astonishing.

"*Don't tell me you've never done that,*" she voxed. "*Sing, that is.*"

"*Well yeah, but not like that! Where'd you learn to do that?*" He immediately regretted it as soon as he said it. Her face went dead. Dammit, Woods, why do you keep doing that, he thought. He was waiting for her to stand up and stalk away again like she did last night.

She didn't. She had heard him, he could tell. But then she seemed to shake it off.

"*We ought to be able to see chiss with this.*" She nodded toward the camera.

Will raised an eyebrow. "*There's probably some couples down in the park on a night like tonight,*" he replied. As Will watched for her response, a buzz of excitement crept up his spine because her face had taken on that same look that first tickled the latent adventure gene inside him. It was her dark hair hanging loosely about her clean features, her mouth tweaked up into that slight half-grin with just a hint of a dimple, and her eyes peering up from under a brow that was pinched down in a devilish way that signaled that something interesting was about to happen.

Without another word, they slid off silently in tandem down to the park. They went to the spot where they knew couples liked to hang out at this time of night. The first couple they spotted turned out to be a waste of time. Their eyes were closed and their faces were suction-cupped together and it looked like it would be a while before they would be unstuck. Will and Blue moved on to another favored spot and discovered a couple that was just sitting and talking quietly.

They found a good spot behind a bush and peered at the couple. Will had a good view of the girl's eyes and he picked up some whispers of *chiss*. What he heard instantly turned his ears blazing. He heard a little gasp and looked over at Blue who had clapped her hand over her mouth. She clearly picked it up, too. They looked at each other uneasily.

"Well, she sure is a leaker," Will voxed.

Blue looked like she was going to choke. "Stop it! I'm going to lose it if you say anything more! Use the camera!"

He put the camera up to his eye. He could see the girl's eyes glow ever so slightly, but couldn't make out the *chiss* through the camera. What came through was just too weak and chopped up.

"I saw the girls eyes. They had a faint glow, but nothing like us. Take a look."

Blue shook her head.

"Don't worry, I couldn't make out her chiss, the camera chops it up too much."

Blue took the camera and pointed it at the couple, but just as she did, their mouths docked and their eyes disappeared.

"Damn I just saw them for a second. I saw a little glow but didn't make out anything." voxed Blue. "How can we hear anything at all from them? I could barely make out any glow."

"My dad said that eyes can see a single photon—the smallest amount of light possible."

"A single photon? But how bright is a single photon?"

"Umm, I'm not actually sure. Not very, though. Probably like the faintest star you can see."

They both sat thoughtfully for a while. The fatigue from the previous late night seemed to have melted away. Will didn't feel like going back just yet. He wondered what else they could try with the camera.

"I wonder if this can see security cameras," voxed Will.

"Security cameras give off infrared light?" she asked.

"Not exactly. Most security cameras use an IR illuminator."

"IR illuminator?"

"Yeah. It's like an infrared flashlight. This camera has one, too."

He flicked the switch for the illuminator but had to double check because it wasn't obvious by just looking at it that the illuminator was actually on. He handed the camera to Blue.

Blue put the camera up to her eye and after a moment whispered, "*Wow, the illuminator really lights things up.*" She lowered the camera again. "*No one would notice our eyes or reflections with this thing on, it's too bright.*"

Will tried out the camera with the illuminator on. "*Yeah, this is pretty amazing. Might make stalking a lot easier, except you can only see a narrow spot.*"

"*But you can take pictures and videos with this thing, right?*" voxed Blue. Her voice had a sudden intensity to it.

"*Yeah . . . and?*" voxed Will.

"*That seems pretty useful, that's all,*" she replied.

"*Useful for what?*" asked Will.

Blue hesitated, and then said, "*Nothing.*" She moved away from him and that weird vibe from the beginning of the evening came back. Will had a sense that she was retreating back into that tight, impenetrable private world of hers. She was silent for a long time. When she finally replied, it was with a flat, business-like tone.

"*I need to borrow the camera,*" she voxed.

Will was floored. "*Blue, this isn't something you can just borrow. I was lucky my dad even let me bring it home for one night!*"

"*I need to borrow it,*" she said again.

"*What for?*"

She didn't answer, she just gave him that wary stare.

"*That's a pretty big favor to ask,*" he voxed.

Blue just kept looking at him.

Will shook his head, partly in frustration and partly in admiration of how single-minded she became when she lapsed into one of these moods. "*Alright, I will ask my dad if you can borrow it sometime, but I don't expect he'll say yes.*"

"*Thanks,*" voxed Blue.

And that was that. She was gone, her thoughts securely hidden behind the castle walls she had built in her mind. They walked silently back to the O'Day house, not exactly together – she walked like he wasn't there and he walked slightly behind to give her some space. She headed to the backyard and disappeared up and through the window without even turning to say goodnight. Will shook his head. She sure didn't make being a friend easy all the time.

On his way home, he thought about how Blue had come out of her shell over the previous few weeks when they had been out practicing night stalking—almost chatty, definitely bossy about teaching him stuff, but also inquisitive and almost warm towards him. There was that one dark spot at the end of the night last night, but there was no way that was the reason for her behavior tonight. Some of tonight was normal but the beginning and end were outright weird. She had treated him like he was a ghost or a zombie or a wild animal. Something had to have happened since last night. Something not good.

18

NO GOING BACK

Blue was angry. She had been shaken badly by the nightmare, and she didn't like it. It had invaded her new life and morphed into a new kind of torture by replacing the cast of characters. It was like it knew it was losing its grasp on her and needed to reinvent itself in order to continue torturing her. It was no longer a dream about a memory, it was a threat to those she cared about now.

Well, she was damned if she was going to let her life be dictated by this cursed nightmare. She was going to defeat it.

She was convinced it wasn't going to go away until she had dealt with the root cause. It would continue morphing and haunting her until then. The cause was the people who did this to her and her family—the same people who now threatened her new family. They were drug dealers, she knew that for sure. She might never know the dealers who killed her family, but it didn't matter now. The drug dealers of her memory were replaced with something much more dangerous, the drug dealers who were threats right here and now. They were in her sights and it was time to stop messing around and start nailing them. She had been forming a plan in her head for a while, and until now it had been more of a good intention. But the infrared camera changed everything. It gave her a secret weapon. Now it was real. She was going to do this. And she knew exactly what the first step was.

Confrontation.

———

Jack was sitting on a bench close to the restrooms this morning. Bronco was gone for a couple of days. Probably stocking up, thought Jack. Bronco didn't tell him much detail about the back end of this whole operation, and Jack didn't really want to know. He was just in it to earn some cash right now and didn't want to get in any deeper than he needed to.

It was a nice morning—a little cooler than earlier in the week, and it was a welcome change. Between the cool temperature and taking a drag on the first cigarette from a fresh pack, he was feeling pretty good and didn't much care if anyone came by today. It was easy work, and the setup was pretty low risk. A kid would come by and give him a nod and then flash a twenty from his pocket. Jack would get up and chat with the kid, and they would walk, and while they walked the kid would slip him the twenty, and he would slip back a small ziplock with five joints. Sometimes, if there were a lot of people in the park, Jack would tell the kid, "Restroom in 5." After the allotted time, Jack would get up and go to the restroom. If the kid was still in there, he would just swap the twenty for the ziplock. If the kid wasn't there, Jack would reach up above the light fixture over the sinks and find the twenty stuck there. He would replace the twenty with a ziplock. Didn't matter who found it. As long as he got his twenty, he was happy. It was low risk either way. There were no surveillance cameras in the restroom and hardly any in the park and the ones that were there were easy to avoid.

If at any time it didn't look good to make a transaction, if it was too crowded at the restroom, or a cop was around, Jack would just shake his head at the prospective customer and then go to a different bench in the park where it was quieter. Everyone knew where to look for him and how to make the exchange. It was pretty safe, too. He never had more than an ounce of pot on him and never took in so much money that he looked rich. If he got busted, it would just be a misdemeanor. But he didn't plan on getting busted.

Sometimes, someone new would come along. He could tell it a mile off—the nervous glances and the hesitation. If there was nobody around, he would just say, "Hi there. You waiting to meet someone?" or something like that to put them at their ease. They'd usually respond with something like, "No. Well yeah, I'm looking for someone named Jack." He'd reply with a smile and say, "Well you found him." He'd then be friendly and say, "Look, nothing bad is going to happen, I've been doing this a long time," and then he would explain how to approach and when to keep walking. "It's easy, no problem." If it looked like it could turn awkward, he would just stand up, pull out his phone as if he had gotten a call, and then walk away, talking into his phone.

Jack was often amazed at how easy it was to read people. This sometimes seemed more of a study of sociology than it was a job selling illegal drugs. Sociology. He smiled to himself. It had been the only class he had really gotten into in high school. Everyone had been shocked when he aced that class.

Yes, people were very predictable, which was why he was a bit puzzled now. A girl was standing in front of him, bold as brass, and he hadn't the faintest clue as to how she got there without him noticing. She was thin yet sturdy and looked young, but could be anywhere from eleven to fifteen. She was looking at him blandly and suddenly started talking.

"A friend of mine said you would sell me some pot," she said simply. "Will you?"

"Whoa, whoa, whoa, there girl. Where did you hear that?" asked Jack, caught off-guard.

"I just said. A friend of mine told me. That's where I heard it.

Can't you hear me? I'll speak up." The girl got ready to repeat herself loudly.

"Wait, wait, wait!" said Jack, and he held up his hand for her to stop. He felt kind of stupid holding his hand up like that to a young girl, so to cover, he put his hand up to his mouth thoughtfully, sat back, and darted a look to the left and right. Jack was ticked at himself. He was acting like a complete amateur. This girl had knocked him out of his rhythm. He sat and rubbed his chin thoughtfully while he recovered his wits.

"Okay, you got me. I do happen to have an extra joint here in my personal stash, and I might be willing to share it," and then he paused. He looked down at the ground and then back up at her face. "But I don't just give it to young kids like you. What are you, twelve? You are way too young to be smoking dope, kid." Jack took a pull on his cigarette. He thought to himself, "*So what if I was ten when I started. With a drunk son-of-a-bitch for a dad like mine, who wouldn't?*"

The girl stared at him for a moment. Jack felt like he was being dissected. "I'm not twelve, I'm fourteen," said the girl, and before he could object she continued, "Look—I've been in and out of a lot of foster homes, group homes, and even a psych ward. There isn't much I haven't seen. I don't think I would've made it without getting stoned now and then to take the edge off."

Jack could see it in her eyes. There was truth behind her words, maybe not the total truth, but enough. He knew exactly what she was talking about, and whether he believed her or not, he had enough of a heart in him to give her the benefit of a doubt, so he said, "I get it. Say no more. This is what we'll do. This one is on me, but we will do it so nobody gets in trouble. I am going to leave a little ziplock packet over the light fixture above the mirror in the boy's room. You go there in about five minutes and reach up and pick it up. You don't have to look, you can just feel for it. You're okay going into the boy's room, right? Nobody's gonna care, just tell 'em you're looking for your dad, okay? You got that?" He looked up at the girl.

She said, "Got it."

"Okay," said Jack, "But remember next time, you bring a twenty dollar bill. Twenty bucks for five joints. Just pat your pocket to show me you've got a twenty, and we'll find a spot to swap. Easy-peasy. You got that, too?"

She said, "Got it. I'll be back in five." She turned and walked off.

"Wait a second," said Jack, and she stopped and turned. "I know you, you're that girl that hangs out with Wu and that other kid, what's his name . . . Will . . . down here at the basketball court, aren't you?"

The girl didn't reply, except for a scowl. He couldn't quite decide if her scowl was because of anger or if that was just a normal look for this girl.

"So you are one of the O'Day foster clan? That Wu is one heck of a basketball player. He is going to be a star. His friend ain't bad either. Look, you be careful, I don't want you to get in trouble, okay?"

The girl's scowl turned into an unmistakable glare. "Mind your own business," she said curtly and then turned and walked off.

Jack shook his head. She was a strange one, without a doubt, he thought. But she had a familiar look in her face—the look of a survivor. He smiled a little. This girl had some gumption in her.

Blue was somewhat bothered. She had planned this approach quite carefully, and it went off almost like she expected it to. Almost. What she hadn't expected was Greazal. She figured he was a low-life psychopath like his older partner, but up close he didn't come off that way at all. Maybe it was because Gronk wasn't around. She had always regarded them as Gronk and Greazal, but now she couldn't ignore the fact that his real name was Jack. She had picked up on that some time ago, but until now, it was much more convenient to think of him as Greazal, the low-life. But, after talking with him, and reading his thoughts, she realized he was more like Jack, the human being.

Well, anyway, she had the joint, which means she had some hard evidence. She wasn't quite sure she knew what to do next. She needed more than the joint. That was small stuff. She had been hoping she might pick up something that would let her know how they dealt the hard stuff. The "candy", the "smack", the "horse", the "junk", the "big H." Heroin.

But she got nothing.

She suspected that Gronk was the key and that she would have to find a way to confront him and catch the *chiss* that would lead her to the answer.

She was walking back home, deep in thought when she passed a couple—young, maybe college students—and she caught a *chiss* "*. . . SCORE SOME SMACK . . .*"

She stopped short. She turned around and caught up to them as casually as she could. She got close enough that she could hear them talking and she even pick up reflections of their *chiss*.

". . . yeah, tomorrow night . . . restrooms . . . it'll be fine . . ." ". . . *SHE WORRIES TOO MUCH. I'VE DONE THIS A MILLION TIMES . . .*" ". . . I've got cash . . ." ". . . *BRONCO CHARGES TOO FUCKING MUCH . . .*"

This was it! These two wanted to buy some heroin. Probably tomorrow night by some restrooms! But—which ones? What time?

Blue took a chance and got a little closer. She stared intently at the backs of their heads and as the guy turned to the girl. Blue could pick up the voice and *chiss* clearly.

". . . like I said, over there—the parking lot next to the restrooms, midnight . . ." The guy gestured toward the park building with the restrooms next to the parking lot, ". . . *REALLY RIDICULOUS, THE POLICE ARE CLUELESS . . .*" "Um, are you looking for someone?"

The guy was looking right at her. Blue turned instantly on her heels and headed back to the house leaving the couple safely behind. But she got the clue she wanted. This was more than a lucky break. It was a sign. She felt like she was meant to nail these guys. She believed for a long time that this moment would come—everything would fall into place and go in her favor. She had a time and a place, and now all she needed to do was get that night vision camera! It had a zoom lens and could take videos, too. That was something she could take to the police . . . and something they couldn't ignore. She knew she could do it. She just needed to borrow that camera from Will somehow.

Tomorrow was Friday and Will didn't have work, so she should be able to meet with him, but could she get the camera? And would Will come with her? He'd be a huge safety factor. She had to convince him somehow. Problem was, she had a hunch that interpreting nightmares was not a convincing argument for Will. And besides, how could she possibly bring up what she saw in her nightmare, especially to him? Plus, she hadn't exactly treated him very well the past couple of nights. Still, the threat of drugs and pushers in their very own park had seemed to resonate with him, and the threat to Rose and Sam was very real. The joint would prove that. If she could get one so easily, how long was it before friends of Rose and Sam were getting stoned? A new wave of disgust and loathing welled up in her. She couldn't forgive Jack, no matter how reasonable he seemed. You don't just give out a joint to a fourteen-year-old. And he had even thought she was younger!

As Blue reached the house, she also reached a new resolve. She was going to do this Will or no Will. It was the right thing to do, whether she could convince Will to help or not. She just hoped she could.

19

———

THE PROPOSITION

Wu handed Will the note and said, "What's up with this, we're back to notes again?"

"I don't know. Has she been acting weird lately?" asked Will.

"Yeah, a little. Ma Beth said she spent the whole day in her room except to go to the park by herself for about half an hour. Why would anyone go to the park for just half an hour? I don't know. She gets in weird moods from time to time."

Will was anxious to read the note, but he was afraid that Wu would want to know the details, especially since he seemed worried about Blue. Will decided he had to take the chance anyway. Blue would have known that he might have to open it in front of Wu.

He opened it and read:

Sorry for being grumpy,
must have been the lack of sleep
from the huMid night. I'd like
to see your dad's Camera you
were telling me about sometime.

That was it. Will smiled, because this was clever. A little corny, but clever enough to work. She knew Wu would be there, and she also got a message across to Will without it being suspicious. Meet at midnight and bring the camera.

He read the whole note out loud to Wu.

Wu seemed relieved. "Yeah, it has been humid the last couple of nights, and being up in that room? She should just go down and sleep on the couch in the rec room. What's this camera she's talking about?"

"It's really cool, a night vision camera, I'll show you." Will still had the camera in his room. When he got it out and demonstrated it, Wu tried to act impressed, but only showed half-hearted interest. Wu was not exactly a science geek.

———

At midnight, Will intercepted Blue as she slipped out the downstairs window of the O'Day's family room.

"*Click, click, click*" voxed Will.

"*Cht, cht, cht!*" Blue voxed back. "*Where are you?*"

Will couldn't help smiling to himself—he must have gotten better at stalking if Blue couldn't find him. "*By the gate,*" he voxed

In a moment Blue materialized next to him. "*You brought the night vision camera,*" she said matter-of-factly. "*Good. Let's go to the park. I don't have much time. I want to get back soon.*"

Well, thought Will, I guess things are back to normal. That is, the familiar minimal words, to-the-point, 'introvert' normal . . . not the 'Hey Will, good to see you' normal.

"*Okay, but why not someplace closer if you need to get back soon?*"

"*The park,*" she voxed with finality.

Great. It was going to be one of those nights again. He sighed. "*What are we waiting for then . . .*"

She looked at him with the tiniest hint of apology in her face, but then it vanished and she took off with a dash—disappearing into the shadows. Will followed her and matched her pace with much more practiced ease than their first night weeks ago. He almost didn't trip on anything.

They quickly reached the park—the route being so familiar they could have each easily reached it with their eyes closed. They only encountered one smooching couple and one car but easily evaded any exposure or detection by melting into the shadows. Will had no idea where Blue was taking him—it wasn't their usual stomping grounds, during the day or at night. It was at the far end where there was a small parking lot and restroom. It was not well lit, only indirectly by a single streetlight down the block. And there was one outstanding feature about this spot: an enormous maple tree.

"*What are we doing here?*" asked Will.

Blue was inspecting the restroom area and studying the tree. She didn't speak for a minute. Then she pulled something out of her pocket and held it near his face. It looked like a ziplock bag. He could smell what was in it before he could actually see it. It had the spicy, fruity fragrance that he had learned to identify in his first year at high school. When his eyes finally focused on the bag and its contents, he wasn't sure what to say. Even though he was expecting something unusual, he wasn't expecting this.

"*Blue, what are you thinking? You could get in so much trouble with this! Where in hell did you get it?*"

And then she dropped the real bombshell. "*You have to keep it,*" and the next thing he knew, she was stuffing the little bag in his pocket. "*And don't open it. It's a bag inside a bag. It's got his prints on the bag inside.*"

"*Whoa, whoa, whoa!*" voxed Will, and he scrambled to take the bag out of his pocket again. He held the bag in his hand awkwardly. He couldn't give it back to her. He really didn't want her to get in trouble, but he couldn't keep it either. "*I can't take this!*"

"*Stop being ridiculous,*" voxed Blue. "*It isn't hard to hide*

SOMETHING LIKE THAT. BESIDES, COPS DON'T WATCH KIDS LIKE YOU. THEY WATCH KIDS LIKE ME. THEY WOULD THROW ME BACK INTO THE SYSTEM."

"WHAT ARE YOU TALKING ABOUT? AND WHY DID YOU BRING ME ALL THE WAY OVER HERE TO SHOW THIS TO ME? AND WHAT ARE YOU DOING NOW?"

Blue had started climbing the tree. She climbed like a cat right up to the lowest branches. *"CAN YOU SEE ME FROM DOWN THERE? WALK AROUND, AND SEE IF YOU CAN SPOT ME."*

Will was starting to feel like he was a trained monkey, and he was getting a little ticked off by it. She's moody all week, then leads him here, hands him a joint in a ziplock, then climbs a tree and tells him to walk around and see how well she is hiding? What was happening? He felt like leaving, like dropping the joint and just going home. But she was a kid—she was his responsibility. He felt like an older brother wrapped around the little finger of a bossy little sister.

"WELL?" came her vox from above.

Will hesitated, but then gave in. He couldn't leave her alone, and if he was going to find out what was going on, he was just going to have to see this evening through.

He looked up from where he stood. The broad canopy of the tree kept the light from the streetlight out and deepened the shadows near the trunk of the tree. Will could make out the silhouette of her head and one shoulder *"I CAN MAKE OUT YOUR HEAD, BUT ONLY BECAUSE I KNOW IT'S THERE."* He saw a light blob bouncing a little bit, *"AND I CAN SEE THE WHITE BOTTOM OF YOUR SHOE."*

"DAMN, I FORGOT ABOUT THESE SNEAKERS. I NEED TO WEAR MY BLACK SLIPPERS. WHAT ABOUT FROM OVER THERE NEAR THE PARKING LOT?"

Will could hear her making some adjustments in her position up in the tree. He walked slowly backward toward the parking lot, moving his head around to see if he could spot anything that was a giveaway.

"WELL?" came a vox from the tree.

"*WELL, I CAN'T SEE YOU FROM HERE, AND I KNOW WHERE YOU ARE. LET ME CHECK IT OUT FROM DIFFERENT ANGLES.*"

Will and Blue spent the next few minutes checking out different angles and different positions. Some were perfect from one angle but not so perfect from another angle. If anyone had been watching, it must have looked like a lost deranged boy was lurching silently around the tree as if he had never seen one before in his life.

Finally, Will voxed, "*I REALLY DOUBT ANYONE WHO DIDN'T KNOW YOU WERE THERE WOULD EVER SPOT YOU. YOU'D HAVE TO MAKE NOISE TO GIVE IT AWAY.*" Then he remembered he had the night vision camera hanging around his neck. "*WAIT A SEC, I WANT TO SEE IF I CAN FIND YOU WITH THIS.*" He powered it up and turned the illuminator on and then held it to his eye. There was Blue, clear as day waving at him. He put the camera down and squinted carefully. Nothing.

"*IS THERE ROOM UP THERE? I'M COMING UP,*" Will said, and he climbed up to join Blue. Now he could see why it was easy for her to hide. It was a very roomy spot where several large branches converged. "*YOU WERE CLEAR AS DAY IN THIS NIGHT VISION CAMERA WITH THE ILLUMINATOR ON, BUT I COULDN'T SEE ANYTHING WITHOUT IT.*"

Blue reached out and nodded her head at the camera. Will took the camera from around his neck and handed it to her. She took it and fiddled expertly with the controls and then held it up to her eye and started scanning the area below.

Will watched her. She was totally engrossed. Hidden under her dark hair and buried somewhere deep was this place she retreated to. In that place, she was dancing to a different drummer, living a different life. Nobody seemed to know what that was. Will decided that he was going no further until he found out. Things were starting to get just a little too weird, and he didn't want to be a partner in madness.

"What's up with the joint, Blue?" he whispered.

She looked at Will. "*IT WAS A TEST. I GOT THE JOINT THIS AFTERNOON. I WENT TO THE PARK AND DECIDED TO SEE IF GREAZAL WOULD*

SELL ME A JOINT. IF HE DID, I DECIDED I WAS GOING TO TAKE THOSE GUYS DOWN. HE DIDN'T SELL IT TO ME, HE GAVE IT TO ME!"

She paused for Will's reaction, but he was silent.

"DON'T YOU GET IT?" she asked.

"NO, I DON'T GET IT, BLUE. YOU ARE TIGHT AS A DRUM. I DON'T KNOW WHAT THE HELL IS GOING ON IN THAT HEAD OF YOURS."

"LOOK," she voxed, *"ON THE WAY BACK HOME I HEARD A MAN AND WOMAN CHISS ABOUT SCORING SOME SMACK—HEROIN! THEY'RE GOING TO MEET A GUY, BRONCO, HERE AT MIDNIGHT TOMORROW NIGHT AND BUY IT FROM HIM! GRONK IS BRONCO! WITH THIS NIGHT VISION CAMERA, WE CAN TAKE THESE GUYS DOWN!"*

"What? Geez Blue, you're not serious! Let's just tell the cops and let them handle it! That's what they are paid to do!" He didn't even try to hide his voice.

"STOP TALKING! FOR CRYING OUT LOUD, YOU WANT TO GIVE AWAY THIS HIDING PLACE!"

"SORRY! FOR SOME REASON I JUST WENT COMPLETELY NUTS, BECAUSE YOU ARE INSANE. FORGIVE ME! FOR GOD'S SAKE, BLUE, I CAN'T KEEP GOING ON THIS CRAZY VENDETTA WITHOUT KNOWING WHAT IS GOING ON IN YOUR HEAD. EVEN THEN, I STILL THINK IT'S CRAZY. WE'RE NOT SUPER-HEROES. YOU CAN'T JUST GO OUT AND SNEAK AROUND CONQUERING BAD GUYS."

Blue looked away from Will. She was looking off into the dark at nothing. She finally spoke in a whisper, "What more do you need to know than the fact that these guys are giving kids drugs—little kids! Me! All they want is easy money, and they don't care about anyone. Do you want Rose or Sam to start smoking dope? Do you think Gronk or Greazal cares what happens if they *did*? Do you think you could prevent Rose and Sam from doing it just by saying 'Don't do it'? Really, how stupid are adults thinking they can just tell kids not to do it and think they won't?"

"That's it then? You don't trust adults? Is that what this is all about? Is that why you don't want to go to the cops? Well, what about me? Do you trust me? Do you think it's stupid for me to tell you not to do this and hope that you won't do it? You think it is stupid for me to care when it's all I can do? It's all I can do because I don't know what is driving you! If I did, I'd try and stop that!"

Blue looked down and was silent. Will waited. She finally looked up at him. He was expecting a look of anger, but instead it was a look of anguish. Even the deep shadows of the tree couldn't hide it.

"*You can't stop it. I'm the only one that can stop it,*" she voxed.

Will could sense that this was the core. Something happened that only she knew about, and she didn't trust telling anyone else, so she was dealing with it on her own.

"*You're wrong. There are people who will listen and help. What about Ma Beth? She'd listen to you. I will listen and help. My Mom would listen and help. She is awesome. She is a psychiatrist, you know.*"

Blue's face became hard. "*You don't know anything about it! They've been trying to tell me how to stop it for years, and they don't have a clue! I honestly don't know why anyone listens to those people. They are so full of crap!*"

"*My mom's not full of crap. She's really good at it,*" voxed Will calmly.

"Therapists! Doctors! Psychiatrists! That's exactly what I'm talking about! I've been to so many of them, and I trusted them, and all their drugs and talking and therapy. Do you know what it did to me? Do you?" hissed Blue in an angry, exasperated whisper. She didn't wait for an answer. "*A psych ward for six weeks! You know what it's like being around crazy people? Best thing that happened to me there was I figured out I wasn't crazy! Half the people in there weren't crazy; they just didn't play the game. I figured it out. I started playing their game. I became 'normal', so I could get out. No drugs, no therapists, just me. 'Ready for reintroduction into society!'*" She turned away and put the camera to her face and started scanning again with renewed intensity. "If you don't want to help me you don't have to. Just go."

Will didn't go. He couldn't move, because he was trying to digest this new information. He decided he wasn't going to give up. "It doesn't mean there aren't people out there that can help. There's me. There's my mom. You've never talked to a psychiatrist that could vox."

Blue pulled the camera from her face and glared at Will. "*I DON'T WANT TO TALK TO YOUR MOM! I DON'T CARE IF SHE'S THE WORLD'S GREATEST PSYCHIATRIST! NO MORE PSYCHIATRISTS! NO MORE ANYONE! FAT LOT OF GOOD TALKING TO YOU HAS DONE ME, TOO!*"

She scrambled down out of the tree and headed back, fast.

He scrambled down after her and followed—though he made sure to give her some space. She ignored him all the way to the hedge outside the O'Day house, until she finally turned and voxed, "*I DON'T WANT YOUR HELP ANYMORE. JUST LEAVE ME ALONE.*" She turned back and plunged through the hedge.

Will didn't follow. He just stood there for a while. He knew he had done the right thing to push her, but now he didn't know quite what to do. If he could talk to his mother about it, she would give him great advice. But he couldn't talk to her—that would betray a confidence between him and Blue. He wasn't ready to do that. It wouldn't be right. He thought his mother would agree on that point.

Finally he turned and went home. He would just have to work it out himself. Just like Blue.

20

MORTAL

It would be midnight soon. Blue was settled comfortably in the big crook of the tree. She had been there at least a half an hour, and she was quite certain no one had seen her climb up silently in the blackness. She let her dark hair and clothes melt into the shadows of the tree, and this time she remembered her dark slippers. She had taken the last-minute extra step of rubbing some ash from the barbecue onto her face just to erase the last pale patches of her skin from possible detection. She even smudged some on the backs of her hands. She had a clear view of the pavement between the parking lot and the restroom where just the slightest streetlight reached through to make long, weak shadows.

The night vision camera hung at the ready around her neck. She and Will had both forgotten that she still had it the night before when they had their tense parting. She didn't notice it until she was climbing back in the second-floor bathroom window, but by then it was too late to take it back, and it would have been too awkward anyway. She would take it back tomorrow, after she had gotten what she needed. She felt a little bad about how she had acquired it, yet she also felt it was another good sign that it wound up in her possession the very night that she needed it.

She was still angry at Will. He just didn't get it, but on the other hand, who ever did? In truth, he was still probably the best thing that had happened to her besides the O'Days. She didn't want to blow it with him. But a psychiatrist! God, if he had to pick one thing she loathed, it was psychiatrists. And up until then she and Will had been working together so well. She sighed. She knew they both would be mad about it for a while and then they both would forget about it. She should forget about it now, but some of his words kept nagging her: *"We're not superheroes. You can't just go out and sneak around conquering bad guys."*

She did want to conquer these guys. It was true. But she wasn't pretending to be a superhero. She was just taking advantage of the skill she was born and raised with. So what if she was trying to conquer something. She was striking back at something that took something from her and continued to threaten her—her family, her friends, her life. It was a just cause. And it wasn't that she felt super-powered, she felt cursed. She wanted to get rid of that curse. Will just didn't get it. She desperately wanted him to get it, though.

She was going to miss him tonight. It would have been great to have him on the ground as a spotter. That was the way she and her dad had hunted and stalked. You didn't have to whisper with vox, it was like talking out loud right in front of your prey and they didn't have a clue. You could talk about them and share observations, and they heard nothing. It almost wasn't fair when there were two of you. But one would be enough for tonight. She wasn't nervous about it. It was a comfortable thing to be doing. This was like getting back to her roots. Frankly, the biggest thing she was worried about was being missed back at the O'Days. She had to leave a little earlier tonight than on the nights she had met with Will. If she were missed, that would be a big problem. It was late enough that everyone would be going to bed, but early enough that someone just might check on her. But she didn't think they would. Things had gotten comfortable enough for her at home that Ma Beth often didn't bother coming up the attic stairs anymore. She would, without fail, however, say softly from the bottom of the stairs, "Goodnight Blue. Sweet dreams!"

Blue wasn't usually a sucker for that kind of sappiness, but from Ma Beth . . . it was nice. Will had said she could trust Ma Beth with this whole issue and Blue knew he was right. She thought about bailing. Just go and tell Ma Beth, and she would take care of things, she thought. Yeah right. The DFC would find out what Blue and Will had been doing, and that would be the end of this happy little life with the O'Days. Besides, she had pledged she was not going to get them involved. She was going to protect them.

She shook her head and admonished herself *"Concentrate!"* This was not the time to second guess anything, it was the time to make sure she was prepared. She went through a mental checklist. Controls, check. Batteries, check. She had practiced with the night vision camera that day and had put in fresh batteries. She knew where the controls were without having to look. She took some practice shots now just to make sure everything was good. It worked perfectly, as if it had been designed for stealth operations like this. She was ready. She would take her pictures and go home, and the next day she would send them with a description of all the activity to Westbury Police Chief Hannah. Blue would send them anonymously, so she wouldn't get in trouble. The police couldn't ignore this. They'd have to follow up and Gronk wouldn't have a clue. They would stake out the same place she was now, and Gronk would be put away for a long time. Maybe Greazal, too, and she felt a little bad about that but not bad enough to let it worry her. He had made his choice.

Now Blue just had to wait. She closed her eyes and listened. It was a warm night, but not too warm, and there was a slight wind. With the wind, the crickets, and the night birds there was enough background noise that Blue had no worries about any sound she might make short of breaking a branch or sneezing.

And now there was some activity down below. A car pulled into the parking lot and stopped, but no one got out, they just sat there.

She couldn't see any faces, but she bet anything it was that couple. It wouldn't be long now.

Soon someone came walking around the restroom. It was Gronk! He paused and lit a cigarette, and she could see his face clearly for a moment in the glare of the match. She looked through the eyepiece of the night vision camera. He was clear as day. She took a picture. She didn't see Greazal, and she should have been disappointed, but deep inside, she was kind of glad. She was starting to think she would be willing to give Greazal a second chance. Not Gronk, though. No way in hell.

Gronk cased the area out. He was very good at it, she had to admit. If you weren't looking for it, you wouldn't know he was doing anything but enjoying a smoke. But she could see how he checked out every angle, every spot where someone could be watching. For just a moment she had a flash of fear that he would see her, in spite of all her confidence and precautions. He looked briefly her way and almost right at her. She held her breath. But he never looked up. They never look up, thought Blue. She took another picture after he looked away. Then she started the video recording.

After about a minute, Gronk made a gesture that must have been a signal. The car doors opened. A girl and a guy got out and walked over to Gronk. They looked like they'd done this before. The exchange was very practiced. Gronk offered the guy a cigarette, but it was more than a cigarette. There was a little package inside the palm of his hand. The guy took the package and the cigarette and took the offered match for his cigarette. He looked around and then stuck his finger in the package, and then sucked on it.

Blue was watching through the viewfinder carefully and quietly. This really was pretty easy. It almost felt like a game.

After a pull on his cigarette, the guy reached into his pocket and pulled out what looked like a roll of bills. The guy nodded and Gronk took a pack of cigarettes out of his pocket and handed it to the guy, only Blue knew it wasn't a pack of cigarettes. She was beginning to have some doubts. They were too good at this. They made it look just like some friends having some smokes. There was the wad of bills, though. A big wad. This must have been a big deal. That had to show up in the video, along with the guy testing the powder with his finger. Blue zoomed in on the guy's face and then the girl just to make sure she got good shots of their faces. Then Blue remembered to zoom over to the car. She could clearly see the license plate number. Good! This was going to work.

The three chatted quietly and naturally for a few minutes. Gronk never stopped looking around, but he made it seem like he wasn't looking around. Blue stopped the video recording. She had what she needed and was anxious for them to get done, so she could get home. Finally, the guy put out his cigarette, crushed the butt with his shoe, nodded at Gronk, and the couple got back in their car and pulled out.

Gronk stood for a moment, and then casually turned around and walked off. She waited until he was well across the park before she finally let out a sigh of relief. It was over. She had done it! Now she had to get home and get in the house without being detected. Then she had to see if the pictures and video were good enough to see all the details. And then she had to get them to Chief Hannah anonymously somehow.

She climbed carefully down the tree, but not as carefully as when she went up. She had nothing really to hide now, no need to be cautious until she got back to the house. If somebody saw her, they'd just think it was someone hanging around the park late at night. She finally hopped onto the ground. A small stick snapped. Instinctively, she looked up.

She was looking right into the face of Gronk.

Time stopped. She wasn't sure she really believed what she was seeing. This just wasn't possible. Gronk had walked across the park. She had watched him, just to make sure. This must be a ghost. But then the ghost started talking. She couldn't really understand what he was saying. Her ears weren't working properly, her conscious mind was shutting down, but she felt her body starting to go into emergency mode. Gronk took a couple of steps towards her. Her mind wasn't sure what to do, but her body reacted for her. It took off like a rocket. She heard Gronk curse and then heard his footsteps pounding behind her. She ran and ran. The footsteps started to fade away behind her, but she didn't stop. She just cared about getting away and getting home. She knew she could do it; she was fast and she knew the park, even in the dark. She just didn't quite sense a low-hanging branch hiding in the deep shadows.

Bronco was feeling pretty good. His trip down south set him up nicely with good stock to sell, and he was still in pretty good with the suppliers in the city. He had worked for them for many years until he moved up here ten months ago. He felt he could set up his own territory in this quiet, virgin Vermont college town. It was small stuff for the big timers down south, but it was a growing business for him here. He knew that if sales went too well here, they would want to move in and control more of it. For now, they were happy to let him have it, but he could tell they were starting to get the scent of opportunity. He wouldn't have much more time with the area all to himself.

Meanwhile, he had it easy—a small, quiet town without much police coverage. There were two police cruisers at most during the day and only one at night. Frankly, the college campus security was tighter than the town police. That's why he did most of his business in town. It was pathetic, really. All he had to do was wait in his car until the night police cruiser sweep went by, and he could head the other direction, knowing it would be half an hour before the cop car would ever be back near the park. Then he would just ring the customer once, and they would show up at the park. They'd make the exchange, and then he would go home richer. Some nights he would do two or three customers. He started letting Jack do the day customers by himself—just joints and small bags of dope. Small change, really, but it brought in new heroin customers. Day work was the risky part, but Jack was good at it, and if he got arrested? He was only 17, he'd probably get let off, Bronco thought, but if he didn't, well, there were plenty of kids to take his place. Didn't matter to Bronco. The real money was heroin. He wasn't going to let Jack handle that or even let him know how the deals went down. If Jack got arrested, Bronco was clean, clean, clean. Jack didn't even know his real name, he only knew him as a phone number and as a guy named "Bronco." Obscurity and anonymity were the keys to his freedom and prosperity. He would kill to keep that.

Tonight, it was just regular customers. Big customers. They always bought 20 or 30 bags at a time. No problem, easy money. He checked the time. Time to go. He dialed a number on a cell phone and let it ring twice then immediately hung up. He got up from the bench and walked calmly and easily toward the restrooms. Behind the restrooms, in the parking lot, he knew he'd find his customers waiting.

He walked over to the parking lot at an easy pace, just enjoying the night, but he was casing out everything. If there was anything suspicious, he would just keep going and wait for another night.

Tonight was quiet. There was nothing he could see, and it looked like another routine deal. Still, the quieter it was, the more uneasy he was. He wondered if he wasn't getting jumpy. His father had warned him not to get jumpy. Didn't matter what happened, always stay cool, his dad had said. It made people more comfortable when you were cool, and when they are comfortable, that is when you have the advantage. Always. "Don't forget that," his father had said. And Bronco hadn't. His dad may have been an abusive, sadistic, bastard-of-a-father, but he was street smart.

Bronco rounded the restroom and lit up a cigarette. It was more suspicious when you tried to conceal yourself. It was better to act like you had nothing to hide. The light of a cigarette actually lowered suspicion rather than raised it. Again, one of his dad's bits of advice.

It was also a signal to the couple in the car. They got out and greeted him like a buddy. The guy even lit a cigarette. They chatted a bit and then they did the exchange, completely natural. He liked these guys. They had money, they never bitched about the price, and they knew the drill.

A little bit of chit chat, and then it was all over. They got in their car and left, and he ground out his cigarette (never look like you're in a hurry to leave, his dad said) and started back across the park to his car. He was completely clean. All he had was a wallet, newly fattened with fresh cash, a pack of cigarettes, a lighter, and car keys. Cops could stop him now, and no worries.

He tapped out another cigarette as he walked and reached into his pocket for his lighter. But it wasn't there. He patted his pockets, looked around on the ground. Damn it, that was a sweet lighter, too —not a disposable one. A real silver-jacketed lighter. He'd had it a long time. It was almost a good luck charm, and he'd hate to lose it. He backtracked toward the parking lot, looking at the ground as he went. When he heard a crack and snap, he stopped and looked up. Standing directly in front of him was a girl dressed all in black.

It was so unexpected he almost thought he was dreaming. Where did she come from? And what the hell was a girl, practically a kid, doing out in the park in the middle of the night? And what was that thing hanging around her neck? And why was she dressed like that?

Act cool, he said to himself. Make her comfortable. "Hey, missy. What are you doing out here so late? Do your parents know where you are?" As he said this he stepped casually towards her. She backed up. He stopped, stunned. He could see what was hanging from her neck—a night vision camera. He looked back up to her face—it was covered in black . . . what . . . soot? Makeup? Shit, this wasn't just an innocent kid sneaking out at night for fun. Was she here when he was doing the deal? Bronco could feel his expression harden, and he was having trouble keeping cool. "Out taking pictures this late are you? Animals? I didn't see any flashes. Is that some sort of . . . fuck!"

That last word came as he lunged out to grab the night vision camera, but the girl was off like a gazelle. "Damn it!" said Bronco, and he went after her. That was definitely a night vision camera. He knew it. His dad had had one like it. That damn girl was spying on him and had nearly gotten away with it. If it hadn't been for his lighter, he would have gone home feeling all secure only to wake up to police banging on his door the next morning.

Bronco was pissed. He didn't care if it was a kid, she had just messed with his business and he was not going to let her get away with it. But he had to get her first. And damn, was she fast! He couldn't believe it, he thought he'd have her in the first 50 feet, and now she was halfway through the park and pulling away from him. A burst of rage at possibly being out-smarted by a little kid gave him a boost of speed, but still, it looked like she was getting away. She was dodging and weaving and going around obstacles he couldn't even see. It was like she had everything memorized.

And then he heard a thwack and an "uh!" The sound of footsteps stopped. He slowed down and moved quietly up to where he had heard the sound. The girl was lying in the shadows on the ground completely knocked out. He stepped closer but had to duck under a branch. She must have run straight into it.

Bronco didn't dwell on his good luck. He took it as a sign that it was simply meant to be. He was oddly superstitious about these things. He took a quick look around to see if there was any witness to what had happened. There was no one. He wasn't surprised. It was after midnight, and the whole chase didn't take more than fifteen seconds. He took a moment to just listen and scan every nook where someone could be hidden. Nothing.

He reached down and pulled the night vision camera from around the girl's neck. She was limp, but breathing. He examined the camera and could just make out the familiar controls using the dim light of a distant streetlight. He turned it on and hit the play-back button. He held the eyepiece up to his face and after another couple of seconds, lowered the camera and hit the stop button.

Shit. This was incriminating. He couldn't just let this go; he had to do something about it. He looked down at the girl. She was limp as a rag doll, but his car was more than 50 yards away. He had been lucky so far, and he was pretty sure there had been no witnesses, but anything or anyone could show up or drive by at just the wrong moment.

He quickly considered his options. He could take the camera or, better yet, erase it and just leave it there. That would leave no evidence. On the other hand, could he really erase it? He knew forensic detectives had a way of looking at erased files. The only way to really erase it was to destroy it, or take it with him. Either way, it was risky. Someone would find her in the morning, if she didn't wake first and go home and call the cops. She would tell them what had happened. They probably wouldn't believe her without hard evidence, and without the images on the night vision camera, she didn't have any. Or did she? Did she have any other evidence? If she took this much trouble to get night camera footage, she must not have felt she had enough evidence without it. But suppose she had a little, and then this incident, too? If they did believe even part of it, at the very least they would try to find him and question him.

He supposed he could just kill her where she lay, and leave her. That would tie the killing to the park, though, and lead to questioning people who came to the park and maybe to his clients and from them maybe to him.

He could take her back to his apartment. That would buy him more time. She would be missed, probably later in the morning, and then there would be a search, but they wouldn't know even where to start to look.

He looked at her again. She had almost gotten away, fair and square. Again, he was oddly superstitious. If he made her a captive instead of killing her outright, it was like he was giving her a sporting chance. That somehow would make it okay to kill her later, if he had to. It also dawned on him that he had the perfect place to keep her, at least for a week if he had to.

He made up his mind, but he was wasting time. A small moan came from the girl. She was starting to regain consciousness. He lifted her off the ground and carried her like she was a sleepy child. If he was stopped by anyone, he could just say he found her lying on the ground and was taking her to the hospital. He took one quick look at the ground to make sure nothing was left behind, and then he sauntered as naturally as he could through the most shadowy parts of the park toward his car. He opened the back door and slid her carefully in, laying her on the back seat. Then he walked around the car and slipped into the driver's seat and closed the door. He reached down under the front seat and pulled out a silver roll of duct tape. He peeled off a piece and leaned over the seat and put it across her mouth. He grabbed a couple of zip ties from under the seat and bound her feet and then her hands behind her back. Always carry duct tape and zip ties, his father said. Always. Bastard knew what he was talking about.

Bronco took a close look at the girl. A nasty bump was rising under a red scrape on her forehead. She was breathing and moaning a little, but she was still out of it. She'd probably stay that way until he got home, he thought. He threw a jacket and newspaper over her to make it not quite so obvious that he had a captive in the back. He thought about putting her in the trunk, but he'd already spent too much time hanging around. No, he was much better off just getting out of there quickly. The less time you mess around, he thought, the less chance you have of being spotted.

He started the car and headed home. He just made one stop—in the restroom parking lot, where he found his lighter on the ground. Bronco lit a cigarette for the ride back.

All Blue could remember were snapshots of things—streetlights going by, cigarette smoke, vinyl car seat. She had an aching forehead and she was woozy and couldn't focus very well. She was aware that she was in a car and that she had tape across her mouth. She could feel that her hands and feet were bound but she was too dizzy to think straight or be afraid. She felt like she was in a fuzzy dream.

The next snapshot was being carried in the dark from the backseat of the car and through the side door of a yellow house.

And then she woke up in a bed in the dark. Her head was on a soft pillow and she had a blanket over her. It was comforting, even though she didn't know where she was. Her hands and feet were still bound and the tape was still across her mouth. Her head ached and she felt dizzy but awake enough to be able to look around her. She tried to pierce the darkness with her eyes but it was hard with the pounding in her head. There was the very faintest glow from a shaded window, the light from the moon making the pane into a white square. She slowly made out the shape of a small bedroom. She identified a dresser on one wall and a nightstand next to the bed. There was a door across from her. It beckoned escape. A little flutter of hope started to well in her chest, but along with it was the growing realization of her predicament. And the danger she was in. Her eyes erupted in a reflexive cry, "*WILL* . . . ?" A sharp pain in her head stopped the vox short.

The pain throbbed for a minute but then subsided. When she could think straight again, she ventured getting out of bed. She moved her legs toward the edge of the bed, but they stopped short, contained by an unyielding tether. At the same time, a sound of movement inside the room brought her wide-awake. She stared hard in the direction of the sound and then froze.

A dark, unidentifiable mass near the door came alive like a living shadow. It grunted, "Hmm, you're finally awake."

The mass expanded up and resolved itself into the shape of a person. It moved over towards her and as it did it leaked *chiss*,

"*Let's see what we have here,*" then spoke, "So I suppose you're wondering where you are, but I bet you can guess who I am."

Of course she knew. Even in the dark, there was no mistaking the voice or the *chiss* she had be surveilling all summer.

He went on, speaking in a reassuring tone but maintaining the slightest undercurrent of menace. "You are in a nice safe, secure spot, for now, and I'm not going to hurt you. At least, I won't hurt you as long as you cooperate."

Bronco squatted down next to the bed, and Blue could finally make out his familiar features.

"So I'd like to think you'll cooperate. Can I count on you to cooperate?" Bronco was looking straight at her. His *chiss* came through loud and clear. A little too loud and clear for Blue. "*Please don't get hysterical on me, little girl, I could break that skinny neck in two seconds if I had to. But I suppose a little H would do for now to keep you sedated.*"

Blue involuntarily jerked her head back and took in a sharp breath. The comfort of the bed and the notion of feeling safe evaporated. Bronco's thoughts were hard and cold, devoid of any empathy or humanity, and they sent a chill down Blue's spine. She suddenly realized that this guy was more dangerous than she had ever imagined.

Bronco acted startled at her reaction. "*Hmmm, maybe I should just go straight to the H . . .*"

Blue started to shake her head, but realized this was the wrong reaction. She switched to nodding her head desperately. She wanted to show that she would cooperate. She realized she had to be extremely careful around this guy.

He gave her a puzzled look. "So, you'll cooperate then?" he asked.

Blue nodded again, more calmly. She relaxed her body and expression a little.

Bronco apparently took this as a sign of assent. "Okay, then. This isn't very hard. I just need you to relax and sleep through until morning. You need sleep after that knock on your head. I know what it's like. I've been knocked in the head." He was speaking in a conspiratorial tone. She could tell he was trying to manipulate her. "It wasn't me that hit you on the head, by the way, you ran into a tree branch. Do you remember?"

Blue shook her head. She remembered up to the point she started running but nothing after that.

"Yep, you ran like the dickens, right into that branch. I nearly hit it myself. So, you get some sleep, and you keep quiet. It'll do you good. But just remember, I'll be listening and watching all the time. I've got a little video camera over there on the dresser and I can check it any time on my phone. You see that?" He pointed up the dresser, "It's got a motion sensor on it, too, so I'll know the minute you start moving around."

There was a small surveillance camera on a tripod. Now she really felt defeated. How could she possibly get away, and if she did, where was she? She wasn't even sure she could stand or run if she did get away. He wasn't wrong. She needed the rest if she was going to be able to make a move later. It would be much easier to run and find help in the daylight anyway, since she didn't know where she was. She fell back onto the pillow, which was starting to feel comforting again.

Bronco was apparently satisfied with her reaction. "Okay then. That's what we like to see. I'll be very close by, so don't dream up anything dramatic." He got up and walked over to the door and then added. "You get dramatic, I get dramatic," he said. "Broken legs and arms are very dramatic. I don't mind breaking arms and legs. I've had plenty of practice." Then he shut the door.

She shuddered. It wasn't what he said. It was the way he said it —without any hint of humanity. She was in deep trouble.

21

SLEEPLESS

Will couldn't sleep. What Blue had said the night before kept him tossing and turning, his head buzzing with thoughts. *Maybe she's right, maybe there are times when you just have to break rules, take drastic action. Maybe I'm just being a coward. No, this is nuts, we are just kids. We need to tell cops . . . adults . . . someone!*

He considered which adult he would tell—Mom? No, she worked at the school and she had a legal obligation to tell the authorities if a kid was involved in any suspected drug activity going on. Blue would be screwed. Who were the 'authorities' anyway? The FBI? The cops? The DFC? Any of them would be bad for Blue. It would probably get the O'Days in trouble, too. The cops? Well, maybe Chief Hannah would overlook Blue's involvement, but even she needed evidence to act on anything.

So here he was back at the beginning. He and Blue needed evidence in order to get anyone's attention and it should be convincing and anonymous. No one listened to kids about serious stuff like this unless something that couldn't be ignored was shoved right under their noses. Will was beginning to convince himself that maybe Blue was right. After all, just about everything she had said and talked about sounded like she was way ahead of him when it came to worldly matters like this. She obviously thought about things like this often and was passionate about them, driven by some deep motivation she felt she couldn't share.

Will tried to think of anything he was passionate about. Basketball? That seemed kind of shallow. Science? That had at least had some merit. But what did that matter beyond his own self? What did he care about outside himself? Well, he cared about his mom and dad. He and Rose were pretty tight, and he cared about her. Blue had said that if these drug dealers didn't get caught, more and more kids were going to have their lives ruined. And Rose was one of those kids that could be affected. Rose, taking drugs? Will shuddered. That seemed way too creepy and depressing. He couldn't imagine Rose as a sullen druggie. Was it possible? He had friends whose sisters or brothers had gotten into drugs. Some he wasn't surprised about, but some were kids Will never guessed would go that way.

So wasn't getting these guys arrested the same as protecting Rose? And didn't his parents say he should always stick up for Rose? And what about Blue? Did he care for her? What about protecting her? He must not have cared enough to go with her tonight. On the other hand, she seemed invincible.

Arrgh! It was too confusing. He felt like he was doing what adults always expected of him—sticking to the rules. It was a safe path. If anything happened, no one would blame him, and everyone would say he made the right choice. But it didn't feel that way. It felt like cowardice. It felt like abandonment. He wanted to change his mind and go, but he just couldn't bring himself to do it. The thought of getting up, going out, and trying to bust some drug dealers was just ridiculous. He was sure that Blue would come to the same conclusion and chicken out, too. At least he hoped so. Morning would bring the answer and reveal that this whole thing had been just a crazy idea and nothing real would come from it. Blue would make more plans, not do them, and just be a wanna-be superhero like every other kid. The sooner Will fell asleep, the sooner morning would come, and this whole crummy feeling he was having would be over.

He laid down in the dark, scrunched up his pillow, closed his eyes and sighed. His mind was still buzzing. What if, what if, what if? Cowardice, abandonment, crazy plans, drug dealers, Rose turning into a drug addict, Blue tackling the drug lord Gronk and tying him up. News headlines declaring Blue a heroine. Heroin, heroine, dope, dopey.

He just could not get to sleep. He tossed, he turned, thought he was asleep, looked at the clock. Still only 1:30. God, it was hours until morning. The drug deal would have already gone down. It was officially too late. Still, he couldn't stand it. He got up in the dark. He could at least sneak out, go across the street, check Blue's window, and if she was awake, check to see if she had gone or not, been successful or not. If she was asleep, it wouldn't matter—at least he would have done something.

Without changing out of his pajamas, Will stuck his sneakers on. He was only going to slip across the street and down the block, and no one was going to see him at that time of night. He opened his window and slipped silently out, just as they had practiced. It was a pretty cool feeling, being able to slip around unnoticed. He crossed the street, keeping to the well-known shadowy spots. He knew the area well now and didn't stub his toe or run into anything in the dark. He crouched at the spot in the O'Day yard where he had the best angle for reflecting vox into her room. It was quiet. There were no police cars or sirens or anything unusual going on. Everything seemed perfectly normal for that time of night.

He did his signature, "CLICK, CLICK, CLICK," and watched for a moment. He waited for her "CHT, CHT, CHT" reply. It didn't come. He did it again, "CLICK, CLICK, CLICK, CLICK." Nothing. He kept at it a few minutes more, but then he gave up. If she was awake, she would have come to the window by then. She had either gone out and come back safely or had never gone out, and he was guessing, the latter, but deep down, he was hoping for the former. It would be pretty cool if she pulled it off. The only way to find out for sure was to sneak into the O'Day house and up to her room. He considered that for a minute but . . . no way. No way could he do something that bold. If he were caught he would have no explanation of what he was doing and why. His parents would flip. The O'Days would flip. Wu would probably be completely miffed. And Nate? Well, getting on the wrong side of Nate was a scary proposition.

Will came to the realization that basically, his excursion tonight had accomplished nothing. But at least he had tried, and that was something. And there were no sirens, only the normal peaceful night sounds. That made him feel a little better.

He quickly slipped back to his room and checked the clock. It was 2 a.m. and this time when his head hit the pillow, he went straight to sleep.

22

BRONCO

He should leave tonight. That's what kept running through Bronco's head after he left the room where the girl was tied up. Leave tonight and I can get out of here clean, he thought. The problem was, the bulk of his "earnings" from the last ten months was sitting in a safe deposit box at the bank and he couldn't get at that until 9 a.m. He was kicking himself for using a safe deposit box, but he knew he had to. Keeping that much money around the house was risky. Nothing worse than a criminal getting criminalized.

He grabbed the police scanner out of his backpack, his bug-out bag. It was stuffed with the critical items he would need in case he had to make a quick escape. He switched on the scanner and set it on the kitchen table. He slid out his laptop and put it on the table, along with his cell phone, and he plugged them both into their chargers. Then he put on some coffee. It was 2 a.m. He wasn't going to get any sleep, and he had a lot of planning to do. He wanted his equipment charged and ready to go and he wanted to be charged and ready to go.

There was no activity on the scanner, at least not yet. He

expected the night cruiser to do a check-in with the dispatcher periodically, and once he heard that, he would know that no one had called in a missing person.

He considered the situation carefully. He recognized this girl. It was a girl he had seen at the park when he was getting Jack started with the dope trade. She was notable because she was a loner—carried a book bag, sat by herself, and did a lot of reading. He had looked for identification on her when she was still half-conscious, but all he found was a name written with a permanent marker on her shirt tag: O'Day. That should be enough for him to find some information on her. If she was from a well-connected family, he would have to consider leaving his safe deposit box behind. He wasn't going to stick around if somebody pulled out all the stops looking for this kid. It wasn't worth it.

On the other hand, the fact that she was a loner kid with a high-tech camera, and that no one had reported her missing yet, meant that she probably "borrowed" the camera and snuck out without telling anyone. This wasn't an activity any parent would sanction, so she was probably on her own. Pretty gutsy kid, but pretty stupid also. On the other hand, he had to give her credit. She had nearly nailed him. The video and the stills she had captured on that night vision camera were good. Good enough to put him in jail. If he hadn't dropped his lighter, that's where he'd be headed. That bugged him. He had nearly gotten caught down in the city a couple of times, but that was by cops, and that was their job. That was why he was up here and why he was being way more careful. But this came out of nowhere. Who in hell would suspect a little kid in a park of being some sort of mini-vigilante, and why would this kid be after him? And most importantly, how did she get the information she had? And who else knew about it?

The wild card was just that. When would the police get the call, and how much had this girl left behind that they could use to catch him? And how the hell did she find out about the rendezvous the previous night? And where the hell did she get that night vision camera? That was not just a consumer night vision camera, this was the kind people bought for jacking deer or spying.

As for the rendezvous, Jack was about the only person who would know, besides his customers. He and Jack had talked it over more than once in public. Could she have overheard when they were in the park? Not likely. Bronco was way too cautious for that. He was sure no one could possibly have heard them, unless they had Superman-like hearing or could read lips. He considered that for a moment. It seemed daft, reading lips—too much like a movie script. It didn't happen in real life. There were lip readers out there, of course, but they were usually deaf and had to focus carefully to understand a person. They'd have to be right in front of you, and this girl had never been even close. And she certainly wasn't deaf.

Maybe one of his customers gave it away, but why would they do that? They would put themselves at risk, too, and why would they tell a kid? Maybe she was a stoner. Maybe Jack had sold her some weed. Maybe she had asked for something more. Jack could have told her about how to get heroin, but even Jack didn't know any details about when or where a deal happened. For any new potential customer, Jack would give Bronco a phone number and some background info. Bronco would call the customer and set up a place and a time, but he would only give them an exact time after he had confirmed that the night police cruiser had passed or was out of range.

It kept coming down to the same thing—it didn't make sense that anyone would give information like that to a kid. And it was clear that no one had talked to the police already. If the police knew, he would be hearing a lot more activity on the scanner. That was the one sure thing. The police did not know about the drug deal. They would never know about the drug deal. His customers did not know his identity. This girl was the one person that could nail him, and the police did not know where she was. He was going to make sure it stayed that way until he was a long way away. He just needed to find out who she was and where she lived. Once he had that information he would have better control of the situation.

He typed "O'Day Westbury Vermont" into Google, and the results relaxed him a little. The whole first page was full of good hits. It looked like there was only one O'Day family in town, and it was a foster family. It looks like his girl might be a foster kid, and that was a good sign. Their first thought would be "runaway" and that was a whole lot better than "abducted." Better for him, anyway.

He made up his mind, he was going to stick around and get his money. That would also give him more time to erase as many of his tracks as possible. This was better. Be smart, take your time, don't look like you're in a hurry, don't look like anything is out of the ordinary. That's how you stay out of jail. Hide in plain sight like what his father had taught him. His father may have been a bastard, but he was damn good at staying out of jail.

Then he had to decide what to do with the girl. His preference was to just leave her behind and then maybe call in an anonymous tip in a couple of days with information on where they could find her alive once he was safely gone. If they found her alive and had no trail to follow, they would give up. It wasn't worth the search, not for a two-bit drug dealer. They would just be happy he disappeared and that they got the girl back safely.

His second choice was to kill her and dump the body. This was not a problem either. He'd helped his dad dump plenty of bodies. It just involved a good location and a lot of digging, which he was not fond of. It would also require the cover of darkness, which meant he would have to wait around until after dark to leave. He had no real reason to kill her yet, except the certainty that anything in that head of hers that could get him nailed would be erased, unequivocally. He doubted a great deal if she knew anything that would help the police to follow him once he had split. But he was going to find out when she woke up.

For now, he had a lot of other things to do in the time before the bank opened. First thing was to find out more about this O'Day family. Bronco poured a cup of coffee and got to work.

23

———

CAPTIVE

Blue kept trying to get some sleep, but between the throbbing in her head, the digging of the zip-ties, and the ache in her shoulders from having her hands bound behind her, she was having little success. She would nod off uncomfortably until the throbbing woke her again, and then she'd try another position, and nod off again, only to wake again moments later. It seemed like forever, but eventually, daylight came and in spite of the hellish night, she felt a little bit rested. She lay there alone in the dimness of the early morning and tried to set aside the pain and discomfort and think of what she could possibly do to get out of there. Unfortunately, a new concern started to dominate all her thoughts. She had to pee. Badly. She couldn't believe that a biological function could trump being kidnapped, but there it was. Time slowed to a crawl and she was getting to the point where she couldn't hold it anymore when she heard a noise outside the room and then watched as the door opened and Bronco stepped into the room. She hated herself for being happy to see him as he was the only one that could save her from her immediate plight.

Bronco looked at her and mistook her pleading look, "Don't worry, girl, I'm not going to break your arms. You cooperated nicely." He walked over, pulled a chair to the bed and sat opposite her. He said the words she was hoping he'd say, but his menacing tone was a reminder of her real predicament, "I'm going to pull the tape off your mouth. Don't even think about shouting for help. You make a single loud sound, and you will not make another. You got that?"

Blue nodded sincerely. She was going to be the cooperative captive as much as she could. At least for now.

He reached over to her face. She felt him tugging at the tape and then felt it slowly release from her skin. As soon as a corner of her mouth was free, she finally ventured her urgent question, "I've really got to pee."

Bronco glared at her. "All right, just don't do it right here. I'll get you to a bathroom."

He released her from the bed frame, but her hands were still bound behind her back. He carried her to a small closet toilet. She was shocked at how clean and tidy it was. Somehow she expected a low-life like Bronco to be a slob. He set her down on her feet and then took out a pocket knife. She stiffened.

"Relax, little girl—I'm just taking the zip tie off your wrists. Turn around."

She hopped herself around on her bound feet and then felt his knife cut through the zip tie. The relief on her shoulders and wrist were instant. He turned her back around and said, "Your feet stayed tied. I'm not taking a chance of you running. You are way too fast. Just sit down and do your business, I'll be standing right outside." And he stood up and stepped out, but kept the door halfway open.

She took a second to move her arms around and to get her hands working again. It felt so good to move them! She managed to get her pants down without falling over and sat down on the toilet. It was hard for her to relax but she managed to 'do her business'. The relief was tremendous. Unfortunately, filling the void that the relief left behind was a sickly feeling in the pit of her stomach. She was a prisoner, she didn't know where she was, and she didn't know what Bronco was going to do to her.

She stood up pulled up her pants and zipped them. She flushed the toilet and whispered, "I'm done." He opened the door all the way and picked her up and carried her back into the room. He wasn't rough, just business-like, carrying her like a piece of furniture. He sat her down in an armchair.

"Sit still for a minute," he said. He picked up a roll of duct tape and reached for her upper arm. She instinctively pulled her arm away, but he grabbed her firmly and said "I said sit still. I need to tie your arms up for a while until we can trust each other. This will be more comfortable than the zip ties, but I can zip tie your hands behind your back again if you'd like." He looked at her. She looked at him. His eyes were dead. His words sounded sympathetic, but they were just words with nothing even human backing them up. It was the most terrifying thing she had ever seen. There was no doubt this guy was a psychopath. She put her arm back and sat very still.

He didn't say anything more. He pulled off a long piece off of duct tape and wrapped it around her upper arm, and around the back rail of the chair. It was snug but her shirt protected her from the aggressive stickiness of the tape. He then taped her forearm to the arm of the chair. He did her other arm the same way, and then cut the zip ties off her ankles and taped them securely to the chair legs. She wiggled them a little and her heart fell. He had used a lot of tape.

"There now," he said. "You can move your arms around a little and scratch your navel if you want, but good luck trying to get out of that." He sat back studying his work with satisfaction.

"Now let's have a little chat. I don't know who you are or what the hell you thought you were doing last night. All I know is that you're a kid that made the mistake of sticking her nose in my business, and now I have to take care of you somehow, like a stray dog."

He stared at his feet and started tapping one foot thoughtfully.

"I took a look at that night vision camera of yours. You recorded a very nice video. I'd like to think it was just an accidental film, just something you thought interesting to shoot, while you were casually walking around dressed in black clothes and blackened face past midnight in the park. I like how you zoomed in on the license plate and the faces. It came out very clear. It's a very nice piece of equipment. I'm wondering where the heck you picked it up."

Shit, Blue thought. He didn't ask her a direct question, but she knew he wanted an answer. The night vision camera—how could she explain it? She didn't want to implicate Will or his family. Bronco was turning out to be very smart. Dangerously smart. She felt herself starting to sweat and at the same time, the throbbing in her head started re-asserting itself. Clearly, the knock on the head was more than just a bruise. She winced as the throbbing started to be punctuated with sharp stabs.

The wince saved her for the moment. Bronco saw it and looked at her forehead.

"You've got a nice little goose egg there. You took quite a knock on the head. Maybe you don't remember it, but I heard it. *Whack!* And you were out cold. You know, you almost got away." He spoke in almost an admiring tone.

Blue wasn't sure what to make of it. Maybe he was giving her some credit—some leeway. Maybe she could milk that for something, but maybe he was just trying to manipulate her. She knew manipulation. She had had plenty of that in her therapy sessions. She was going to have to be very careful with this guy, but she was having a hard time concentrating. Her head really did hurt. She did another convincing wince. It was convincing because it was real.

"Okay, I'm going to give you some acetaminophen—Tylenol," said Bronco. He was being nice to her. He was trying to soften her up, she thought. "That's better for this than the other stuff. Trust me, I've been hit in the head a lot. But before I do, I want to know, where is that camera from?"

He wasn't going to let her off, but she had managed to think of a good answer.

"I kinda borrowed it," she said, knowing this was bending the truth, but she bent it back, ". . . kinda without telling anyone I was borrowing it. I was going to put it back."

She caught his *chiss*. *"I buy that,"* Bronco thought. *"I've 'borrowed' plenty of stuff. Doesn't everyone?"* "Fair enough," he said. "Does this person know why you 'borrowed' it?" Bronco may have bought it, but he wasn't letting up on her.

She reeled from a sudden excruciating stab of pain and croaked out "No, no, no, ow, oh!" and closed her eyes to the pain. She was saying no to the pain, not to answer the question.

Bronco sat dispassionately, but apparently it was good enough for him. "All right, let's take care of that pain." He went out of the room and came back with a glass of water and two white pills. She took them gratefully and waited, hoping they would work soon. She kept her eyes closed partly because of the pain and partly because she just didn't want to hear what Bronco was thinking right now. It didn't stop his voice, though.

"We'll let this Tylenol do its stuff, and I'll be back in a while. I've got some errands to do. We'll chat again later. While you're sitting here, though, I want you to consider that it will be a lot better for both of us if you come clean with your story. A little honesty, and we'll work something out." His words sounded sincere, but she knew bullshit when she heard it.

"Sorry about this, but I have to tape your mouth up again." He tore off a piece of duct tape and put it across her mouth with feigned care. "There, is that a little more comfortable than before?"

Blue nodded cooperatively. It wasn't comfortable at all.

"Good." He patted her hand and got up. He started toward the door and then paused and turned. "Oh, and just a little something to consider while I'm gone. If you are thinking about trying to escape, don't forget about the camera," and he held up his phone and pointed to the camera on the dresser. "And if I ever check this camera, and you are not sitting nicely in this chair, well . . ." He looked at her with a deadly expression, "I wouldn't want anything to happen to Wu or Sam or Nate."

Those names hovered in the air between them for a ghastly moment and then shot through the fog of pain and exploded into shards that shot through her whole body. The room started to spin. She felt like she was falling. He had lied! He *did* know who she was! How did he get those names? She had made sure she didn't have any ID on her, didn't she? Through the spinning, Bronco's face came into focus. It had a wicked smile on it. "Oh and I almost forgot, we can't overlook those friends of yours—Will and Rose."

Everything came to a stop, the spinning, the falling, her breathing, her heart. There was a pause as if the universe itself had stopped turning, and in that silence, the only sounds were her shrill, panicked thoughts. This was not possible! How could he have learned all this? How much more did he know? What would he do to them?

The questions were left unanswered because the pain and spinning returned with a suddenness and ferocity that would have knocked her off the chair if she hadn't been bound to it. The throbbing pain hammered like a drum—doom, doom, doom—driving home with every beat the realization that somehow she had caused an unspeakable nightmare to be unleashed on the people around her who had done nothing but accept her and support her. It was exactly what she was trying to protect them from. Instead, she *made* it happen. *She* was the cause, the curse, the bane, the Jonah.

Bronco's self-satisfied voice went on, "Well, I'd love to keep chatting, but I've got some errands to run. Have a nice day, and I'll see you later." She caught a glimpse of his face as he turned, and she wished she hadn't. It showed the smugness of someone who knew very well that they had complete control.

Bronco stepped out. The door closed. He was gone. And behind him, in a dimly lit room, strapped to a chair in a house that was god-knows-where, a broken girl cried for real, for the first time in a long, long time.

24

STORM

Will had a dream that he was on the deck of a ship that was lurching unpredictably as storm waves tossed it about. It was one of those half-awake dreams where you know you are dreaming but can't quite wake up. A voice was hissing at him, "Will, wake up! WAKE UP!" Will opened his eyes groggily. It was light out —had he actually slept through to morning? Rose was shaking him back and forth and whispering as loud as she could and still call it a whisper, "Will, would you please WAKE UP! Blue is missing! Would you wake up?"

Will sat up, not sure if he heard right, but shocked enough that he was wide awake. He couldn't have heard right. He matched Rose's loud whisper, "Did you just say Blue is missing?"

"Yessss!" she said emphatically, "And you are impossible to wake up! Mom and Dad got a phone call just a few minutes ago from the O'Days. They were asking if Blue was here. Is she here Will?"

Why would she be here? "No, of course not!"

"If she isn't here and she's not at the O'Days . . ." she trailed off.

Will's heart sank. This was exactly what wasn't supposed to happen! Things were always better in the morning, it was almost a rule. Instead, it seemed things had gone horribly wrong. There must be some explanation. Things had to be okay. Blue had to be somewhere safe, he reasoned. There was no other possibility he even wanted to consider.

"Will," said Rose, "Where could she be? She has to be somewhere, right?" It was a pleading kind of nonsense question, not wanting to ask the real question that was nagging at Will's mind, too. *She has to be somewhere safe and not . . . the other thing* which was "not safe" and just not possible. There had to be an explanation.

Will jumped up and started pulling on his clothes. "*Rosie, I'll be right back. There's one place she might be, but don't tell anyone yet, okay? I have to check first! I don't want her to get in trouble!*"

"*I wanna go with you!*" voxed Rose.

"*Hey, little Meerkat, you can't. I don't want you to get in trouble.*" Will knelt down and held Rose by the shoulders and looked her in the face. He knew she'd like being called meerkat, but she wasn't grinning this time. "*Okay?*"

"*Okay,*" she replied, "*But where are you going?*"

"*I'll tell you when I get back, but promise not to say anything. Just tell Mom and Dad I was already up and gone, okay?*" And with that, Will slipped out his window.

Rose whispered after him, "Okay, but I can't lie if they ask me!"

Will just gave her the thumbs up as he went around the back of the garage, slipped in the side door, grabbed his bike, and shot off down the hill to the park. He didn't know what he was expecting to find, but he couldn't think of anything else to do. If she wasn't at the O'Days and she wasn't at his house, then she had to be there—asleep on a bench, or in a bush, or in that tree or something!

He headed straight for the parking lot by the restrooms. It looked entirely different during the day. He studied the tree they had climbed. It looked like it couldn't possibly hide anything. He wondered how they could have convinced themselves that it was a good hiding place. They had checked it carefully at night, but seeing it during the day, it just didn't seem possible.

He checked all around, in the bushes and in both restrooms, hoping that he would find her asleep somewhere. Nothing. He scanned the ground around the restrooms and tree but didn't know what he was looking for. A discarded piece of clothing, a lock of hair, a shoe, blood? There was nothing but grass, dirt, a few bits of trash and a lot of cigarette butts.

Will pedaled despondently back up the hill, thinking hard. This was not good, not good at all. There was nothing, absolutely nothing at the park to tell him whether she had been there or not. He was trying to think of alternative places. He looked left and right as he rode, checking the spots they had hidden in or spied from. He was desperate to see her sleeping in the bushes, or hiding somewhere, just to jump him when he passed by. He kept up a steady, "CLICK, CLICK, CLICK. . ." ever hopeful that he would hear that reassuring "CHT, CHT, CHT . . . GOT YOU!"

He was almost to his house and his hope was draining out and being replaced with a slowly forming ominous possibility. Before he could ponder that possibility, though, Rose spotted him and came running out in the yard. "MOM'S BEEN LOOKING FOR YOU. I DIDN'T TELL, AND I DIDN'T LIE! YOU SHOULD HURRY INSIDE, THOUGH."

"THANKS, ROSIE. YOU'RE THE BEST SISTER," voxed Will.

"I'M YOUR ONLY SISTER," she voxed but without the usual smile at the old joke.

Will parked his bike and walked into the house. His mom was sitting at the table and had just hung up the phone. She had a list of names in front of her and about half of them were crossed off.

Her lips were pressed tight and her face full of concern. "Will, I'm glad you're home. We got a call this morning and . . ."

"Blue's missing. I know Rose told me. What's going on Mom?" Will asked. He decided to play dumb, so he could get the full story from his mom.

"Ma Beth said that they had breakfast around nine this

morning and Blue didn't come down, which wasn't that unusual to them, I guess. But when it got to be ten, and Blue still hadn't come down Ma Beth decided to check on her. When she went to her bedroom, Blue wasn't there. Her bed was made as if she'd gotten up already. Ma Beth said they checked everywhere in the house and didn't find her. None of the boys knew where she was or where she might be, so she started calling other places Blue could be." Will's Mom paused and then looked intently at Will. "*Do you know where she could be? Did she visit here last night?*"

Will voxed back, "*She wasn't here last night! Why would she be here?*" He wondered why she would have asked that. He looked sideways at Rose but Rose looked back at him and shrugged.

His mom said, "Okay, but do you know where she could be?"

Will hesitated. He could tell her that she might have gone to the park last night. She would've been back by now, unless something went wrong, but he still wanted to believe that it couldn't have, that something else was going on. "I don't know, really Mom," and then he decided to add, "She does like to be out at night, but she never stays out!"

"Okay," she said. "Then maybe we can at least start looking for her outside. She might have fallen asleep somewhere. It is still early. They say 90% of runaways are usually found somewhere right around home."

Will realized that his mom did not want to consider the bad possibilities either. She was calling Blue a runaway, and Will was trying to believe that, too.

"I'll start looking around the neighborhood for places we hung out. I bet she'll be asleep in a bush somewhere," said Will.

Rose said, "I'll come, too!"

But their Mom said, "No honey. You need to stay here."

Rose looked crushed, but Mom just said, "No pouty faces!"

Rose voxed to Will, "*I hope YOU find her, and soon!*"

"*Yeah, me too, little Rose,*" and he smiled. "*No problem.*" But inside, a hot pressure was starting to develop, an inkling of dread that he was not going to find Blue or that he would find something he did not want to find. He tried to brush it off, but just like last night, he was feeling like his body was being more truthful to him than his mind was. What his body was telling him was that something bad had happened and there wasn't much time.

25

MOVING DAY

Bronco had a lot to do, and he wanted to get it done quickly. He was confident that Blue wouldn't cause trouble for the moment. She also wouldn't be in the way. He reflected on his luck that the neighbors were out of town on vacation for another week and that they had left their keys with him so he could water their plants. Bronco had left the house with his little hostage secure in their back bedroom and returned to his apartment, but not before he had watered all the plants. Then he brewed a fresh pot of coffee and started going down the checklist he had carefully prepared in his mind. First thing was to collect all his local assets. Although he had transferred most of the assets from his dad's estate to his bank in New York City, he still had close to $90,000 of his earnings in gold and cash in his safe deposit box here. It was just before 9 a.m. now, so by the time he finished his coffee, the bank would be open.

There had been no alarming traffic on the police scanner all night, which was encouraging. It was a Saturday morning, and it could be a long time before someone in the O'Day household got around to saying, "Anyone seen Blue this morning?" After that, there would be a search, phone calls to neighbors, yadda yadda yadda. He'd seen it happen when his friends ran away—when he ran away. He was guessing it would be noon before the cops were called and then to them she would just be a runaway, unless someone came up with something very credible to convince them otherwise. He was guessing not. That was part of his gamble, and that was what he was going to pry out of the little lone ranger when he got back. Meanwhile, he had time to get the first part of his list done. He drained the last bit of coffee out of his cup, stepped out of the apartment with a quick glance at the shaded window in the house next door, and then got in his car and headed to the bank.

As he drove, he reviewed his plan. He figured he had about a day before the police got involved and made some connection with him and this car and his apartment. A day if they were good. But when they did, they'd discover it belonged to his current persona, Bob Kelly. By then, Bob Kelly would have vanished from the face of the earth, because he had never really existed. Bob Kelly owned the car and he had a genuine Vermont drivers license and an authentic birth certificate. He even voted in the last election. But it was all a fraud. It was an insider built-up ID, very reliable. You couldn't just buy an ID like that, unless you knew someone. It was expensive, but it had already paid for itself ten-fold. And now it was going to pay off even more. He was going to leave Bob Kelly behind in this little college town and if the police ever tied any drug deals or killings to Bronco and then tied that to Bob Kelly, well, Bob Kelly was fiction. No one in this town knew Bronco's real identity; he'd been very careful of that. His customers didn't even know about Bob Kelly, they only knew him as Bronco. Double protection.

Now Bob Kelly was going to go to his bank and access his safe deposit box, and he would even exchange some pleasantries with the staff to make everything look normal and innocent. Of course, he was going to wipe his prints from the safe deposit box at the same time. Then he was going back to his apartment to scrub it down and make sure there were no obvious tracks left behind. They would find something eventually, sure, but it wouldn't be enough, and it wouldn't be in time. And it would all be tied to the wrong person.

The last item on his list was a final interview with the little detective. That would give him the information he needed to make his final exit plans. He was starting to get in a better mood now that he had a plan and was committed to it. He was going to have a busy day, and he was actually looking forward to maybe playing hide-and-seek with the cops later on. He was hoping they would make it interesting, though he doubted it. The police were loaded down with procedure and law, and he was not. They knew very little, and he knew everything. Situational knowledge was everything, and they were starting from scratch. He almost felt sorry for them. Well, not completely sorry. He still needed to win the game and until that was accomplished, he was going to make it as difficult as possible for them to follow him. And since this was his last time, he was going to give it his all. After this, it was retirement—a nice rich retirement somewhere else, somewhere warm, somewhere that was not New York and not New England. Maybe Costa Rica . . . .

26

SEED OF PANIC

As soon as he started the search around the neighborhood, Will knew it was pointless. He felt sure he wasn't going to find her here, but he had to at least eliminate the possibility, plus it gave him time to think. He was in such a panic when he got out of bed that he just went into automatic, going down to the park without thinking it through. He was starting to realize that the only thing that made sense was that Blue had somehow gotten caught by Gronk or Greazal, or maybe the couple who was buying the drugs.

Will considered the idea that it might have been something totally unrelated, like maybe she was mugged because of the night vision camera, since it was pretty valuable. He was starting to regret that he hadn't immediately gone over to the O'Day's and asked for it back yesterday. He had let it go partly because of the way he and Blue had parted, and partly because he was implicitly loaning it to her so she could follow through with her plan. That made him a partial accomplice.

He didn't think a mugging was likely, though. Blue was far too skilled to let something like that happen. Even if it had, she still would have returned home. Unless the unthinkable happened. He pushed that out of his mind.

He ran into Nate, who was going around to the neighbor's houses and knocking on doors. Nate had a paper in his hand that had a picture of Blue—an ID picture from her file. She looked a lot younger, but just as serious. "Hey Will, I just got a call. The police are at our house and Ma Beth wants us all to come back, so they can interview us."

Will went back to his house where his mom and Rose were waiting for him. Together, they walked quickly down to the O'Day's house. There were two police cars outside, and the whole O'Day family was out in the front yard. Nate was already busy talking to the police. Will spotted Wu and Sam, and he and Rose went over to meet them, while his mom went on to join the group of adults.

"Will! Rose!" yelled Wu. As they walked over he immediately launched into explaining the situation. "Ma Beth called for Blue when she didn't come down for breakfast this morning and then she went up to check, and she wasn't there. So we all started looking. We turned the house upside down, I mean *upside down*, and then we turned it upside down again while Ma Beth started calling the neighbors. She finally called the cops, and they just got here. I've been looking all around the yard in case she fell asleep outside or something, but she would have been awake by now."

While Wu was blurting out the details, Sam was nodding his head in agreement. Wu went into a loud whisper, looking over his shoulder first to make sure he wouldn't be overheard, "Will, did she sneak over to your house last night? I know she has been doing it, but I never told anyone!" Wu had grabbed Will by the shoulders firmly with a flash of desperation and a little bit of anger in his eyes.

Will looked back in surprise and said completely sincerely, "No, Wu, she didn't come over last night, honest. Believe me, I wouldn't lie to you about this." Wu relaxed his grip and his glare. Will added, "And thanks for not telling anyone. How did you guys know?"

Sam had been wiggling to get a word in edgewise, and he finally piped up, "I know she went out last night—she thinks she can get by everyone else." He looked at Wu, "But I know how she does it, and I figured out how to..." Sam trailed off, because Wu was signaling him to hush. A female police officer was walking over to the small group.

Wu said, "Hey Chief Hannah, can you tell us what's up?" Will recognized the officer—she was the police liaison officer at school, so a lot of kids knew her.

"Hey Wu," she said. "And this is Will, right? And who are you, miss?" directing this last question at Rose.

"I'm Will's sister. My name is Rose" she said boldly.

"Nice to meet you, Rose," Chief Hannah said with a kindly smile. Then her face became more business-like but still kindly. "Okay, I am going to be straight with all of you kids. We are considering this a runaway right at the moment. There is nothing to indicate that it is anything else. You may have heard that most runaways are found close to home. This is true. It is also true that as time goes by, the chances of finding the person drop very rapidly. We think that Blue has been missing for about 12 hours, which is not good." She paused to gauge the effect of what she was saying to her young audience. They were all somber, but not panicking. She decided to go on.

"What helps a lot—and I mean a lot—is information. Information about where she might have gone, if she left on her own, and it seems that she left on her own. If any of you know anything about why she left or where she was going, it would increase our chances a great deal." She paused. "Look, I know a lot goes on that you'd rather not let adults know about—I was a kid once, believe it or not. Right now, however, is not a good time to play this game. Adults and kids need to be honest. No one is going to get in trouble if it leads to finding Blue. Is there anything you want to share now?"

Wu, Will, and Sam couldn't help but squirm and glance at each other a little bit. Rose was cool as a cucumber. So was Chief Hannah. She was watching them carefully. She looked at each of them and then said, "Okay, but if any of you think of something, the sooner the better, and come right to me, right? Here is my card—you can contact me any time, and I mean any time—even if it is the middle of the night, okay?" She handed out business cards to everyone.

They all nodded their heads. Chief Hannah nodded back and then said, "Okay. Don't hesitate to call, I mean it." And with one last meaningful glance, she walked back to the group of officers talking to the adults.

Wu, Will, Sam, and Rose watched her go, and then immediately started talking intensely among themselves.

Wu was the first to speak, "Will, it's time to 'fess up right now. Why have you and Blue been meeting at night? It's got to have something to do with what's going on right now. We all have to know, even Rose and Sam."

Sam and Rose gave Wu a half sour look, but Rose piped right up "Blue came to our house the first time after our sleepover. She thought everyone would be asleep."

Will was shocked, "You knew about that? Why didn't you say something?"

"I won't tattle on you, and that's that," said Rose. She continued, "And they've both gone out at night a few times since then."

Will felt defeated, but resolved, "It's been more like four or five times." "*ROSIE, I WANT TO KNOW HOW YOU FOUND OUT!*" Wu was starting to look angry and ready to pop. "Look, Wu, it was totally innocent—don't get worked up about it. We weren't 'doing' anything!"

Wu finally let it out, "Then what the hell WERE you doing? What girl is crazy enough to get up secretly in the middle of the night and go meet a boy unless they are 'doing' something!" He could barely contain himself.

Sam said quietly, "It's because they have 'powers.'"

This time not only Wu, but Will and Rose turned in shock to Sam.

"Sam, what in hell . . . heck . . . are you talking about?" Wu was almost apoplectic. Will checked to see if adults had noticed this sudden, heated discussion, but they all seemed absorbed in a sober conversation.

Sam repeated, "They have superpowers. I know it. Haven't you noticed how Blue can read your thoughts sometimes?"

Wu sat on the ground and put his head in his hands and shook it back and forth. "I don't believe this. Blue is missing and you are talking about goofy nonsense. Sam, this is not the time!"

Will looked at his friend, and then at Sam, and then at Rose. Rose seemed to be the wisest person right at the moment and she was looking back at Will. She nodded her head slowly and voxed, *"We should tell them. They're our best friends."*

Sam was watching them with a knowing look. Wu was still shaking his head, looking at the ground.

Will didn't know what to do. Everything they had been taught was telling him that they should keep vox a secret. But he also knew his parents had already trusted certain friends. He knew there would come a time when he could trust a friend. Now seemed like the time, and who was better than Wu. And Sam?

"Do you trust Sam?" he asked Rose.

Rose nodded.

Will took a deep breath, made his decision and said, "It's true. Wu, what Sam said is true . . . sort of."

"Ha ha, not a very good time to be joking," replied Wu, still holding his head in his hands. He seemed to be wrestling with several emotions at once.

Rose said, "It's true. It's not really a super-power, though."

"Well then, what good is it? Is it going to help us find Blue?" Wu asked. "You guys are talking about super-powers when Blue is missing. How about just coming out and telling us what you were doing, so we can get some real truth and maybe find her still alive!"

This last part kind of woke them all up. Will and Rose had gotten caught up in the moment. They hadn't expected such a dismissive response to their revelation. And the suggestion that Blue might be dead, well . . . when someone said it out loud, it was kind of sobering.

Will felt he had to explain. "Look, Wu, the reason Blue came that first night—remember all the notes and stuff?"

"Yeah," said Wu starting to pay attention.

"Well it was because I suspected she could vox," said Will.

"She could what?" said Wu in new exasperation.

"She can vox, Wu," said Rose. "I can, too. It means we can talk to each other without using our voices."

Wu stared at her.

"I know, biz-arre, right?" Rose continued.

Sam nearly jumped out of his skin, "I KNEW it! I knew it, I knew it," and he capered around in a jerky victory dance chanting, "I knew it, I knew it, I knew it . . ."

"Sam!" hissed Rose. The adults had looked around at them a little disapprovingly.

Sam calmed down. "Sorry!" he said and stood still as a post.

Wu, however, was still sitting on the ground, stock still. He said, "What does this mean, 'Talk without using your voice'? If not your voice, what are you using? Do you mean you are telepathic or something?"

Will felt he finally had Wu's serious attention, and he jumped in quickly to explain in a rapid, hushed whisper. "It's not telepathy. It's our eyes. You know how a cat's eyes shine in the dark when you turn a flashlight on them? It's something like that. We are sensitive to infrared light, and we can communicate with it."

Wu took this in and then thought for a moment. "Wait, how can you communicate with light—you have to generate light or something like that. Are you saying your eyes are like flashlights?" Wu said, suddenly all concentration.

"Infrared flashlights," said Will, "Well, not really flashlights, more like infrared glow sticks. Something like fireflies, only it's not visible."

Sam just went "Whoa!" and they were all silent for a long moment. A very long moment.

"Bullshit," said Wu, but not convincingly.

Rose stepped over to Wu and said, "Whisper something in my ear—anything."

Wu hesitated but then said, "Okay." Rose bent down to Wu's mouth and Wu cupped his hands around her ear and whispered.

Rose looked at Will. Will smiled and repeated, "You said, 'Stop screwing around so we can get busy and look for Blue.'"

Wu just sat there stunned. Sam was jumping excitedly and saying, "Let me try, let me try!"

But Rose warned them very gravely, "You guys cannot tell anyone!"

Will suddenly remembered the seriousness of what they had just done and said, "Really, you can't tell anyone. We trusted you guys with this. It may seem unbelievable to you guys, but for us, it's like a curse sometimes. You would not believe what people would do to you if they find out you could do something like this."

"Like the Salem witch trials," said Rose.

"I get it," said Sam seriously. "I know what it's like, a little." Will remembered Rose telling him that Sam was often picked on at school.

Will looked at Wu. His harelip scar was often the victim of cruel side comments and jokes. He was silent, though. Will realized it was time to get to the point. "Blue came over because she hasn't had anyone to vox—talk—with since her family . . . well . . ." and he trailed off. He could never really say they 'died.' He just went on "Anyway, so she snuck over to my window one night and scared the crap out of me. But then we just talked. I think it was a big help for her. Since then, we've met to just talk, but she's also been teaching me how to hunt at night! I know that sounds weird, but I guess her family was really good at hunting at night, and they practiced it. She is really amazing how she can move around at night. With our voxing, we can communicate at night even when we are far apart, and no one can hear us or see us."

Rose jumped on Will, "And you never took me along!" She crossed her arms.

"Rosie, I know you hate it, but we were taking a big risk ourselves doing this. I didn't want to get you in trouble. Mom and Dad would kill me if they found out we took you along. Well they'd kill me if they knew Blue and I were sneaking out at night. I really did it because I thought it was helping Blue come out of her shell."

Wu and Sam were just listening somewhat dumbstruck, but Wu finally said, "So where IS she? What does this have to do with why she is missing?"

Then Sam jumped in. "That's what I was trying to tell you before. I think she climbs down the trellis outside the bathroom. One night, really late, like after midnight, I got up to go to the bathroom and when I got to the door, I thought I heard someone moving inside, so I waited. But then I noticed that the bathroom light wasn't on. Then I heard the trellis creaking. It was scary, but I had to go, so I peeked in the bathroom and it was empty." Sam turned to Will, "It happened again last night, but it wasn't that late —only, like, 11:30."

Will felt like things were moving too fast now. He wasn't sure how much he should say. He wanted to say enough that it wouldn't impede them finding Blue, but not so much that she would get in trouble after she was found. She had trusted him, and they both knew how important it was to keep this secret, but he also felt that there was a middle ground. Time was running out, and as his dad said, you can't think too long before deciding to jump out of the way of an oncoming freight train. Will's decision seemed to come out of nowhere, but he was confident it was the right one.

"Okay, look, you have to trust me. Let's go talk to Chief Hannah, but let me do all the talking. I'm going to tell her the truth, but not everything. We can NOT tell her about voxing. Rose and I have been doing this a long time and I know how to tell people the truth

without bringing it up. It's something we have learned to live with."
He looked at Wu and Sam and went on, "But afterward, we four are
going to come up with our own plan to help. Because Rose and I
and my parents can vox, we may be the only ones to hear Blue if
she is voxing for help."

Sam agreed right away. Wu seemed reluctant, but then
shrugged and said, "Well let's get going then."

As a group, they headed over to Chief Hannah with Will
leading them.

27

STILL CAPTIVE

Blue had finally gotten control of her emotions. It had taken a while. With her hands too far away to dry them, her tears had woven their way down across the contours of her cheeks, dripping onto her shirt, leaving cool tracks crisscrossing her skin. They were drying now. The feeling of dried tears on her cheeks was an almost forgotten sensation.

She was angry with herself because she had let Bronco get to her. She wasn't going to let him do that again. His threat was not empty; he was clearly a dangerous man. She would do as he said to protect her family and friends, but she would not let him break her. The anger made her feel better, and with that, and the quiet of the house, the immediacy of her predicament faded a little, and she could relax somewhat. Her head felt better, too. The Tylenol must have worked. For the first time, she felt like she was more herself. Until that moment, she hadn't even had a chance to look around carefully at her prison. She started to slowly scan the room, taking note of all the detail.

There was one window, which had a roller shade pulled all the way down. In spite of the surveillance camera, she tried hopping her chair over to it, but there was no way she could get enough body movement to hop the chair. It was heavy and she was expertly bound. She looked at her feet bindings—several wraps of duct tape around the legs of the chair. She would've slumped in defeat, but the bindings kept her too upright for that. She could move her hands and wrists, and that was somewhat of a comfort. Bronco was right, about all she could do was scratch her navel.

She continued her scan of the room. There was the little closet bathroom. There was a chair with a side table and lamp on it, and a chest of drawers with a mirror on the top, and a ceiling fan with a light. Both lights were off. The only light in the room was coming from the translucent roller shade. It cast a yellowish pale light. And there was the bed she had been tied to. That was it. That was her world right now.

She suddenly wondered what time it was. She had no idea how long she had been there. She had been so distracted by the pain and fear and disorientation that she had lost track of time. It could be early morning. It could be noon. It may not even have been the same day. Maybe she'd been out more than 24 hours.

Either way, she must have been missed by now. She had a sick feeling when she realized that even if she had been missed, they didn't even know where to look for her. She didn't even know where she was. She could be anywhere, though her first guess was that she was in Bronco's apartment. Or was she? He was smart. Maybe he didn't take her to his place.

Will knew, or probably guessed, that she went to the park to follow through with her plan. He would tell them, thank God, about her plan because he was too straight an arrow to not confess. That would cause problems for her down the road, but she realized that that was not important right now. She just wanted to survive so she could have any road to go down at all.

If Will told people about their plan, then they would eventually get around to checking out Bronco. The problem was they didn't know who Bronco really was. Jack might know, so they would probably question him first. But how long would that take? Then they would have to find Bronco. By the time the police figured out who he was and where he lived, hours could have passed. Even then, they would have to find evidence or get a warrant to search . . . search what? His apartment? Maybe that's where Bronco went, back to his apartment to come up 'clean.' Maybe make an alibi. If that was the case, then where *was* she? She had been too fuzzy-headed while in the back of the car to notice how long they had been driving, or where. She couldn't see anything because she was covered up, but the few times she was semi-conscious, she could tell they were passing street lights and making turns.

No, she was pretty sure they were somewhere in town, or very near town. She had not traveled much in the town and she didn't know a lot of details about where things were or which streets led where. And why did it seem so important to figure out where she was? What good would it do? There was no way for her to tell anyone or signal them anyway.

She stared at the window for a minute. Actually, there was a way to signal. Bronco had said that no one could hear her, so that meant she was a ways away from any nearby house and probably back from any road. The thing about vox is that you can *hear* it from a long distance. She knew from her childhood games and their experiments with the night vision camera that her eyes made a faint beam of light that could be directed to things. All she had to do was shine her eyes on the shade. If she voxed while she was looking at the shade, Will or someone else in his family could prob-ably hear it even if they were not close. The shade was translucent which meant that it would pass the light from her eyes and show on the outside, just the reverse of the moonlight on the shade last night. It would even spread it out like a light on a movie screen.

That was her only chance. If all four of Will's family were to walk around town, and she was in town, they just might walk by this place.

A little well of hope rose up and she suddenly found herself voxing at full tilt at the window, *"Help, help, help! Please help!"*

She paused to listen for a response. She waited, and waited. Nothing. She tried again. Still nothing. And then again. Nothing. Each time the sense of futility grew and grew inside her to the point where a worm of fear and panic started crawling inside her. She felt hot tears surging into her eyes again, and she fought hard against it. She could not let it get a hold of her again. She had to maintain control this time. She panted and suppressed the hard sobs that were struggling to get out until she started to calm down.

As she calmed down, her mind got going again and she decided she should keep trying. She would just pace herself. She would concentrate on voxing hard at regular intervals to maximize the chance that she could catch someone in that brief moment that they might be looking her way. She wasn't sure how long she could keep it up, but it was the only thing she could think of to do right now.

28

THE HUNT REALLY BEGINS

What Will told Chief Hannah was the truth and it was enough information to help but nothing that would reveal their secret. At least, that was his gamble. He told her about Blue's obsession with the supposed dealers in the park and told her that she called them Gronk and Greazal but their real names were Bronco and Jack. But that was all he knew. He told her how Blue was skilled at night stalking and had taught Will a little bit. He also floated the idea that Blue might be willing to go out at night and try and trap these guys, but that he had warned her against it. What Will didn't say was that he was supposed to go with Blue but didn't. He did tell the Chief something important, which was that Blue thought she overheard a location for a drug deal and that they had checked it out. That might have been where she went last night.

Chief Hannah listened patiently while Will spoke. After Will finished there was a long pause. Will, Rose, Wu, and Sam were looking at each other. How would Chief Hannah react? Would they be in trouble?

"Thank you, Will. This is disturbing news" She hesitated as she saw the worry grow on their faces, "But, telling me was the right thing to do. I believe you."

Chief Hannah looked at each one of them and then said, "I promise you I will follow up on all of this information. I think I know who Jack is, and I think that he would not be involved with this, but he might know something." *"At least I hope he's not involved with this . . ."*

Will caught her *chiss*. He wondered why she would be thinking that. He also wondered why Chief Hannah was looking right at him when she thought that.

Chief Hannah turned back to the rest of the group. "This information changes the whole situation from our standpoint. Before you came forward, we had to consider this a runaway situation, but now we are going to change it to a different category." She didn't say what that category was, but they all knew. "What it means is that we can get more resources to help look for Blue, and it means that we will set up a search headquarters and coordinate volunteers for an all-out effort."

Sam piped up, "What can we do?"

Chief Hannah thought for a minute. "What you can do is think hard about what might have happened last night, or anything you find out about Bronco or Jack. Let me know any of your ideas. You have my mobile phone number—don't hesitate to use it. There isn't much time. Every minute counts." She then looked at each of them again and said, "Look, I know what you want to do. You want to search on your own. I can't keep you from doing what you're going to do, but I do *not* want to be looking for more than one person today! Whatever you do, be safe and do not go anywhere where there aren't plenty of people around, okay? And do not go off on your own. Make sure you have someone with you at all times." She gave them all a stern look. "Do I have your word?"

They all nodded, but Will knew that he, for one, was not being sincere.

"Okay, I have to go now and get things rolling the right direction. Will, you need to stay right here. I'll be back in two minutes, and then you can show me the area where you think she might have gone last night. We need to tape that off for the detective. The rest of you, work with the search coordinators, please. We will set that up as soon as we can and let you or your parents know more about what you can do. Keep me informed, okay?" Chief Hannah gave them one last significant look, and then she walked back to the group of parents.

"What are we going to do now? We can't just wait around," said Rose.

Will knew exactly what to do. "We have to search *now*. And especially me and my parents, because we have a better chance of hearing a call for help. We shouldn't wait until they have the coordinated search set up, but we shouldn't be stupid about it, either. We have to all have phones and stay in touch. Rose, you and Sam have to stay here because our parents would freak out if you two were to go searching. Wu and I are older . . . don't look at me like that!" Rose and Sam were both giving Will a sour look. "You know it's true and we can't have parents freaking out right now, or they won't even let Wu and I start looking."

Rose and Sam looked down at the ground—they were both kicking at stones, which meant they got it but weren't happy about it.

"Wu, you should ask around—you know a lot more kids in high school than I do, maybe one of them knows where Jack lives or even Bronco. I've got my bike and I'll start cruising the neighborhoods and listening for Blue as soon as I'm finished helping Chief Hannah.

Wu looked lost. "You think you can . . . hear her or whatever . . . during the day? I thought infrared was best in the dark."

"Yeah, it's better at night, but not that much different. You guys let me know if you get any clues where I should look." Will realized this is the first time that he had come to the conclusion that Blue had been kidnapped or taken against her will. He wasn't really pretending that she had fallen asleep in the bushes anymore.

Sam said, "I am going to get on the computer and start digging for dirt on Jack and see if I can figure out who Bronco is. Rose can come with me." Sam grabbed Rose by the hand and said, "C'mon, let's get to my computer!"

Wu was the only one that still seemed at a loss for what to do. Will could see he was still trying to process everything.

"Hey Wu, it's going to be fine," Will said. "I know this vox stuff sounds weird. We'll sort it out later, after we've found Blue."

Wu shook his head, "Yeah, well, I'll figure it out. I know some kids who might know who this Bronco guy is."

Chief Hannah walked back over to Will.

"Ready to go, Will?"

"Yeah, the sooner the better"

The reality was really starting to sink in. He was going to help them tape off a crime scene. It didn't seem right; they only did that with murders in the movies. It all seemed so surreal, like they were in a play or doing an emergency drill. But it was real. His friend was gone, and by now she could be anywhere. She could be dead.

29

FINAL INTERVIEW

Bronco unlocked the side door of the house and went in, closing the door behind him. He walked down the hall to the guest bedroom and opened the door. The girl was glaring defiantly straight at him, and he could see where tears had streamed from her bloodshot eyes.

"Upset you earlier, did I? Sorry about that. I brought you something to make up for it," and he held up a paper bag. "You're probably hungry and thirsty. I'll give you a bite, and then we can continue our little chat. You remember what I said last time I took the tape off?"

She nodded at him. She looked beaten. Good time to talk.

He pulled the tape off her mouth—as carefully as he did the first time, almost tenderly. He gave her a drink and she gulped it down thirstily. He fed her a granola bar and she chewed it dutifully but did not seem particularly hungry.

"Okay, let's get down to business now, Blue," he started.

She gave a halfhearted glare.

"Yes, I know your name now, obviously. Wasn't hard to find. I know quite a bit about your friends and family, too. The internet is a wonderful thing, don't you think?"

Glare.

"What I couldn't find on the internet, though, is why the hell you decided to stick your little nose into my business. I don't get it. I haven't done anything to you or your friends or family, but here you come uninvited into my life and screw things up. Now can you explain that to me?" He tried to put a little bit of authority in his voice. "Well?"

She looked down. The glare was gone. "I'm sorry," was all she said.

"Well, I accept your apology, but you haven't answered the question. Why did you stick your nose in my business?" He put a little more spice into his inquisition this time.

She whispered, "You sell drugs."

"Yes, I do sell drugs," he replied, "And so does the corner drug store and so does your doctor. And food companies put drugs in foods, and there are drugs in cigarettes. Do you take videos of people who sell those?"

"Your drugs are *illegal*, and they ruin lives," she replied with a little more energy in her voice.

Now he was getting somewhere. "People ruin their own lives, little girl, and they will find ways to do it whether it is legal or not. Now, do you take drugs?"

"Of course not!" she said with a little more fire.

"There you go! Good job! Neither do I, except these fine legal cigarettes, unfortunately. They kill more people than guns do. Freedom of choice, I say. Don't you think freedom of choice is a good thing?" He could see she was starting to get angry. Good.

"Little kids shouldn't be allowed to get drugs! Jack gave me a joint! I'm only fourteen!" She was getting worked up now.

"Why shouldn't kids have freedom of choice? You seem to have chosen to come down at midnight and spy on me. You seem to have chosen to 'borrow' an expensive night vision camera. Did you really take a joint from Jack? You could have refused it. So you get to have freedom of choice, but other kids don't? Sounds like you're a bit of a hypocrite there, kid." Bronco could see the emotions playing on her face. "Look, I don't go out of my way to sell to kids. I don't advertise on TV on children's shows like all those crap cereal companies that have turned half the kids into diabetics. I run a quiet business and only grown-ups contact me. In fact, I have no idea how you found out about me. Remember, you were the one busting into my business. Not the other way around, right? Right?"

She looked down again. "Yes," she said in a cowed voice.

"I didn't go out and find you and say 'Hey kid, you want some smack?' did I?"

"No," she whispered.

"Okay, so you should be angry at the person that told you that I sold drugs. If they hadn't, we wouldn't be in this mess, right?"

"Nobody told me," she said quietly.

"Jack didn't tell you?"

"No."

"Well, how in hell did you find out about me then?" Bronco was almost at the crux now.

She was quiet for almost a full minute. Bronco was patient, but finally said "Well?"

"I overheard someone at the park. They didn't know I was listening. I think they were a customer of yours."

"There now," said Bronco "A little honesty feels good, doesn't it? So it was all your freedom of choice to take that information and do what you wanted with it, and you decided to play little detective and snoop around at night. Man, don't your foster parents have any discipline? They let you roam around all you want, like a little wild animal? Even at night? It seems to me it's their fault that you and I are in this pickle."

"They had nothing to do with it!" Blue said angrily. "I didn't tell anyone! They are good foster parents. I would have got in more trouble than you know if anyone found out!"

Ah, and there we have it, thought Bronco. This was truth. She hadn't told anyone. He relaxed. "Okay, calm down, calm down. I wasn't saying anything bad about your foster parents. But it just seems strange to me then—you would take all this risk, all on your own, just to try and do what? Catch me, and turn me into the police? Are you kidding? You're just a kid. Be happy, grow up, forget this." He was relieved. He could just leave her there, alive, and call in a tip in a day or two. That meant he could get out of town right now.

"Your drugs KILL people and DESTROY families!" she shouted angrily.

The suddenness of the loud outburst triggered something in him. He smacked her. It was instinctive. She was too loud, someone could have heard.

"Don't you shout like that again!" he said to her in a fierce whisper. He grabbed her chin, looked hard into her eyes and said very slowly, "Do you remember what I said I would do if you shouted for help?"

She nodded. A little blood was trickling out of her nose, and her right cheek was bright red.

"Look, little detective, people die all the time for all kinds of stupid reasons. Kids fall down stairs, they pull boiling water off the stove, they run into the street, they fall out of trees! And some stick their noses into business that is way over their head!"

Now Bronco was getting worked up. This little kid hadn't seen anything like what he had seen. She had no clue as to what his life had been like. Visions of his own childhood and his brother's death, and of his own revenge played back through his mind in a familiar flash of history. He just stared at her. "At least people who die of drugs do it of their own choice."

The girl gasped. She stared at him, her eyes wide in shock. "Your father killed your brother!" She gasped again.

Bronco was dumbstruck. What had she just said? How could she know that? What just happened? "Jesus, Mary, and Joseph, who are you? What are you?" He stood up and backed away. She had actually read his mind! There was no doubt about it. That would explain everything, how she knew about him and when his drug deal was. She had lied to him. "How could you know that? What the hell else do you know, you little demon?"

He didn't wait for an answer. He ripped off another long piece of tape and wrapped it hard over her mouth. He didn't care if it was uncomfortable now. He was not dealing with a human, he was dealing with a devil. She might know everything. He had to get out of that room, now.

"You make a single peep now, and I will come in here and break your neck! Have you got that? Have you got that?" he pointed his finger violently at her. He was shaking.

She stared at him frantically and nodded.

He got out of the room and shut the door and stood in the hallway to get his breath. Okay, change of plan. He was not going to leave right now. He was going to hunker down and wait until nightfall. Not a problem. Just not his first choice. But this girl, if she really was a girl and not some sort of witch, had really left him no choice.

Blue sat stunned in the sudden silence. Her cheek was throbbing where Bronco had struck her and one nostril was screeching from her panting through the coagulating blood. She was still reeling from the combined emotion of her anger and Bronco's violent reaction. Her eyes stared through the wall and off into infinity, and her mind replayed what just happened hoping, please-God-please hoping, that it would be different the second time through. It wasn't. She had seen what she had seen and said what she had said.

What she had seen was something unbelievable, something she couldn't quite get a handle on. She had *seen* someone else's thoughts. Not just sounds, but actual visions. It was like having a vivid dream, but a dream while she was wide awake instead of half asleep. Bronco's words and thoughts had projected intense flashbacks of his own life in *her* head! She had *seen* Bronco's father push his brother down the stairs. She had *seen* Bronco suffocating his father. And before she realized she was repeating these visions out loud, it was too late. She had doomed herself. She had doomed everyone.

30

THE POWER OF SIX BRAINS

Chief Hannah hoped that she had maintained her professionalism when she interviewed those kids, but inside her chest, her heart had taken a tumble. Her cop brain told her that the situation was bad. If there was any hope, she had to move fast. That realization is what kicked her cop training into top gear.

She took her new information and headed straight to the station to get her team moving in a new direction. On her way she called a detective she knew in up in Burlington. They didn't have a detective in their small town, and she was desperate to tap some deeper expertise.

"John, this is Summer Hannah. You got a minute?"

"Sure, Summer, how are things going? I haven't heard from you in a while. Nothing bad I hope," said John

"I hope nothing bad, but I've got a feeling, and it's not good. I've got a missing juvenile—girl, fourteen, foster home—possible runaway, but I just got some new credible information that it is likely an abduction. It happened sometime last night. Girl probably left the home on her own—she liked to slip out at night and hang with a friend. The friend is the one with the credible information. I know the kid and the family. Apparently, she had a bit of vigilante obsession with some characters in town that are possible drug dealers. We know one of them—a high schooler, probably sells marijuana—we've been watching him for a while. But the other is unidentified and likely dealing in heroin. We are going to start canvassing for witnesses. These two alleged dealers were apparently seen frequently at the local park. The park is close to the victim's home. Just tell me if you think I am justified in cranking this up to probable abduction."

There was a pause and then John said, *"If you say she left on her own then it would be a Type C runaway, but given the circumstances, I think you have to assume Type E which assumes abduction and possible foul play. You said she was fourteen?"*

"Yes she's fourteen, and I agree, we need to assume possible foul play." She didn't want to make that assumption on her own because of the awful implications, but it was her job to. She didn't have to call John to know this, but it sure helped to get his confirmation.

"If she is fourteen and she left on her own, then ordinarily the risk factor is not consider as high as it is with a thirteen-year-old or younger. We assume fourteen and older know the risks of leaving home. However, in this case, I think it is wisest to assume high-risk factor—that is, she was ignorant of the risks of what she was doing."

"Thanks, John. Do you think it is too early to call for outside help?"

"Well, calling me, you've called for help. I can help you get information into the NCIC Missing Persons file. As you know, the law says there is no waiting period for missing children, you can file immediately. There is also Amber Alert when you are ready to go public. How long did you say she has been missing?"

Chief Hannah checked her watch. It was noon. The O'Days said she went to bed about 10 o'clock last night. "Fourteen hours," she said into the phone. As she said it her heart sank.

John was silent for a moment. *"That is not good. Fourteen hours is forever. Jesus, Summer, time is running out. Look, send me all the information you know to date, and make sure you have phone numbers and addresses of the foster parents, the parents of the high schooler, and the parents of the girl's friend. It is never too early to pull out all the stops for missing children. Tape off the girl's bedroom, and I'll send a detective down. Do all you can, and if you need more help, let me know. Good luck! These are the toughest cases."*

Chief Hannah hung up the phone. Talking to someone who knew what the hell they were talking about was better than a decade of academy classes. And John knew what the hell he was talking about. Now she knew what had to be done. She took a deep breath and then kicked her high gear into higher gear.

Rose and Sam headed for Sam's room to log into his computer. Sam was chattering all the way. "If she was kidnapped . . ."

"Sam!" said Rose sharply.

". . . I'm just saying if she *was* kidnapped, we should figure out how far away they could be by now and then search inside that circle. I think she went out around ten or eleven."

"I don't think she was kidnapped," said Rose. "I just think she is out to walk and get away from everyone for a while. I think we should draw a circle that shows how far she could have walked instead."

"Okay, we can do both. We'll draw two circles and we can tell Will to search inside the small one first and then the big one, okay?"

They reached Sam and Wu's room and Sam slid down in front of his computer and instantly started tapping away like the keyboard was an extension of his arms.

"Okay, let's look up how fast someone can walk," Sam said as he typed, ". . . and it says here, about 3 miles per hour. It's 10 o'clock now so she's been gone about 12 hours. The first circle is going to be . . . Crap."

"What?" said Rose.

"Jeezum—it's about 36 miles. She couldn't have walked 36 miles. That's, like, more than a marathon. She couldn't have walked that far."

"Well how far do you think she could walk?" asked Rose.

"I don't know. Maybe four or five miles. Does that sound about right?" asked Sam.

"We went for a hike in Colorado once that was about five miles. My legs nearly fell off. Will seemed okay though and he was about fourteen then. I bet Blue could walk that."

"All right we'll go with that. I've got a town map here and I'll just take a ruler . . ." Sam got busy flattening the map out on his bed and drawing a circle five miles in every direction. He couldn't believe what he saw, though. "Crap."

"What now?" asked Rose. She was at the computer herself, looking stuff up.

"It's the whole town," said Sam in exasperation. "I mean the *whole town*. The village and everything around it. It's halfway to Hanksburg. She could be anywhere."

And then Sam froze. He sat down. "Holy crap, in 12 hours in a car she could be . . ."

"As far as Boston?" said Rose.

"Or New York. Anywhere. ANYwhere! We're never going to find her," he said in despair.

Rose was concentrating on the computer. "Will thinks she went to the park, right? Maybe they have some webcams there or something."

Sam perked up, "Yeah, that's true. They must have some surveillance cams there! But how would we ever be able to look at them? We're just kids but the police could! Chief Hannah said to call anytime!"

Rose called the number Chief Hannah had given them and told her their idea. Chief Hannah thanked her and said that it was an excellent idea and that she would check into it.

Rose blushed as she hung up. "I like Chief Hannah. I know she is going to find Blue."

"Yeah, I hope so," said Sam, "But I wish there was more we could think of." And they sat there thinking, waiting for some other inspiration to come along.

Rose was thinking about where she would walk, and Sam was thinking about where he would hide somebody if he kidnapped someone.

At first, Wu was at a complete loss for what to do next. His mind was absolutely spinning with what was happening, and what Will and Rose had said about … voxing? That's what they called it. Talking with their eyes. And Blue could do it, too? And Blue and Will were meeting at night? And on top of that all, Will had pulled him aside just before he went off with Chief Hannah and told him that Blue had gotten a joint from Jack in order to try and get evidence on Jack and Bronco.

Wu kicked the nearest convenient fence post. He was angry and frustrated, about what? That Will had kept a secret from him? That Will and Blue were hanging together? That this whole thing was happening at all?

"Get a grip Wu!" he said to himself. "Blue is in trouble, we know that, and we have to find her."

He started pacing back and forth, slapping his arms against his side. It was his thinking stride. Will said Wu should try and find Jack. Wu knew a few of the kids that smoked dope. He even knew where a couple of them lived. That was the next place to look. He was pretty sure that these kids would trust him when they wouldn't trust anyone else, especially a cop—even if it was Chief Hannah, who everyone at school liked and most kids respected. Probably one of them knew Jack or where he lived or at least his last name, so Wu could start tracking him down.

The first kid on the list in his head lived very close, between here and the park. Wu thought about calling him, but it would be quicker to run there anyway. At last, something he knew how to do. Wu bolted from the yard and headed as fast as his feet would take him to that first possible clue.

"Dad, I'm out on my bike looking for Blue," said Will on his phone. He had helped the police tape off the area around the tree and parking lot where he and Blue had scoped out the hiding place in the tree. He had then gone home, grabbed his bike, and taken off before anyone noticed. He knew that his parents might not have allowed him to go alone, but if he was already on his way, they might relent. At least his father would.

"*Who is with you?*" asked his dad.

"I'm by myself, Dad. So is Wu, but Sam and Rose are together at the O'Days. Look, Dad, we have to spread out if we are going to have a chance of finding Blue. Please don't make me come back and team up with someone. I've got the phone, and I'll be careful."

There was a pause on the other end of the line. He could almost hear his dad making his mind up about something.

"*Okay, Will, but be safe. If what you told Chief Hannah about this man, Bronco, is true, don't go anywhere near him, right? Just call the police, or us. And Will . . . you do know there is not a very big chance that you will find her. If she was abducted, and we still hope and pray she wasn't and that she just ran away, then she is likely very well hidden or miles away.*"

"Yeah I know, Dad, but if she is nearby, we can find her. I wanted to tell you this before, but you've got to know now. Blue can vox! If she is near a window, we can hear her! Bronco can't know that, so what if he just put her in a room with blinds drawn or cellar or something like that. We've got a much better chance of finding her than anyone really knows!"

There was silence on the other end of the line.

"Dad?"

"I'm still here, son. A curious time to be telling me this is all. So Blue can vox! Interesting. Mom and I will take advantage of that information. We are already out looking, you know. Like you, we couldn't just sit around and wait for the police to get organized."

Will was relieved, not only that his dad wasn't angry that he had taken off on his own, but that he had finally shared with his dad the news that Blue could vox. Or was it news? His dad didn't sound that surprised. This thought was interrupted because his dad was speaking again.

"And Will, call Pa Bill and let him know where you have searched. He is setting up a map to track who has covered what territory until the police search center is set up. So check in with him as you go along, okay?"

"Got it. And thanks, Dad," replied Will. "I am headed down toward the south end on Birch Street. I'll call Pa Bill. And Dad, bonam fortunam!"

His dad chuckled *"Audentes fortuna iuvat, Will!"*

"Hmm, I don't know that one Dad."

"Hah! Then I'll have to tell you when I see you. Bye!"

Will was relieved. His dad was on his side and that made him all the more determined. And now his parents were on the hunt, too. This was better. This was some hope. As soon as Will checked in with Pa Bill, he was back on his bike, pedaling faster than seemed possible or safe, dancing and weaving through traffic while scanning side to side, looking for something. Something. What it would be, he had no clue, he just hoped it was there and that he would recognize it in time.

Chief Hannah was busy making phone calls. She had considered the possibility of calling for roadblocks, but it was a drastic measure and she had to have a lot more evidence than what she had so far in order to justify the action. It wasn't a good use of the manpower she had. She was just going to have to be creative.

George had come in on his day off and was setting up a search headquarters, where they could recruit volunteers and do a methodical, coordinated search. She sent Eddie down to monitor the taped off area in the park until the detectives arrived. She called a K9 unit to help search there. They also already knew about Jack, and she was going to go pay a visit to his house to question him. There were others in the high-school marijuana trading group that she knew she could track down and at least question. It was the best bet for turning up a clue.

She took her list of names and addresses, logged in with the dispatcher, and headed out in her cruiser for Jack's house.

Sam and Rose had gotten tired waiting for something to come to them, and Rose had the idea of putting up posters. Sam thought that was a great idea, and he started going through his album of pictures.

"This is crazy," he said after a while of looking. "I can't find a single decent picture that has Blue in it, not even a phone picture!"

"Wait," said Rose. "I think I have one on this phone. We share this phone at home and everyone's always taking pictures with it. Look, here's one." Rose held up the phone.

"Whoa, look at this," said Sam. "Look at her eyes. Can you see something funny about her eyes?"

Rose looked at it and said, "Well have you ever looked at my eyes? Is it the same thing you see in my eyes?" She stared wide-eyed at him.

Sam squinted and looked back at her. Then he looked at his own eyes in the mirror. He looked back at Rose.

"Wow, I mean you don't notice it unless you're looking right at it, at the right angle, but you've got kind of a . . . a . . . like a ring around your iris, and your iris is kind of wrinkly.

"Really? You don't notice it in other people?" asked Rose. She had never really thought about it, that 'normal' people would see her eyes differently than what she saw.

"I don't think so," said Sam honestly, "but I haven't been looking for it. I'm going to be looking for it now, though."

"But Sam, you really, really, really have to keep this a secret," said Rose. There was a tinge of real concern and a bit of fear in her voice. She was starting to feel a little regret about having revealed their secret.

"Hey, don't worry. Really. I promise," and he held his hand over his heart. "Over my dead body, I won't tell anyone."

Will was getting hot and sore and frustrated. He had ridden who-knows-how-many ragged miles with lots of stops and side-tracks into alleyways and long driveways. He also had talked to a lot of people. He got a lot of sympathy and concern and offers of help, but he didn't know what to tell them other than suggesting they just go to the police if they think of or see anything or want to help search. There was a chance that would help—the more eyes on the look-out, the more likelihood of a tip. He wished he had brought a picture of Blue with him.

Will looked at his phone. It was 2:30 already. More than 16 hours since Blue had disappeared. Sixteen hours. Jesus. He called Rose to see if they had heard anything. She said they were going to put up posters of Blue.

"Did you put a phone number on it?" he asked her.

"*Yeah, this one!*" she replied.

Will groaned. Great, now they were going to get crank calls from now until doomsday. "All right, maybe not the best idea. Can you check with Chief Hannah for a better phone number to put on the poster? Just make sure you call me if you get any clues at all, okay?"

"Okay," said Rose *"And don't worry. I think you are going to find her and she is going to be fine, because you are the best brother ever, okay?"*

Will smiled. She always knew how to get a smile from him in the worst situation. "Okay little Meerkat, I love you too," and he hung up. He looked at his bike. His legs were not anxious to get back on. Tough luck, legs, he said to himself. No rest for the weary. He took a deep breath and willed a protesting limb over the bar, settled his sore butt onto the inadequate padding of the seat and pressed on.

Wu had talked to the first two people on his list, but had come up empty. The two kids both knew Jack and about "the other guy", but that's all. That's all anyone knew about Bronco. Either this guy was a genius or a ghost. He was beginning to think the latter. But at least Jack was real. This he knew. And he knew Jack's phone number now. He had tried it but no answer.

Now all he had was the third kid on his list. He wasn't sure what he would do next if this one didn't pan out. Wu had gotten a phone number for him, but this kid didn't answer either. It took Wu about three miles of running, knocking on doors, and searching stores. It was like a scavenger hunt—the kid wasn't at home, he was at a friend's house, and then at the friend's friend's house, then apparently they had gone off into town. It seemed endless. But in the end, Wu finally spotted him with another kid as they went into the hardware store downtown. He ran to catch up to them but before he got to the door to the hardware store, Jack came walking around the corner.

A whiplash of emotion drove over Wu as he experienced a wave of relief followed immediately by an eruption of suppressed anger. He wanted nothing more than to run up to the guy and punch him in the face. He did run up to him, but kept his fists in check. He needed information right now, not bruised knuckles.

"Jack, I need to talk to you."

Jack kept walking but turned around coolly to look at Wu. "Hey, what's up? Hey, you're the basketball phenom' Wu, right?"

Wu brushed off the compliment and the recognition and got right to the point. "My sister is missing and I want to know where she is!" And then he added in a loud hissing whisper, "You sold a joint to her and she is only fourteen years old, you bastard!" Wu could barely contain himself.

The hostility was not lost on Jack. "Whoa, whoa, whoa, calm down, Wu. I'm not sure what you're talking about. Let's just discuss this—maybe where we aren't around so many people."

"No way, man I don't trust you one second. I want answers right here and right now!"

"Look, Wu, I heard you. Your sister is lost, and I want to help, seriously, but if you want some answers I am not going to talk about it right here in front of God and everyone. Let's go in the coffee shop and find a booth, all right? Just be cool, man."

Wu glared at Jack, but was calmed down a little. Jack wasn't as unreasonable as he anticipated he'd be. "All right, but I need answers quick. She's been gone 16 hours now."

"Sixteen hours? Man. That's bad. Let's go in here, they have a nice quiet booth in the back."

They stepped into the coffee shop and found an isolated booth and sat. Jack spoke first. "So you're talking about that dark-haired girl that hangs with you and Will in the park? She's your sister? I thought you guys were all, you know, orphans and such."

"We're a foster family, not orphans. Just because we're a foster family it doesn't mean we don't think of each other as brother and sister! Yes, she's my sister! How the hell do you think you can just sell drugs to little kids? You are sick! And now she's missing, and we think your buddy is involved!"

"Hey slow down, Wu. I didn't *sell* her a joint. Look I don't sell to little kids. Your sister, though, she's different. Did she tell you she already smoked?"

"What? Don't give me that crap! I've never seen her get high. She would never have had the chance! I'm sick of this. Who is your partner—we need to talk to him now!" Wu was starting to get louder.

"Look, she told me she got high now and then to help her through some rough times. Maybe she doesn't smoke now, or maybe she wasn't telling me the exact truth, but that's what she told me. I'm not lying about that, man. But she wasn't lying about having it tough either. I could see it. I know what it's like to have it tough. And I didn't sell her a joint. I gave her one. I felt sorry for her. Look, I want to help, but if you want my help you have to promise you aren't going to tell anyone how you got this information. You good with that?"

Wu didn't answer. He just glared at Jack, but finally, he nodded.

"Okay. Look, if you think that this guy, who is not my partner, he's just a supplier, is involved, I will tell you how to contact him, but he can't find out how you found out, or I am in big trouble. I mean *serious* trouble, not just law trouble. More like breathing trouble. Got it? Everyone knows him as 'Bronco' but I heard someone call him Bob once." Jack stopped for a minute as the waitress came over and put a coffee down in front of him. Jack asked the waitress for a pen and then wrote down a number on a napkin. He paused and took a sip before he went on. "All I've got is this phone number. If I need something, I call it, if he needs me, he calls me. That's it, that's all I know. That's all he wants me to know."

Jack must have seen the anger growing in Wu's face. "Hey, I'm sorry she's missing, man. Maybe she just ran off for a while, and she'll come back. I liked her, man. She's got guts. I know some places she might hang out if she ran away and needed some space. I'll check them out."

Wu stood up. He was angry, but he needed to get this information to Chief Hannah right away, and to everyone else, too. "She did

NOT run away! She was fine!" Then he dropped to a loud whisper, ". . . and there is no way she smokes dope!" Wu headed out of the cafe, pulling out his phone as he went.

"Whatever, man," said Jack to Wu's back. "I'm sure everything at home was just fine." He said this with the slightest touch of sarcasm.

Wu heard him. Even though he was angry, he couldn't help but wonder if maybe Jack had a point. Maybe Blue had run away. Maybe I'm overlooking something, he thought. She had been acting overly quiet the past few days. He actually kind of hoped that was the problem, because that was something they could fix. Still, he had to assume the worst until they found her. Wu had a possible first name, Bob, which was pretty useless, but he also had a phone number. That was crucial information. They'd surely be able to track Bronco down with a phone number. Wu held his phone and punched in the number for Chief Hannah. As he did, he noticed the time. 4 pm.

Jack sat in the coffee shop for a while, thinking. He was inclined to believe that the girl ran away and would show up before the end of the day, but Bronco being involved with something more sinister wasn't out of the question. Bronco had treated him fairly and seemed like an okay guy, but he had this menacing aspect to him that Jack was very wary of. He knew all too well how two-faced people can be, but Bronco only told him what he needed to know, and Jack was not inclined to take it beyond that.

Wu hadn't suggested abduction outright, but that also was not out of the question. It troubled Jack to think that a kid like that would be abducted. He had instantly liked the girl and felt a connection with her. Kids like that have enough trouble in their life. Kids like him.

Jack paid for his coffee and left the coffee shop. He tried to ignore the whole thing and get on with his day, but it kept nagging him. All he had wanted to do was make some money selling dope to people who would get it from somebody else if it wasn't him, so he didn't feel bad about it. Bronco made it very clear that Jack was to mind his own business and that the hard stuff was off limits for him. Jack knew that's where the real money was, but he didn't care. He didn't want to get that involved, he just wanted to earn extra money and get some good weed cheap. Abduction, though, and a little kid, well . . . that not-so-little fourteen-year-old he had given the joint to? He really didn't want to believe it.

He decided to go down to his hideout haunts and see if the girl had found them just the way he had when he had run away so many times. It was possible. He would not have been surprised at all to see her down by the river, good and stoned, staring at the water.

Jack started walking down to the river, but on the way, he decided to wander over to the park and see if he had any customers. It was late Saturday afternoon, and he usually started getting calls from his regulars wanting something for Saturday night partying. As he reached the park, however, he instinctively turned on his heel and headed the other way. Cop cars. Not only cop cars, but yellow tape. Something had happened here.

"Hey Jack, wait up!"

It was a familiar voice, one of his regulars. Jack stopped and waited for him catch up.

"Hey man, you got any dope, I need, like, a quarter ounce."

Jack pulled a bag out of his pocket and exchanged it for two twenties in the wink of an eye.

"So what's going on in the park, man?" Jack asked.

"I dunno, some sort of kidnapping or something. One of the O'Day kids is missing. They have tracking hounds there, man, I wouldn't get near the place. They'll smell your dope a mile away man. In fact, I'm outta here. Thanks for the quarter, man. See ya."

"Yeah, see ya."

Jack looked back at the park and the fluttering yellow tape. He could see one of the dogs and dog handlers. The dog seemed intent on something. He turned away and started walking. He didn't know where he was going to go next, but wherever it was it was going to take a lot of walking because he needed to do a lot of thinking. The sight of an actual crime scene complete with tape, uniforms, and howling bloodhounds suddenly made him very uncomfortable.

Will had never known Wu to be so worried and anxious before. Then again, he and Wu had never been in a situation like this. But still, Will was surprised at Wu's deep anguish. They were checking in with each other on their cell phones, and the despair came across loud and clear.

"*I called Chief Hannah with the phone number that Jack gave me. She checked it out, and it is untraceable! It's one of those damned pre-paid phones! And there is no answer. He must have thrown it away by now. How can they sell those phones! They're only useful for crooks and drug dealers! No wonder there's a drug epidemic! This Bronco guy can operate completely undetected! Jesus! How the hell can we find this guy! It's been 18 hours, and nobody has gotten anywhere! What can we do?*"

"What about the friends of Jack's you talked to? Do they know Bronco? Do any of them buy heroin from him? Maybe they know where he lives."

"*Yeah, everyone knows who he is, but nobody knows where he lives. It's like Jack said—all they know is his name and his dead-end phone number. Bronco, Bob, whatever. Neither of those is probably even his real name. The only place they see him is at the park or up on the edge of the college campus and maybe walking around town sometimes. God, Will, she could be dead by now! If I ever see that bastard, I am going to kill him!*"

"Whoa, Wu. Calm down. We're going to find her. We just have

to keep cool and think harder. What about Jack? You said he was going to look for her. Has he contacted you?"

"No! And he doesn't answer his phone. I was so sure all we needed was that phone number to find Bronco. God, Will, I blew it!"

"It's okay Wu, don't worry about it." It was weird. Will never felt like he was the more level-headed of the two of them, but Wu's despair seemed to focus Will's mind and made him concentrate better. "Can you go find Jack again and see what he found out? I would think he would call someone if he had found her, for sure, but maybe not. Maybe he's worried about being arrested."

"I went back to the cafe to try and find him again, but he was gone. He said he was going to look in his hideouts. He's probably hiding out in one of them himself! Jesus, I should have stuck with him! I shouldn't have let him go!"

"It's okay, Wu, it's okay. Look, I screwed up in the first place by not talking Blue out of going. We can't worry about that now. We have to keep looking, right? See if you can find Jack again. Jack must have to meet Bronco somewhere, they can't just do that out in the open. Jack must not have told you everything. Maybe if he tells you where they meet that can be a clue."

"Yeah, okay, you're right. I'll try and find him again. It just took me hours to find him in the first place. I can't believe I let him go. Damn it, damn it, damn it!"

Will was starting to worry about Wu now. He wasn't sure what to say. He just tried to focus his friend. "Wu, we can't stop looking. Don't stop until you find Jack. I won't stop until we find Blue. okay? We are going to find her. I promise." He felt stupid saying that, because he knew he couldn't promise anything. But for some reason promising it seemed to help keep hope alive. It seemed to work for Wu, anyway.

"You're right. Thanks," said Wu after a minute of silence. *"We'll find her. You go. I will find Jack if it takes me all night. I'll call you as soon as I find him."*

"Okay, and I'll call you if I find anything or if I see Jack first. And Wu?"

"Yeah?"

"Bonam fortunam—it means good luck in Latin."

"Hey, you too, man. Thanks."

They hung up. That was better. Wu had calmed down, but some of his worries had rubbed off on Will. He couldn't help feeling a little bit of despair. Wu was not unjustified in his worries. It was getting late and would be dark soon. He had thought they would have found her by now, or at least found Bronco. Now he had to take his own advice and start looking again. Of course he wasn't going to stop until they found her, but now that was looking like a very long road.

Jack was cranky. It was starting to get dark. He had spent all afternoon checking all his hideout haunts and even asked a couple of the street people he knew if they had seen anything. Nothing. Now, after smoking too many cigarettes and only eating half a sandwich for dinner, he had made a decision. He had to go over to Bronco's apartment. He didn't know what he'd do once he got there, but just going there seemed like the only path that would quiet his mind about this whole Blue business. He was now thinking that he should have been more upfront with Wu. He hadn't told him that he knew where Bronco lived. Of course, Wu hadn't asked, but still, he had lied a little bit when he said that the name and number were all he knew. He figured they could find him using the phone number, and that was the same as telling them where he lived. Unless the phone was a burner. He hadn't thought of that.

Maybe this visit would make up for it. It would prove that Bronco wasn't involved. In his mind, what would happen was that he'd knock, Bronco would be there, he'd say hi and that he needed more dope. Bronco would say c'mon in. Jack would ask hey, did you hear about the missing kid? Bronco would say yeah, too bad, hope they find her. See ya later, and Jack would leave.

And that would be that. The girl would show up at home after having run away for a day.

So if that was the likely scenario, why did he feel like he had to go to Bronco's? It was the other scenario that he had to clear out of his mind. And what scenario was that? Bronco would show off his hostage? Bronco would be there holding a bloody ax? Bronco would be raping her? Jack didn't know. Those just weren't even likely. If anything weird was happening, he would just take off and maybe phone the police. He didn't want to think this out too much, so he just started walking towards Bronco's apartment.

31

CARRIED AWAY

It was dark. The sun had set and dusk was over. It was time. Bronco didn't want to wait any longer. He had monitored the police traffic on the scanner all day. They had turned this into an abduction earlier than he thought, but they didn't seem to be getting anywhere. He wasn't going to let that lull him into a false sense of security. He was sure they were using cell phones, too. They weren't idiots. Still, he could read a lot from the radio traffic. They couldn't hide the fact that they were stalled and frustrated. He wanted to keep it that way and that meant getting this done and getting gone. It was time. His apartment was buttoned up and his car was clean and ready to go with only what he needed in the trunk: a roll of heavy-duty garbage bags, a pick, a shovel, towels, nitrile gloves, and alcohol wipes. In the back seat he had just one duffel bag and his bug-out bag. His bug-out bag had a nice comforting heft to it with the six pounds of gold coins and a fat roll of twenties weighing it down. The only thing not in the car was his messenger bag and a package of weed he had missed when he was flushing the rest of his stock down the toilet. It was tough dumping all that money down the toilet, but there was no question it was the right thing to do. Now, other than the stray bag of weed, and one last kit, he was clean, clean, clean. The last kit was for the last item on his checklist. And now it was time for that, and he was ready except for one thing—he was still spooked by that girl.

He had been watching her all afternoon and evening on the surveillance camera, but didn't dare go back into the house. He'd just left her there by herself. At one point, he had a paranoid thought that she might be able to read his mind when he was watching her through the camera. He knew it was stupid, but he tried beaming a thought to her while he was watching. No reaction. She was pretty out of it. It didn't change his mind about her, though. There was no doubt she could read his mind. Nobody knew about his brother. Nobody except him and his dad, and his dad was dead. He suspected that she knew about that, too, because he had been thinking about that at the same time he was thinking about his brother. And who knew what else she had picked up while he was with her? There was no question about letting her go now. He was just going to go in and take care of business.

He grabbed the kit and stepped out of the apartment, got in his car, and started it up. He backed it out of his driveway onto the street, and then, instead of turning around, just kept backing up to the driveway of the yellow house next door, and then he backed into that driveway. He wanted the trunk as close to the side door of that house as possible. He set the brake, got out of the car, unlocked the door to the house and stepped in. He paused in the doorway, letting his eyes adjust to the darkness. He stared down the hallway until the outline of the bedroom door slowly appeared. He stepped quietly to the door and reached for the doorknob, but stopped just short of grasping it and looked at his hand. It was shaking. Jesus, get hold of yourself, he thought. He waited just a moment more and then took a breath and opened the door.

A waft of acrid odor greeted him. He flipped on the lamp. What the light revealed sent a shiver down his spine. It wasn't a little girl sitting there, it was a nightmarish character come-to-life from some warped fantasy horror film. Her jeans were dark from where she had been sitting in her own pee. Tracks of dried tears crossed her soot-darkened cheeks radiating in a spider-like pattern from her squinting, bloodshot eyes. Trickles of dried blood from her nose painted ruddy maroon stripes across her silver-taped mouth and chin. Whether or not she was an actual devil, she sure looked like one now.

The sudden brightness of the lamp sent a shock through Blue's body like a lightning bolt. Her body started shivering uncontrollably. She tried weakly to stop it but couldn't. She couldn't control anything now. Her muscles, her emotions, her courage, her sanity. For hours now she had tried. Tried to get Blue back. The survivor Blue. The invincible Blue. But she was gone—lost to the dark thoughts that eat away at you when you know that you have put everyone you ever cared about in danger, and you are powerless, strapped to a chair, in the dark, in a house that was god-knows-where. And there was no one there to stop you from blaming yourself again and again and again. Soon she would be dead and any last hope to warn them would die with her. Bronco had won. She had lost. Not just lost—she had made him more dangerous than ever.

Bronco, the killer. The images came to her again and again—a rubber sheet stretched tight over a man's face, Bronco's father, obliterating all his features except the unyielding structures of the nose, forehead, and writhing mouth wearing the haunting, animated look of desperation—desperation that then morphed into realization, and then acceptance. Death. She had witnessed the murder of a person who knew what was happening and could do nothing about it. She knew it was a preview of her own death.

She had screamed, as much as you can scream behind a thick layer of duct tape. She struggled against bonds that didn't give her the satisfaction of being able to hurt herself. The chair back wasn't even high enough to let her bash her brain into oblivion. All she could do was scream a muffled scream again and again and again. She would scream and cry herself to exhaustion and then do it again. And again. And again.

Darkness came to make it impossibly more nightmarish. This was how she was going to die. Alone in the darkness. With what energy she had left, she moaned and cried herself to half consciousness until the sudden, harsh, bitter light brought reality back. The reality was Bronco.

"Hmm, had to pee did you? Sorry about that. I brought you a present to make up for it." Bronco pulled a paper bag out of his messenger bag and held it up for her to see. "It's probably not what you think. You're gonna like it, though. Most people do. In fact, most people pay a lot of money for what I am about to give you."

Blue stared blankly at the bag while her brain tried to do some sort of groggy analysis of what it was seeing *"Too small for a rubber sheet,"* it thought. *"Maybe he's going to suffocate me with a paper bag,"* it continued. *"Stop it, brain. You're being stupid."*

Bronco put the bag down and took something out. It wasn't a rubber sheet. It was an alcohol wipe, followed by a spoon, a lighter, a little white bag, and some blue gloves. Her brain slowly came out of its stupor as it recognized the objects. When it finally put them all together, her body twitched so suddenly and violently, the chair jumped off the floor. A sound like a whimper tried to force its way through the duct tape.

"Hey, relax, this is no big deal, it's just going to calm you down a little. A lot, really. You look like you could use some calming down."

He put on the blue gloves and knelt down next to her and unbound her left hand. Then he rolled up the sleeve on her left arm. She pulled her hand away from him, but he patiently and firmly pulled it back. He took a piece of rubber tubing from his bag and wrapped it around her upper arm. He tied the tube firmly around her arm, and she could feel the blocked blood vessels start to throb. The throbbing was rapid. Frantic.

"You really are too jumpy. I am serious when I say you are going to be happier if you let me do this." He pulled a flat plastic package from his bag and tore the top off, revealing a fresh hypodermic syringe. "See?" he said. "Nothing to worry about. Just like at a doctor's office—a sterile fresh needle, and a shot and you are going to feel just fine." He turned his back on her so she couldn't see what he did next. He seemed to be preparing something. After a minute an aroma started to fill the room—somewhat sweet and molasses-like. When he turned back around, he had the syringe in his hand and it had a golden liquid in it.

He reached over and grabbed her wrist to pull her arm back, but she pulled it away again. He sighed and then looked calmly into her eyes and said, "You will put your arm back over here on your own or I will break it. I haven't got time for this. Which is it going to be?"

Blue knew she had no choice. She actually wanted to give into his voice. He said that this was just something to calm her down, and she would like it. It wasn't a rubber sheet, so maybe he wasn't going to kill her now. She really wanted to believe that. She didn't even try to spy on his thoughts to see if he was lying. It seemed that he had stopped leaking them anyway. How could he know how to do this? She didn't care anymore. She was too weak to care. God knows, she could use something to calm her down. He had her. She put out her arm.

"There we go. Good girl. This isn't going to hurt that much— you've gotten shots before. This is no different. And here, I can do it very professionally—I'm swabbing your arm with alcohol, so you don't get an infection. That's the worst thing, when people are stupid and don't disinfect the injection site. So stupid."

Blue let herself get sucked in by Bronco's calming demeanor. She knew it was all an act, but she didn't fight it. What did she have left to fight with? Her vox? Vox seemed to be nothing but a lethal disease. A curse.

He finished swabbing, then looked for a good vein, and artfully stuck the needle in. It pinched a little, but Blue was so numb to anything she didn't even wince. He pushed down on the syringe plunger and released the tubing at the same time with his free hand. Then he looked straight at her.

"Goodbye, little demon. Sorry it had to end this way, but that's the way it goes. I should have just killed you in the park, but for some reason you got under my skin."

She stopped breathing. Her addled brain was having trouble grasping what it had just heard. He *was* killing her! From some reserve deep in her core, an uncontrollable power surged up through her like a volcano. The sound that burst behind her taped up mouth and escaped through her bloodied nose was so shocking and eerie that it made Bronco jump back with a look of fear and panic in his eyes. At the exact same time, a scream slammed through her eyes with such power that it felt like they might explode. *"NOOOOO I DON'T WAANNN . . ."*

And then *BAM!* Her irises slammed shut and reflected her vox scream right back at her, and the power of it snapped her head back. She felt like she was going to vomit, and then the drug hit her like a hot wave. There was a roaring in her ears, and she had the sensation that she was being swept into the air on top of the wave.

She was dying! Deep inside, there was a part of her that started crying uncontrollably, because this was death and that part of her knew she should be upset. But there was no pain. There was no fear, no terror. The hot wave dissipated gradually, magically, leaving behind a warm, peaceful flow which carried her gently on its soft current. She gradually floated away from the wailing cries of her internal despair. She didn't mind. That was okay. She settled more and more into the comforting folds of the warm waves and let the soothing undulations lull her slowly towards the realization that this was the calmest she had been in her life. It was relief. It felt like a final reward for putting up with everything she had been through. Death seemed better than life. It was comforting. It was peaceful. There didn't seem any reason to fight it. No reason at all. So she settled back and relaxed.

And she let it take her.

32

———

KEY DECISIONS

Will just kept riding. Riding, riding, riding. Why? He wasn't sure anymore. It was dark, and he was exhausted. His legs had barely enough energy to push the pedals. It all seemed so pointless. The search was going nowhere and all he was doing was visiting spots he'd been to a thousand times already. The only thing that was keeping him from collapsing was a fragile thread of hope, but hope for what? That he would spot Bronco? He was long gone by now for sure. Maybe spot Jack? As if that would do any good now. To see Blue skipping down the sidewalk? That was just a dead dream now.

He kept riding anyway. Riding and watching. As he watched, his mind started playing tricks on him. The darkness and exhaustion had turned trees into giant trolls, staring at him with angry bark faces, reaching out with their branches to slap him. He rode past houses that looked at him with their glowing, square eyes, like cubist owls, hooting, *"Who, who, who are you looking for?"* The concrete sidewalk flowed under his tires like a river of quicksand. It was as if he was standing still and the town was rotating underneath him. Under a bush, he imagined a body with flies buzzing around it. He looked away. Across the street, he saw another crumpled body leaned up against a trashcan. It was just a black trash bag. He saw a ghostlike apparition walking toward him on the sidewalk, glowing faintly. Emanating from the ghost's eyes was an accusatory voice, *"If only you'd come with me . . ."* He swerved nervously away from the ghost. It was just a woman dressed in white, walking her dog. He shook his head, trying to banish these weird visions, but that only made his head buzz. Buzz, buzz, buzz. Buzz, buzz, buzz.

Shit. It was his phone. He stopped and pulled it out, staring dumbly at it as he slowly came back to reality. He had missed a call. There was a message. His heart leaped, but he wasn't sure which way it was leaping – toward hope or despair? He hesitated, his finger hovering over the play button. He sucked in a breath and then pushed the button. But it was just his dad saying, *"Come home and get some dinner, mom worries about you."* He let his breath out slowly, trying to give himself time to sort out his jumbled emotions. No good news. No bad news. His parents are worried about him. He's exhausted. He's hungry. He's starting to hallucinate. He should keep going. He should go home. Fuck.

He closed his eyes, tilted his head back, and let his mind drain. A breeze rustled through the leaves over his head. In the distance, a dog barked. A hiss of tires marked a car passing by. The world was going about its business, heedless to the plight of a lost girl, and a boy, straddling a bike, on a street, in a small town, his thoughts in tatters.

He finally opened his eyes. Nothing had changed. Nothing was going to change, no matter how many times he rode around that damn town. He ached to go home and try and find some escape from this nightmare. At least find some solace.

But he knew he couldn't. This wasn't going to be over until it was over. He had to keep going. He lifted his foot onto the pedal. He eased his aching butt back onto the bike seat. He started to push off . . . but was stopped short.

"NOOIIIDOONNWANN . . ."

Jesus, he thought. That wasn't a hallucination. That was real. It was barely detectable but it was *definitely* a vox.

He looked around quickly. There was no one nearby. It was faint, so, it had to be from a distance, but what direction? He stared hard for another sound that might give him a clue. Nothing. Where was he, anyway? He was at an intersection. He looked at the road signs. The vox could have reflected from that. The cross street was Pine Street. It was as good a guess as any. He took off down the block scanning side to side, but he saw and heard nothing. He reached the end of the block and stopped. There was no way the vox came from any farther away. His only choice was to go back and try another street. Just as he started to turn around, he spotted someone walking towards him.

Jesus, it was Jack! Will started to call out, but caught himself. There was a chance that Jack would recognize him and bolt. He ducked into a driveway and hid behind a hedge. He peeked over the hedge and saw Jack stop in front of an apartment building. Will quietly laid his bike down and crept along the hedge until he was directly across the street from Jack. Jack stood in front of the apartment looking down its sidewalk at the front door.

This was more than coincidence. The vox and then Jack standing in front of an apartment? Will was having a hard time containing a growing excitement that he may have found where Blue was. But what should he do now? Should he wait? Was Jack going to go into the apartment? Apparently not because Jack suddenly turned on his heel and headed back down the street the way he came. Damn! Now where was he going? Will started to follow when he spotted another person coming down the driveway of the house next door to the apartment building.

Jesus. It was Bronco.

"Hey Jack," said Bronco, as casual as could be.

Jack turned and saw Bronco come down the driveway. "Hey, Br– Hey man, what's happening," "*SHIT, I CAN'T BACK OUT NOW.*" Will picked up Jack's *chiss*. What did Jack want to back out of?

"Not much, you want to come in and have a drink?" said Bronco.

"Okay, sure. Thanks, man."

Bronco took Jack by the shoulder, like an old buddy and led him back down the sidewalk to the apartment. He opened the apartment door, and the light from the hallway poured out onto the walk. Will tried to get a look at what was inside, but Jack and Bronco blocked the view. The door shut and then Will was alone outside once again.

Shit! This had to be it! He had to get the police here. Will fumbled for his phone, dropped it, and panicked as he felt around in the grass. God damn it, this was not the time to fuck up, he told himself. He felt a huge rush of relief as his fingers touched the hard plastic case. He opened the phone and tried to get his shaking fingers to tap out the message. He almost screamed in frustration, but he finally forced them to type, "Bronco, 59A Pine Street, hurry." He hit the send button, watched it go, and then looked up. Nothing had changed, thank God. The scene was the same as before.

It all seemed so surreal—like a game, and he was almost ready to play the winning card. But winning meant the police getting there and finding Blue safe. How long would it take them to get there? Was she even in the apartment? If she was, what had Bronco done with her, and why did he invite Jack into the apartment? Was Jack in on this? What did Jack mean when he leaked, *"I can't back out now?"* Back out of what? What were they going to do?

Damn it! He had to do something. He was supposed to wait for the police. It was the safe path, for him, but what could happen in that time? What had already happened? He felt exactly like he had the previous night. He had stayed put and let Blue go alone. He had pretended it was all a game and that everything would be okay by morning. Here he was again, but he couldn't hope everything was going to turn out fine. He wouldn't do it this time. He was going to do something. Now.

As soon as he had made this decision, it was like the noise in his head stopped. His head was clear. He was calm. He could think logically. And like magic, it came to him—a distraction—something to get Bronco and Jack out of the apartment. He would run up to the door and bang on it to get their attention and then he would try and get them to chase him. That would at least delay or interrupt whatever they were doing.

Will moved quickly across the street and found himself at the end of the driveway Bronco had come down. He took a glance up the driveway and noticed that there was a car there, backed in. Somewhere in his head, a brain cell or two were observing that it was odd to back a car into a driveway. The rest of his brain was too busy getting ready to sprint across to the apartment door to pay it much mind. He noted the obstacles between him and the apartment door, looking for a clear path, and then it dawned on him. There was no car in his way. There was no car in Bronco's driveway. There was one in the house next door and it had been backed in.

That was Bronco's car! Blue wasn't in the apartment, she was in the house! That's why Bronco was coming from here when he greeted Jack! That's why he didn't hesitate to invite Jack into his apartment!

Will turned and sprinted up the driveway of the house. He glanced in the car as he dashed past it. He could see nothing but a backpack and a duffel bag. He looked at the house. The windows were all dark. It looked like no one was home. He spotted the side entrance and ran up to it. Through the small window in the door, he could see a bit of light creeping out from the bottom of a doorway in a hallway, just inside the entrance.

He tried the door handle. It was unlocked. He held his breath as he opened it and slipped into the house. He moved quietly down the hallway to the door where the light gleamed underneath. He opened the door as quietly as he could and peeked inside, and took in a sharp breath. It was Blue, there was no doubt about it, but she was slumped unnaturally in a chair, in fact, he couldn't understand why she was still upright, and then he saw the tape wrapped around every limb, strapping her to the chair as if some medieval surgery was about to take place. He dropped to his knees in front of her and grabbed her by the shoulders. "Blue!" he hissed, "wake up!" She didn't move. Her face was pointed toward the floor. He reached up and tilted her head back with one hand and used his other hand to push against her chest to get her more upright. It was like trying to move a wet bag of sand, but he could see her face clearly now. What he saw made his heart drop right through the floor. Her eyes were barely open and her face looked like she had been painted for some sick ritual. Her mouth was covered with duct tape and her nose was crusted with blood. There was so much terribly wrong here he was having trouble getting his thoughts to go in a straight line. What was wrong with her? Why wasn't she waking up? A little glint of light drew his eyes toward a table. There, under the soft light of the table lamp, were a couple of empty packets, a lighter, a silver spoon, and an empty syringe.

Bronco had let Jack in the apartment without any hesitation, so Jack was already getting a feeling like the first scenario—the one where he was going to find nothing—was going to be the right one.

"So you need more dope?" asked Bronco once they were inside and the door was closed.

That's not why Jack was really there, but he decided he better make it seem like that was why he was there.

"Yeah, man. Not much, though, I've only got a hundred bucks."

"No problem." Bronco reached behind him and then put a fat envelope on the table. Jack thought briefly that it seemed odd that Bronco would have all that dope that handy, but he let it go. He just wanted to get a sense that Bronco was not involved with the kidnapping and then get out of there. Bronco handed him the envelope and Jack looked inside. It was a lot of dope.

"All this for a hundred bucks?"

"Yeah, why not. It's your bonus."

"Well, I won't need to see you for a while then," said Jack.

"Why? Is business slow?" asked Bronco.

"Maybe. I went to the park today but couldn't do any business. There were police all over the place, and a spot was marked off with yellow tape. Looks like the park might be off limits for a while."

Bronco appeared unmoved and just said, "Huh, that's a surprise. Nothing really happens in this town. Was it a murder?"

"Nah, someone said it was a kidnapping. I didn't stick around to check it out. They had bloodhounds. I was afraid they'd smell the dope."

Bronco sat there nodding, "Yeah, good move. Just wait 'till they've figured that one out. You should probably move your business somewhere else."

"Yeah, but the park is the best. Listen, thanks for the extra dope, but I gotta go."

"You don't want to stay for a beer?" asked Bronco.

"No, but thanks. My old man is expecting me and he is a total ass if I'm late."

"I get it," said Bronco. He got up and walked Jack to the door. "You're doing good—being smart. Keep being smart."

Right, thought Jack, like getting out of there.

"Yeah, thanks. Later."

"Later."

Jack walked away relieved. Happy, actually. Bronco had eased his mind. He hadn't reacted at all when Jack mentioned the kidnapping, and there was nothing unusual going on in his apartment. It seemed completely empty. Almost un-lived-in. No bloody murder scene or hostage drama. And on top of it all, Bronco had given him extra dope. That was like giving him free money. Bronco must have been doing pretty well for himself with his business.

Jack turned and headed down the sidewalk the way Bronco had come and then remembered how Bronco had come out of nowhere. He looked to the right at the house next door. There was light coming from one shaded window in the back. As he passed the house, he saw a car backed into the driveway. That car looked familiar. It was like one that Bronco usually had in his driveway.

Jack kept walking, but he was uneasy. He got to the corner and stopped under the streetlight. Bronco might have come from next door when he saw him. That might be Bronco's car in the driveway. Of course, it could be anyone's car, it was a silver Toyota. Only about a million of those around. But if it was Bronco's, what was it doing next door?

He should just forget it, but he couldn't. There was just something that didn't feel right . . .

Will stared at the syringe. The end of the needle had a drop of blood on it. He looked at Blue's arm. There was a needle mark with a trickle of drying blood twisting its way down her skin. He looked back up at Blue's face. It was completely lax. He looked down at his hand pressed against her chest. It wasn't moving. Somewhere in his mind was a voice saying, "she's dead." He shook his head and said, "No!"

He ripped the duct tape off her mouth, leaving behind a crimson rectangle on her skin. Then he tilted her head back and parted her lips with his thumb. He held his cheek near her mouth but felt not even the slightest movement of air. Without hesitation, he took in a breath, sealed his lips over hers and blew. Some air squeaked out of her nose, but it felt like some went into her lungs. He tried again but this time pinched her open nostril closed with his right forefinger. It was like blowing into a wet air mattress with someone lying on it, but her chest moved so he knew air was going in. He pulled his face back from hers and he could feel a gentle waft of breath, and it was warm! It *felt* alive. He gave her three more breaths, waiting for her exhale between each, and then just before he gave her a fourth, she breathed in on her own! He watched her chest expand slightly, and then another soft breath. It was only then that he noticed the slight bluish tinge in her lips. He felt for her pulse in her neck. It seemed fast and weak, but steady. Oh God, oh God, oh God, thank you, he thought. Just keep breathing!

He went to work on the tape holding her to the chair. If he got it off, he could lift her and get her out the door, down the hall and out. She wasn't heavy but she would be dead weight. Once they were out, he could carry her through the backyards, and stay hidden, at least until the police got there. Why weren't they there already? Had things happened that fast?

Shit, peeling the tape was taking too long. It was wound around multiple times. He gave up trying to unwind it and just started tearing it off. He looked around the room again for something that he could use to cut it and saw a camera on a tripod on the dresser. Shit! She was being monitored! Bronco could be watching him right now! He jumped over to the dresser and turned the camera around. Maybe Bronco would think it fell over or something. Now he knew he didn't have any time to waste. He started tearing at the tape so hard that soon there was blood coming from his fingers. He only noticed because it was making everything slippery. He got one of her arms free, but as soon as it was free, she slumped even worse. He cursed himself for not starting with the ankles. He tried to prop her up while he worked on her left ankle. It was impossible. She kept slumping over and he had to push her back up and try and hold her with his shoulder. He kept checking to see that she was breathing, and it seemed that she was but it was so weak. He gave her another mouth-to-mouth hoping that would help. He reached down to work on the ankle but she slumped over again!

"*Blue, wake up, I need your help!*" He looked at her barely open eyes but they were vacant– a hundred miles away and her pupils were tiny—like pinpoints.

Will was starting to panic. He had no idea how long it would be before Bronco came back. He tried to free the ankle again, but this time she overbalanced the chair and it started to tip. Will tried to catch the chair and right it, but he was at an awkward angle and all he could do was slow down the fall so Blue didn't smack her head on the floor.

Will cursed but stopped halfway through the curse. That had solved his problem. She was on the floor on her side, and now he could work at her ankles without her slumping all over him. She also seemed to breathe easier. He cursed again. He was an idiot for not thinking of that earlier and now he was running out of time.

———

Jack looked back down the street. No sign of Bronco. It wouldn't hurt to just take a quick look, he thought. He walked carefully back the way he came. When he got to the house, he cautiously walked up the drive. He could see that he had an escape route out the back yard of the house if he needed it. There was a side entrance to the house next to the driveway. Jack looked through the windows of the house. He didn't see a light or activity, except a light coming from a half-open door in the hallway behind the side entrance. He tried the side entrance. It was open.

This was stupid. What was he doing? Breaking and entering! He didn't need that. He should just turn around and keep on walking. He hesitated for a moment but instead of turning around and leaving, he opened the door, slipped in quietly and listened. He could hear activity in the back room, probably the room with the lighted window. He crept cautiously down the hall, ready to run. He leaned his head carefully through the half-open door and then froze. He wasn't quite prepared for the scene that met his eyes. "Will? What the hell . . . ?"

———

Will froze. He felt his heart stop as he looked up and stared right into the face of Jack. Jesus! It looked like Jack *was* in on this.

Jack suddenly stumbled into the room as if pushed and behind him came Bronco. Bronco took one step inside, looked at the scene in front of him and grunted. He took his shoulder bag off, squatted down and started to fiddle with something inside it.

Will didn't know what to do. It looked like Jack didn't either. Jack seemed as confused by everything as Will was. Will glanced at the door. Jack had been pushed clear, leaving an inviting escape route. For an instant, Will realized he had the opportunity to make a run for it. He crouched, ready to spring, but he knew there was no choice. He couldn't go. He wasn't going to leave Blue behind. He wasn't going to do that again. Ever. All he could do was to wait for the next thing to happen.

And the next thing to happen was a strange sound, like a soda can opening, and at exactly the same time, he felt like someone gave him a punch in the chest just below his left shoulder. It knocked him off balance, causing him to rock back from his crouch, landing on his butt. He looked at Jack, but Jack was exactly where he was before, except now he was staring at Bronco's hands. A strange burning was starting to surge through Will's chest and shoulder and he gasped reflexively as the burning gave way to searing pain. He barely perceived what happened next. He was blinded by the sudden pain but he knew that Jack had taken a lunge at Bronco, knocked him over, and then Jack was gone, out the door. Bronco looked at Will gasping on the floor, hesitated for a moment, and then took off out the door after Jack.

Will didn't care! All he could focus on was the pain. It was growing unbearable! He struggled to breathe. He wanted to figure out what happened, but he couldn't think straight. He must have been shot by Bronco but there had been no sound like a gunshot. Maybe it was a taser or something else. He was hoping it wasn't a gun, but when he could focus enough, he brought his right hand away from his upper chest, where it had involuntary gone in a protective move. He saw blood.

Will's eyes started to lose focus and he felt himself rolling onto his right side, holding his right hand to his upper left chest. He didn't want to pass out. Rolling to his side seemed to help, but the pain was still enormous! He sat there gasping in agony for a minute, or ten minutes, or forever . . . he had no idea how long. But slowly, the pain peaked, turned a corner, and moved imperceptibly from being unbelievably unbearable to being nearly bearable. Will started to breathe more evenly instead of in gasps. He tried to sit up but decided that wasn't a good idea just yet. His eyes focused a little better, and then he saw Blue's feet in his field of vision. She wasn't free, but Will thought he could slide over and start working on the tape again, as long as he didn't sit up right away. He slid himself over and used his right hand to work the rest of the tape off her right arm. He looked down. She was still breathing weakly, but the blue tinge in her lips had gone down—they looked pinker. He started working on her right ankle—it was hard with just one hand and the blood and sweat and pain. It didn't matter though—having a mission was clearing his head and helping him focus on something else other than the pain. He felt like he could sit up a little and get a better angle on her ankle.

He didn't know how much time had passed, but he suddenly realized he had unbound her ankle. She was free. He eased her away from the chair. He was determined to get her out of there. He could do it as long as no one came back right away. Anything to buy time until the police came. The police! He had completely forgotten about them. He had heard noises outside—people yelling, a car door slamming, the crack of a real gun, and a car driving off . . . they must have come but where were they? Maybe they didn't know to come to this house. He had to get them out of there and into the open where they could be found.

He dragged Blue little by little toward the door. He didn't feel like he could stand yet so he sat on the floor and scooted them both inch by inch. Before they had even gone a foot, he heard the back door open and steps in the hallway. Shit! He looked for something to throw. He wasn't going without a fight.

"Blue! Are you here?"

Will couldn't believe his ears. It was Chief Hannah! It was the sweetest sound he had ever heard in his life.

"Chief Hannah! In here!" His voice sounded hoarse. He looked toward the door just as Chief Hannah eased herself through it, gun drawn looking this way and that.

"Will!" she said in surprise. "Is there anyone else here? Are you alone?"

"Just me and Blue, I think," he croaked.

Chief Hannah appeared to relax a little. She stopped scanning the room and turned her attention to Will and Blue and as she did, Will saw her eyes grow wide and heard her gasp, "Jesus, Mary, and Joseph!"

After Jack had left the apartment, Bronco sat back and relaxed. He was actually glad that Jack had shown up. If Jack was questioned, the fact that he'd visited Bronco and didn't see anything suspicious would divert suspicion away from him. Plus, he learned more about how the search was going. And as a bonus, he'd gotten rid of the rest of his dope. All in all, it couldn't have worked out better.

Bloodhounds? Well, the police were smarter than he'd thought. That could be bad news if he didn't get the little demon out of there soon and start working on the next step of his plan. That was fine, he was ready to go. Time to say goodbye to this apartment and head out. He had watched Jack go out the drive and walk down the block. He should be gone by now.

Bronco pulled his phone out of his pocket. It had buzzed a couple of times while Jack was there, but Bronco ignored them until Jack was gone. It could only be the surveillance camera motion alerts because no one knew this new phone number. They were motion alerts. It was possible that the girl was going into convulsions. That happened sometimes when people were dying.

He didn't bother to look at the surveillance recordings. He was headed over there now anyway.

He picked up his shoulder bag, took one last look around, and locked the door behind him. He walked casually over to the house, confident that Blue would be dead or near enough to it. He would just double bag her, then put her in the trunk, and get out of there.

Bronco walked in the door and stepped into the hallway and knew immediately that something was wrong. The guest room door was open, and a shadow of someone standing just inside the door was projected across the floor and onto the hallway wall.

Bronco stepped down the hallway and instantly recognized the silhouette of Jack. Damn it! Well, it was nothing that couldn't be taken care of. It would just be messier now. He shoved Jack out of the way and stepped in the room, and then what he saw really pissed him off. That boy, Will, was there, too! He had the girl half untied, and the tape was off her mouth. Damn it. Now there were two problems he had to take care of. This was going to be a lot of work.

He opened his shoulder bag, and instinctively turned on the red dot sight of his Browning Buck Mark. He congratulated himself on having mounted the silencer already, then he pulled back on the slide, slid the gun out of the bag and put one bullet into the boy.

The boy was knocked back. Good thing. He was pretty athletic and Bronco didn't want to mess with him. He turned to do the same with Jack, but just as he did, Jack knocked the gun hand away, pushed Bronco hard onto the floor and then bolted out the door.

Damn it again! Now there was a third problem! Now he was totally pissed. Jack was quick! That surprised him. He looked at the two kids; they weren't going anywhere. He had to get after Jack. He jumped up and ran out the door, down the driveway and out into the street to see which way Jack had gone. At that instant, the scene transformed into a bizarre stroboscopic blue landscape. Jesus Christ, the boy must have called the police. A loudspeaker crackled to life, and headlights illuminated him.

"Sir, please stand right there. I need to talk to you." It was a female voice he recognized—the chief of police.

Bronco was now beyond pissed, he was dangerously angry. His mind cleared. The game was really on now, and he was going to win.

He turned slowly and cooperatively, smiling. He looked at the police car, squinting through the headlight glare to see if she was alone. She was, and he could tell she was radioing someone. He waited patiently. He knew she would get out of the car and at least stand behind the door before she came over to talk to him. She might not come over, it was her judgment call, but he wanted to make her feel comfortable.

There she goes, he thought, she's opening the door and getting out of the car. Bronco put one hand under the flap of his messenger bag.

"Sir, I need to see both of your hands, please," said the chief. This time, her voice came from over the top of her car door instead of the loudspeaker. Perfect.

Bronco reacted apologetically and started to slowly withdraw his hand and then he made his move. With one swift movement, he pulled the Browning expertly into shooting position and with two trigger pulls, knocked out the headlights on the police cruiser. He then ran to his car, jumped in, and peeled out of the driveway. He punched the accelerator as he exited the driveway and made a hard right, skidding his rear end into the street. At the exact same time, he heard a low crack that he instantly recognized as the sound of a 9mm, and then a sharp punch on the right side of his butt. He didn't stop to ruminate on this, he held the accelerator to the floor and pushed the little car to excessive speed, waiting for a second crack that never came. He knew now that he was going to get away. He was still in charge of this game. The first part was just a lot messier than he had planned.

33

KNIFE EDGE

"Ed! Come in Ed! This is Summer, do you copy?" Chief Hannah had recovered from her initial shock of finding Blue and Will in the guest room, and she quickly moved into full crisis mode. This was her arena. She was built for this situation. "Ed, for Chrissakes, come in! Are you asleep at the wheel? I will crucify you if you are!"

"I read you, Summer! Over!" came the crackle from the radio.

"Listen carefully, Ed." She spoke clearly and steadily into the microphone, "We have a situation. We have two seriously injured at 61 Pine Street. We need an ambulance, code 99. It looks like one gunshot wound and one drug overdose. Have the ambulance radio me directly on this channel, and keep this channel open! I will give them vital signs. Ed, do you copy this?"

"Geez Summer, what happened? I mean yeah I copy! Gunshot wound and drug overdose. I'm getting Emergency on the line now!" Ed sounded like he was caught off guard. *"Over!"* he remembered to add.

"Good, but I'm not done yet. This is extremely important. We have an armed assailant on the loose. Armed and extremely dangerous. I received unprovoked gunfire from the assailant, so approach him with extreme caution. The assailant left the scene in a 2000-ish Toyota, silver paint. I got a partial on the plate, first three numbers 725. One taillight is out. He left heading south on Pine Street and possibly turned west onto Elm. The time approximately 8:42 pm. Do you copy this, Ed?"

There was a pause before the radio crackled again *"Yeah, I've got that all down. Geez Summer, are you okay? Hold on, I've got emergency on the line . . ."* There was another pause and then, *"Okay, Ed here again. They are on their way, ETA about 5 minutes. Are you okay Summer? Over"*

"Yeah, I'm okay Ed, thanks for asking. Listen, we have to call State in on this. We can't find this guy alone. He should be considered a drive-off and fugitive. Get Frank on the line, and have him drive over and watch the Interstate exit and you can take the second cruiser and get over to Bank street as soon as you have State moving. We need all the manpower we can get, so whatever they want to do is okay with me. I've got to sign off now, I'm going to have my hand's full keeping these kids alive." While she was talking, Chief Hannah had checked Blue's vital signs and then turned to Will.

"How is Blue?" Will asked weakly. He looked exhausted and fading. "Is she breathing?"

"She is breathing, barely, but her pulse is steady. She is better off than you are right now. I want you to lay down and put as much pressure here as you can stand." She held his right hand to his upper left chest "I'm going to lie you on your back. That will help put pressure on the exit wound." She rolled him carefully onto his back. Will grimaced the whole time.

"It's heroin, I think," Will said when Chief Hannah turned to examine Blue's arm and the paraphernalia on the table. "I think he overdosed her. Can you suck it out or something? Can you keep her alive?"

Chief Hannah let a softness penetrate her professional voice when she replied, "You just stay still, Will. I'll keep her alive, I promise. Are you sure it's heroin? Did you hear them actually say heroin?"

"He's a dealer . . . heroin . . . Blue overheard them talking at the park . . . Blue saw something and . . . Bronco caught her so . . . so she wouldn't go to the police." Will seemed to be losing consciousness. Now she started to be more than worried.

"Will, stay with me." She added her hand to Will's and pressed hard. The stab of pain woke him up again, and he gasped, "Ahh! It hurts!"

"I know bud, but we gotta keep pressure on it." And then she saw the pool of blood Will was lying in. His body had blocked the sight of it when he was sitting up. The amount of blood on the floor was far more than there should have been and it frightened her. She realized she had spent too much time talking to Ed and checking out Blue; she should have checked Will more quickly. It must be an artery, she thought. Nothing else would cause so much blood so fast. "Just lie still. This is going to hurt like hell but I'm not letting up."

Will's eyes were starting to flutter. Fear was starting to rise in Chief Hannah's chest, but she kept it out of her voice. "Stay with me, bud," she said. "Do you know the pledge of allegiance? Say it for me. C'mon you can do it."

"I pledge allegiance . . . to the flag . . . of the United . . . AHHH!" Chief Hannah had renewed her hand position.

"C'mon Will, it's not the 'United-AHH.' What is it?" she prompted.

"God . . . stop moving around . . . it hurts when you do that. United States . . . of AHH . . . merica!"

Chief Hannah couldn't help a small smile even if the rest of her face was grim. "Yeah, you're going to be just fine kid," she said. "Keep going, I hear a siren now. You have to keep talking to me until they get here. C'mon now let's do something easier—let's do the days of the week—start with Monday." As she said that, she looked over at Blue again, and her optimism ebbed. It was hard to tell if the girl's lips and nails were getting bluer or pinker. She didn't dare let pressure off of Will's chest. It was clear he had lost a lot of blood and if he lost any more ... "Will! C'mon start with Monday ... let's hear it. Monday ..."

Will spoke like he was half awake "Mon ... day ..."

"What's next buddy? What's after Monday?" She was almost shouting. At the same time, she reached over and pressed down on Blue's chest in the hope she could boost Blue's respirations. She slapped Blue on the cheek, but the girl was completely out of it. Yet Chief Hannah thought she could hear a slight inhale so she pressed on Blue's chest again.

"Tue ... Tue ... Tuesday." Will's voice was getting farther and farther away. The sirens were getting closer but not fast enough.

Chief Summer Hannah felt like she had two lives, one in each hand, and each one balanced on a knife's edge.

Jack ran. He ran and he ran and he ran. He ran from the blue flashing lights of the police car that pulled up as he flew out of Bronco's house. He ran from the *"puh-smash! Puh-smash!"* of Broncos silenced pistol firing and striking . . . something—Jack didn't know what, and he didn't have time to think about it right now, he was just glad it wasn't striking him. He ran, and then found himself groveling flat on the ground after a frightening, *"POW-smash!"* that he recognized as a serious piece of firepower. Jack picked himself up and went into overdrive. He didn't think he could run any faster, but somehow he did.

He kept running well after he knew he was safe from pursuit. He was running from something worse than bullets or Bronco or blue lights. He was running from what he had just witnessed. That was the girl who had been missing. The girl with gumption that he had admired and had given the joint to. The fourteen-year-old. Blue.

And Will was there, too. How he had managed to find this place, Jack had no idea, but it was clear Will had come to rescue Blue. Jack had been paralyzed by the scene. Will had seemed paralyzed, too, and they were both unable to do anything but watch as Bronco calmly took in the situation, reached into his bag, pulled out a pistol and shot Will almost point blank—like Will was nothing more than a bag of sawdust.

Jack couldn't believe it. Bronco had kidnapped Blue—though Jack had no idea why. But Bronco wasn't just a kidnapper, he was also a killer and a psycho. Jack knew about psychos all too well. It hadn't taken him more than a fraction of a second to know what was coming next. He had instantly come out of his paralysis and reacted instinctively with practiced speed; he shoved Bronco onto the floor and ran for his life.

34

LOW TIDE

Blue was floating in a warm sea, rocking gently back and forth on dry soft waves. There were voices drifting about above her, saying things that in another world, she would have cared about, but in this world, meant nothing. She was sure she was already dead. She was not surprised to find that her mind was still alive even though her body was not. She wondered why everyone was so afraid of this. Death. If only she could tell them it was okay, but it didn't really matter. They would find out themselves someday.

She had floated up from the deeper, darker, dry water, where earlier she had almost sunk to the bottom. It was dark down there, but quiet, and peaceful. She was ready to fall into the most pleasant deep sleep she had ever had. She was bobbing, deeper, deeper, deeper, looking forward to resting on the bottom. But then there was a warm feeling in her chest and it expanded, being inflated by some magical force that was warm around her mouth. Maybe this was the kiss of death? It felt very pleasant, and she was pleased when it returned a second time. With the added buoyancy of this warm swelling in her chest, she had started floating upwards again, and the light was returning brighter and brighter. And then she had the sensation of falling—but falling gently and then landing on her side without any pain. She hadn't fallen back onto the dark ocean floor, because it was light here. It was the ocean surface. Maybe she had passed over to the other side—heaven or hell—or eternity. She was jostled about as playful sea creatures pushed her around on the ocean surface, and one of them had splashed her with a bitter spray which almost made her wake up—and that had annoyed her—but they had gone away now, replaced by the soft drifting voices and the gentle rock of the dry waves. She saw little shadows and lights pass above her from time to time, slowly getting brighter and then rushing away as if they were in a hurry. What is your hurry, she thought. This is forever. Stop and stay awhile.

Things came to Will in fuzzy flashes. He could sense he was lying on his back, rocking back and forth like he was on a train. Next, he could sense lights going by, but he couldn't quite open his eyes. Time seemed to go by, but he couldn't tell how much time. His left side and arm felt numb and aching. It was hard to breathe because of pressure on his chest. When he did breathe, the air was sweet and cool and fresh. It was delicious. He could hear a motor, and tires on the road, and voices. His eyes finally opened in small slits. Why was he having so much trouble opening his eyes? Then a voice, a man's voice, was close by and clear. He realized it was directed at him.

"Hey, look who has decided to join the party! Will, how you doing buddy?" said the man's voice.

Will tried to say 'okay' but all that managed to come out was a hoarse ". . . kay." He tried to say 'been better' but gave up after it came out "beh . . . b . . . er." His voice sounded bottled up and he realized he had a mask over his face.

"That's awesome, you are doing great! Good to hear your voice, man. Bet you're finding it hard to talk. We've got a mask with some oxygen on you. My name is Pete, and over there we have the lovely

Sarah. In case you haven't figured it out yet, we are in an ambulance on our way to the hospital, where they are going to take great care of you."

"Hey Will," said Sarah. Will tried to look over but he winced in pain.

"Yeah, that's going to hurt," said Pete. "Just relax and take it easy. We gave you some pain meds, but the heavy duty stuff will have to wait until you're at the hospital. Those meds can make you kind of fuzzy and spaced out, and we can't have that right now. We need to be able to talk with you."

Will was starting to come around a little. The oxygen was helping a lot. He gulped it down thirstily. And then he remembered how he got here, and the situation started coming back to him in a rush. He instinctively tried to sit up and look around but cried out in pain.

"Hey, it's okay, Will. Don't try to move around. I've got to keep this pressure on your chest to keep it from bleeding again. Just talk to me, okay?" said Pete in a calming voice.

The pain subsided but his shoulder and chest were throbbing from the movement. "Blue?" he managed to say clearly. "Where's Blue? Is she okay?" He looked urgently at Pete who was leaning close over Will.

Pete slowly smiled and said, "If you promise to look at me and lie still, I will tell you that she is pretty sleepy and out of it but is completely safe and breathing strong and steady. Oh, and she is lying about six inches from your left elbow on the folding stretcher. Is that what you were hoping to hear?"

Will couldn't help himself, he started to look to the left in spite of the pain, but Pete was way ahead of him and had Will's head held firmly with his free hand. "Hey, hey, hey, what did I just tell you? You're breaking the deal. Lie still! Now, if you just calm down, I will help you turn head slowly so you can see, and we won't risk opening up these wounds Sarah and I worked so hard on, okay? But I'm not going to do it until you relax. Are you relaxed?"

Will nodded ever so slightly and tried to relax. Pete gently tilted Will's head to the left, and Will could see Blue's profile. She was lying still with her eyes mostly closed, and clearly not fully awake. She was rocking with the motion of the ambulance just as they all were, like an involuntary pantomime. The light in the ambulance was dimmed, and the passing streetlights made a lively wave of light and shadow which played over the still ravaged, but peaceful face underneath.

Pete looked at Sarah with a grin and nodded his head at the pair. He turned back to Will and said, "She is going to be fine. She'll probably be up and about long before you are, actually. All we had to do was give her some oxygen and bag her with this." Pete held up a clear plastic bag with a face-mask on one side. "This helps her breathe. It's like mouth-to-mouth resuscitation but without the mouth. You know what mouth-to-mouth resuscitation is, right Will?"

Will wondered if they knew that he had given Blue mouth-to-mouth. Even with all the blood he lost, he felt himself blushing, but Pete didn't seem to notice.

"We also gave her a spritz of Narcan, which helped boost her respiration rate. She should be fine now. We just have to wait until she comes down off the heroin." Pete must have seen the look of concern on Will's face because he spoke up quickly. "Hey, don't worry, it won't last. She'll be fine as soon as it is all out of her system. You don't need to worry anymore, okay? You're in our ambulance and we don't let anything bad happen once you're in our ambulance. You have both been through the worst already, and you're going to get patched up by the best doctors on the planet. Got that?"

"Got it," said Will, finally giving in to the reassuring rhythm of Pete's voice and words. Will tried to make a thumbs-up with both hands, but his left hand felt like it was asleep. His right hand worked, though.

Pete gave him the thumbs up back and said, "I saw your left hand trying. That's good!"

Will did feel like they were both safe now, and that thought was a powerful sedative. He let his eyes slowly shut again with the rocking of the ambulance and the ebb and flow of light that passed through the window.

35

PARADOX

Bronco had been driving about an hour when he finally had to pull over. The pain in his leg was getting excruciating, and he had to do something about it. He wanted to put some miles behind him, though, so he had endured the wound as much as he could.

He had pulled over into a parking turnout next to a lake. He was in upstate New York now—sparsely populated, full of lakes and mountains and trees, and not much traffic. He dug into his bug-out bag and pulled out a Percocet and a water bottle. He had a pretty good pharmacy in his bug-out bag. The Percocet would hit in a few minutes and then he could continue driving. Back at the garage when he switched cars, he applied a dressing on the wound and it seemed to be doing its job, so he left it alone. He sighed and sat back and waited for the drug to kick in.

Those damn police had found the apartment a lot faster than he had expected them to. And then there was that damn kid, Will. And Jack! What the hell led up to that?

Didn't matter now. It meant that they had discovered Bob Kelly, too. Not a problem, though—he had ditched Bob Kelly's car back in Bob Kelly's rented garage where he had been keeping his other car. The APB they sent out was for Bob Kelly's car. They weren't looking for what he was driving now—his black Camaro with New York plates, under his real name.

Bronco laughed. He had still beaten them, even though they were better than he expected, and even though that damned police chief had shot out his tail light. He was impressed—it was a good shot, and it marked his car. It was a lot easier to spot a car with a missing taillight. It stuck out like a beacon, and he was feeling very exposed by it until he got it safely parked in the rented garage.

The garage was a stroke of genius. At first, he thought he was being overly cautious, but now it looked brilliant. He had rented it at the same time he rented the apartment about 10 months earlier. He got it so that he could preserve Bob Kelly's identity. When he had gone to New York, he'd switched to this car and his real ID, and when he came back, he switched back to Bob Kelly's car and ID. The garage was located in an old busted farm. It wasn't even a garage—more of an unused shed big enough for two cars. The retired farmer was looking for extra income, and he didn't ask questions, and he insisted on cash payment for the rental. That suited Bronco just fine. He could switch cars there without anyone observing him and cash left no record for someone to follow. To the farmer, he just was some guy who liked cars. It would probably be a couple of months before the farmer even noticed the rent wasn't being paid.

Tonight, Bronco managed to get to the shed without being pursued, and as soon as he got in and shut the door, he knew he was safe. He took some time to clean up his wound, dress it, and change into some clean pants. The wound wasn't bleeding badly, but it hurt like hell, and he didn't want to be walking around in pants soaked in blood. The police woman's bullet had passed through the taillight and the back of the car, through the trunk, backseat, and front seat and parked itself somewhere in his right butt cheek. All he had to do was make it to New York City, and he knew a guy that could patch him up and would keep his mouth shut.

Hell, if a bullet in the butt was the price for his freedom, he would take it. He was free. He had made it out of there with his money and his anonymity and now his only problem was deciding which southern paradise he wanted to settle in. He started to feel pretty good as these thoughts, and the Percocet, kicked in, so he started the car and got back on the road. He was going to drive the speed limit the whole way. No getting pulled over now.

As he drove, he went over what had happened. It was that damned girl—her and her friend. That was one thing he never factored into his plans, a kid coming in and messing things up. Never underestimate a kid. Especially that girl, Blue. He still got the shivers thinking about her. He believed in clairvoyance and ESP, but he never expected to run into it in real life. It was spooky. He was glad to be miles away from that kid.

At least she wouldn't be talking and giving the police any more help. He'd seen dozens of overdoses in his life and he could tell the girl was on her way out—blue tinge, no movement. And the boy? Well, Bronco wished now that he had put a second bullet in him, but he'd been rushed by that other wild card, Jack. And then that policewoman. Damn, that timing was bad. If it wasn't for the cop, Bronco would've taken care of the whole problem —all three of them. He would still be on the road like he was, but with no living witnesses, and without a bullet in his behind. But on the bright side, he didn't have to do any digging that night. Three bodies and three graves would have been a worse pain in the ass.

Before long, Bronco had put dozens of miles of Adirondack mountain roads behind him, and he was relaxed—at least as relaxed as his wound would allow. All his money was secure, he had plenty of cash with him and his two guns. His Glock was in the backpack and his Browning Buck Mark was in the messenger bag. The Glock was fine for an all-out gun battle, but the long barreled Browning with a red-dot sight and silencer was far better for quiet killing work. It was like having a small, quiet sniper rifle. The best part was the barrel. It was replaceable. The gun was registered and totally legal, but a ballistics report could still tie a gun to a shooting, unless you got rid of the barrel. The barrel of the Browning had no serial number on it, the serial number was on the gun frame. He had replaced the barrel with the nice new one he had in his bug-out bag, and the one he shot the boy and the police car with was now at the bottom of a lake, never to be found.

There were so many ways to beat the system.

His leg wasn't as cooperative as he'd like, however. He was having trouble getting it to do what he wanted. It wasn't the pain, the Percocet was taking care of that, it was something else, like muscle cramps. This was one time he was glad the car was an automatic, as driving the winding roads through the mountains was starting to get more difficult with all the tight turns and braking and accelerating. If he could just get to the interstate, he could put it on cruise control and manage it the rest of the way.

He got a scare as the road bent sharply to the right and he should have slowed down but he couldn't get his foot off the gas pedal fast enough. He took the turn way too fast, tires squawking threateningly. He started braking with his left foot, but he still had to use his right for the gas.

"Slow down, Bronco," he told himself, "Easy does it. You are too close to blow it now." A sign for the next town emerged into his headlight beams—Paradox. Funny name for a town, he thought, but he knew now that he wasn't far from the interstate.

Another sharp curve was coming up, turning to the left this time. It was a turn onto a bridge crossing a very narrow bay of a mountain lake. He moved his leg to ease off the gas and bleed off some speed. But his leg wouldn't behave. He tried again harder, but instead of letting up, his leg seized up in a massive muscle spasm and did exactly the opposite. It suddenly straightened itself with a jerk and slammed on the gas pedal.

The Camaro leaped forward with a surge of power as it down-shifted, anticipating that the driver was anxious to pass someone. He braked as hard as he could with his left foot, but the car wasn't slowing down. The turn was coming way too fast. He hammered on his right leg with his fist. Get. That. Damned. Leg. Off. Now! He slammed the transmission into neutral to stop the acceleration, and the engine screamed to a dangerously high pitch. The car stopped accelerating, but it was already too late. He steered into the turn, but it was too sharp, too fast. The tires wouldn't hold the car. They lost their grip on the road.

The car slammed sideways into the guardrail. The inertia of the sleek black Camaro overwhelmed the ancient guardrail posts, designed half a century ago for cars half as powerful as this. They gave way with hardly a protest, leaving the bulk of the impact to be absorbed by the newer silver steel railing, which held on gallantly but couldn't contain the energy of the impact. The railing held on only just enough to flip the car over, leaving nothing between the tumbling car and the calm, moonlit lake that the guardrail was meant to protect.

Bronco had a sensation of the car whipping around and lifting and flipping over, the violent maneuver throwing him out of his seat and slamming him around the inside of the car. Then there was a brief moment of silence as the Camaro sailed through the air toward the lake. It was just enough time for Bronco's mind to have one last thought before the car hit the water—as long as he had his bug-out bag and wasn't too banged up by this, he could still make it to New York....

Jack was on his second joint of the night. He usually didn't get this stoned, but he did not want to face reality just yet. He was in the safest spot he knew, out on an unused railroad bridge over the river. This was where he went when it was too early to go home. Too early was when his father was roaring drunk and still awake and ready to beat the crap out of him for being late. And lazy. And useless. And a moron. The litany of degrading terms had grown long and familiar to Jack, and he'd grown accustomed to enduring the beating—both physical and mental. He usually could make it to his room now without getting too beat up. His dad would get exhausted yelling and beating on the door and would fall asleep collapsed on the couch or the stairs or sometimes on the floor outside his door, where Jack would find him in the morning, unconscious and non-threatening.

But Jack always preferred to avoid the drama. He just hung out here on the bridge until he knew his dad was passed out. It was quiet on the bridge, except for the bubbling of the water against the piers and the distant sound of cars on the road that ran along the river. The lights of the town marched up the dark hill to the skyline where they reflected in the low clouds. There were two or three other people that used the bridge late at night —mostly to cross the river, one or two to do the same thing he was doing. Hanging out, killing time, getting stoned. He recognized them all but knew none of them. It didn't matter, they all got what they wanted, which was a little peace and quiet. He had spent the night there a few times when it was nice out. He wasn't going to, tonight, however. It began to drizzle, and he was still uncertain whether Bronco would be coming after him—even though it had been hours since he had run from . . . run from that.

Jack had heard sirens from time to time throughout the night. He had no idea what might have happened after he left, and he didn't even want to guess, but sirens meant bad things had happened. He just wanted to go home, step over his passed-out father, and then lock his door and sink into oblivion. But he had to wait. He had a good sense for when it was safe to go, and it was still too early. Until then he had to stay conscious. And because he was conscious, he couldn't prevent his thoughts from continuing, fuzzy as they were.

He was thinking about what he was. He was a coward. He could accept that, but he couldn't accept that he had been working with a kidnapper and a killer. And he couldn't accept the fact that he may have just witnessed a double murder. Two kids. Two kids he knew.

He was really stoned, but it didn't seem enough. He lit another joint. He swayed a little bit and watched the water moving slowly far beneath his dangling feet. He considered what it would be like to just fall into the water and let it carry him away.

The coffee wasn't doing anything except keeping her hands warm. Caffeine had reached that point where it had exhausted its powers and become nothing more than a bitter taste in a hot liquid. Ed looked exhausted, so Chief Hannah could only imagine what she looked like. Ed was a good officer, and he had done everything right during a night that seemed to go otherwise horribly wrong.

"Hey Ed," she said.

He looked up with tired eyes. "Hey Summer," he replied slowly. "What a night, eh?"

"You did good," she said sincerely. "Yeah, what a night, all right. You think anything more could happen?"

Besides getting shot at and then having to shoot back, and desperately trying to save the lives of two kids who were far too young to have this shit happen to them, she had to answer a call of domestic abuse at 3 a.m. to wrestle and handcuff a manic drunk off his son before he murdered him. The son was Jack Menhoff, the boy she had been trying to find and interview. Jack and his troubles weren't unfamiliar to her. She knew the family, and she knew this would happen someday, but she was powerless to prevent it. On the other hand, she might have been the cause. When she had gone to the Menhoff's to interview Jack during the search, Jack wasn't there, but his father was. By the time she left he was clearly on the edge. The suggestion that Jack might know something about a missing juvenile appeared to trigger an ominous anger reaction from him. He was nearly speechless with rage. He might have even been drunk at the time, but what could she do? Arrest a man for being angry and drunk in his own home? No, she couldn't, but she had set the stage for what came later that night. But maybe that was needed. Maybe that was the one good thing that came from this night. Now maybe the DFC could get Jack and his mother away from the abusive father. Chief Hannah hoped so. She did not want to answer any more calls like that, or any of the calls she made that night. She'd reached her quota for the year. Perhaps the decade.

One thing kept nagging at her, however. How did Will find Blue? She had a hunch and if that hunch were true, she needed to have a talk, off the record, with Will as soon as he woke up.

"Ed," she said, "Call Sam now and get him down here to relieve you. You look like hell."

Ed grinned and said, "I bet I look better than you do. You better go home yourself. You go ahead, I'll get Sam down here."

"I'm going to take you up on that," she replied. She knew there was still a lot of work ahead the next day. It actually was the next day already, but there were still a couple of hours of darkness left and she was going to use that time to get some sleep. She wanted to be sharp in the morning.

36

PICKING UP THE PIECES

It started as a little nudge, like someone was trying to wake her in the middle of the night. Blue didn't want to wake up. She was very comfortable right where she was. Why was someone doing that? She ignored it, but then it came again, only this time it was from inside her, as if her body was fighting her brain. Her brain was saying, "Stay asleep! You don't want to wake up!" And her body was saying, "I'm waking up anyway!" Her eyes were opening of their own accord. Where was she? Why was it so bright? Her brain was fuzzy and she was starting to feel dizzy.

A hand was holding her forehead and pulling on her eyebrow. Another hand held a small light that was shining in her eye. She looked disapprovingly at the owner of the hands. There was a woman hovering over her. It looked like a doctor or a nurse who was looking at her intently but kindly. The woman spoke in a steady voice, "Blue, you are safe. You are okay. You are in a hospital, and you are fine. I just woke you up with some medicine." The waking feeling was starting to turn into nausea. Blue was afraid she was going to throw up. She was fine before, so why did they have to wake her up? She was angry. She started to breathe rapidly. She didn't know if it was the anger or nausea or both. The nurse stroked

Blue's forehead with a cool damp cloth. That helped with the nausea but not the anger.

"Just look at me, Blue. Look at me and breathe evenly. You'll be okay in a second. This medicine can make you feel a little rocky sometimes. Look at me," she repeated.

The doctor's quiet, rhythmic voice was soothing, and the nausea subsided. Slowly Blue got control of her breathing and started to calm down. She could look at the doctor now, "Okay, okay, I think I'm okay."

"Good! You sound better already." The doctor smiled. "This will pass in just a minute or two, and then you'll feel a lot better. Believe me, this isn't the worst reaction I've seen. You're handling it well."

"Where am I? What happened?" Blue felt at a complete loss. She still couldn't think straight quite yet. And then she remembered. "It was heroin," she croaked. The pieces weren't all back together yet, but she was starting to remember parts.

"Yes it was heroin," said the doctor, "but I want you to know that you'll be okay. You won't have any lasting effects from this. There is still some in your system, but the shot I gave you will help. You also have an IV in your arm and that is where we have been giving you liquids to help keep you hydrated and help flush it all out."

"Blue?" said a familiar voice right next to her. Blue turned towards the voice. It was Ma Beth. She looked very tired but very happy. She had tears in her eyes. Blue had never seen Ma Beth cry before. Seeing her brought Blue back to reality and she was suddenly frightened.

"Ma Beth! I am so, so sorry." She looked down, not wanting to face her. Ma Beth reached out and pulled Blue to her in a surprisingly strong hug. Blue gave into the hug and let the comfort of it flow through her. It seemed to be bringing life and sanity back to her.

But it also got her brain working again, and the warmth of the hug and the tightness of Ma Beth's arms couldn't suppress what she was thinking. She had blown it! She wasn't going to be able to stay with the O'Days anymore. This incident was sure to have repercussions. "I don't want to leave you!" she said in a panic. "This is all my fault. They'll take me away from you!"

Ma Beth gave her a squeeze and then took her firmly by the shoulders, held her back, and looked steadily into her face. "*THE HELL THEY WILL!*" rang clear as a bell in Blue's head. Only the strongest feelings sounded like that from non-vox. Then Ma Beth spoke in a stern, no-nonsense voice, "No one is going to take you from the O'Day family young lady. You are a part of it now. Don't you worry! Every single one of us is overjoyed to have you back safe, and we wouldn't think of letting you go again!"

Blue reached around Ma Beth and hugged her. She was tired of her brain working again, and she wanted to sink back into the mindlessness of sleep or whatever it was that the heroin was doing.

The doctor interrupted, "I'm sorry, Blue, but I have to do a few checks, and then we will let you get some rest. It will take a couple of more hours before the opiate wears off. Ma Beth needs to sleep, too, you know. It's two o'clock in the morning, and she hasn't slept a bit."

Two in the morning? Was it still the same night? It seemed to Blue that it had been days. She suddenly felt exhausted again, but she let the doctor shine a light in her eyes again and test her reflexes and check her blood pressure, and then Blue sank back into the sheets and closed her eyes. She tried to settle into some sort of oblivion where she didn't have to think of anything for a while.

Sam was the one to wake up Rose. She was curled comfortably in a waiting room chair. Someone had brought out some pillows and blankets and tucked her in.

"Hey Rose. Wake up, we can go see Blue," said Sam.

"She's awake?" said Rose sleepily.

"No, she's asleep but Ma Beth said they woke her up to see if she was okay and then let her go back to sleep."

"Okay. What about Will?" she said, getting up.

"He is still in surgery. Don't worry Rose. He is going to be fine," said Sam seeing the sadness in Rose's face. "Let's go see Blue."

Ma Beth had come out to the waiting room and said that the doctor would allow her to take everyone in to see Blue but only if they were very quiet and let her sleep. Everyone was in the waiting room—Sam, Rose, Wu, Nate, Pa Bill, and Mr. and Mrs. Woods.

They slipped quietly into the room. Blue was curled on her side facing toward them with the bed back slightly up. She looked relaxed and peaceful, which was comforting to Rose. Except for one thing.

"What happened to her face?" whispered Rose.

"What are all those tubes?" whispered Sam.

"Shhhh Rosie, Sam. Not so loud," hushed Wu.

"It's okay," said Ma Beth quietly, "I will tell you when we are back in the waiting room."

After the second group had gone in to see Blue, Ma Beth explained what she knew. "They don't know how she got the bruise on her forehead, but the redness around her mouth is where it was taped so she wouldn't cry for help. The bruise on her face and her bloody nose are where they think she was hit by the man that was holding her."

This was tough for Rose. "Why would he hit her? Why would a man want to hit a girl? Have they caught him yet? I want to punch him when they catch him."

"Hey Rosie, I think you spoke for all of us," said Wu quietly, and he reached over and gave her a hug. Rose let him hug her but she was still angry.

They were all hoping for news about Will. He had been in surgery for about two hours. They didn't have to wait long, though, as a nurse came into the room and said, "He is in recovery now. Everything went really well. Mr. and Mrs. Woods, you can go in and see him. He will be pretty groggy, but he looks good!"

Everyone was relieved. Ma Beth said, "I think it is time for the rest of you to go home and get some sleep. You can all come back first thing in the morning, and then both Will and Blue will be awake."

Wu protested, "Please, may I stay? Will is my best friend, and I know he wouldn't leave if I were in the same spot."

"Okay, Wu, you can stay. But the rest of you have to go home now. No complaints! We can all rest easier now."

It felt like morning, but what day it was, or how long he had been there, he couldn't tell. Will was lying in a hospital bed. The back was slightly elevated and his head was tilted toward the hospital room window where the sunlight was engulfing his bed with a cozy layer of warmth. The window framed a picture of nothing but blue sky with puffy white clouds. He felt like he had just been through a hurricane and come out on the other side into a transformed world.

He was a little spacey and didn't feel like moving his head much, so he just watched the clouds. As he did he started to put the pieces together of what happened. He remembered waking up in the ambulance and seeing Blue, seeing that she was safe. He remembered waking again in the emergency room and then getting moved to a gurney which they wheeled down the hall. Then he remembered waking up in what must have been an operating room —he must have passed out a lot, or maybe it was anesthesia.

Then he saw Mom and Dad and Rose in recovery, but he couldn't remember what he said or what they said. He knew he had tried to make a joke, but couldn't remember it. And then a couple of times when it was still dark out, a nurse came in and checked on him. At one point in the night, the pain his shoulder started coming back, and at about the time it became so excruciating and he didn't think he could bear it anymore, the nurse came rushing in and put a shot of something in his IV. It was miraculous. The pain subsided immediately. The nurse showed him the call button, so he could call if the pain got bad again. That was comforting. He did not want that to happen again.

He held up his right arm. It had an IV in it and was attached to a pouch on a stand next to his bed. It was dripping something into his bloodstream. There was a monitor next to him, too, and he still had wires for an EKG hooked up to him and a sensor on his finger. There was a tube coming out from under the dressing on his shoulder and chest and into a bag hanging by his bed.

He didn't try lifting his left arm just yet. He started with his left hand instead, just wiggling his fingers. They moved just fine, but he could also feel things tugging and tweaking all the way up in his shoulder and chest like they never did before. He tried twisting his arm back and forth. It worked, but it was painful, and it felt like his arm was swollen and the skin pulled at what were probably stitches.

"Testing things out are we?"

Will turned his head too quickly and winced—that was actual pain. "Mom! I didn't know you were here!" She looked tired and red-eyed, even though she was smiling. "*Mom, you look . . . are you okay?*"

Tears leaked out her eyes and she leaned over and hugged Will tightly in reply. "Now I am more than fine," she said softly and then sat back smiling. "*Dad and Rose were here too, until I sent them back to the waiting room. They've been here all night. So has Wu. He is just about jumping out of his skin to see you. Do you want to see them?*"

"*You're kidding me, right? Of course!*" Will replied.

His Mother smiled, "*Just checking, I see my old Will is back!*" "Be back in a flash," she said and started to leave, but she almost ran into Rose and Wu barging in. Rose was dragging Wu by the hand.

Rose let out a squeak of delight when she saw Will and ran over to the bed. "*WILLY! WILLY, WILLY, WILLY!*"

"Hey Rosie! Hey, be careful of my arm!" She had come up to give him a big hug, but her arm barely reached across his chest anyway and she was so little, it didn't hurt too much. "*AND DON'T YOU DARE CALL ME WILLY AGAIN!*" he voxed.

"*OKAY, WILLY,*" she replied. "Wow, look at the bandages. You look like a part-mummy!"

"Hey Will," Wu said. "Good to see you awake. You gave us a big scare there man," "*HOLY SHIT, WHAT HAPPENED TO HIS ARM?*"

Will caught Wu's *chiss*. "Hey Wu, thanks. Yeah, my arm looks pretty terrible, but I think it is going to be all right," said Will.

Wu looked like he wanted to say something more, but stopped short with a puzzled look on his face.

"I'll talk to you later about it," said Will. "Hey, Dad."

"Hey there, son. You're looking a lot more chipper than last night. All is going well. The doctor says your arm will look like that for a while from all the fluid buildup and internal bleeding—it causes bruising that can look quite shocking. This will most likely lead to an overabundance of sympathy from friends and family. I'm certain that you will take the noble path and avoid taking advantage of all this sympathy?" Mr. Woods was looking over his glasses.

"Oh absolutely!" said Will, "*YEAH, RIGHT DAD. I'M GOING TO MILK IT FOR ALL IT'S WORTH!*"

Rosie jumped in, "You've got all the same hoses and monitors and stuff hooked to you that Blue has! Does it hurt having this big needle stuck in your arm?"

"No, my shoulder kind of out-pains everything else. A needle in my arm isn't a big deal," said Will. He looked up at Wu with renewed concern. "How is she? Is everything okay?"

"She's fine. Ma Beth talked to her for a bit early this morning when they woke her up for some tests and she says she sounds just like Blue, just really sleepy. We got to see her when she was asleep. I'll tell you her face looks a bit of a mess. She has a bump on her head and a cut on her nose and red marks around her mouth. But the doctor says that's all just superficial and will heal up fine. They are worried about the bump on her head and want to monitor her for a day to make sure she doesn't have a concussion."

"The red marks are probably from the tape. I pulled it off fast. I wasn't really worried about her complexion at that point." The visions of what happened were starting to replay in his head. "And yeah, I saw the bump . . ." started Will, but Wu interrupted.

"Will!" Wu said.

Will stopped. He looked at Wu.

There seemed to be a battle of emotions in Wu's face as he said, "Will, man, I mean . . ." he stammered, ". . . I mean . . . you saved her life! You took a bullet for her!"

Will wasn't sure what to say. Wu was making it sound like he did something spectacular. "Hey, Wu, I just did what anyone else would do—I mean you would have done the same, probably better than I did. I was pretty stupid trying to pick the tape off. If I'd thought of tearing it first, it would have gone a lot faster, and I should have laid the chair back first thing . . ."

"Will!" It was his mom this time. "To do any better without training would have been impossible. And no one can train for that situation. You showed amazing presence of mind," "AND YOU SHOULD STOP TALKING NOW, WU SEEMS UPSET."

"WHAT DID I SAY?"

"NOTHING, IT'S JUST BEEN A LONG NIGHT FOR US ALL," voxed his mom.

Will paused. He looked at Wu. He looked tired, too. Will felt a sudden surge of warmth towards his friend. "Yeah, well, thanks, Wu. I'm just glad everyone is okay."

Just then a nurse stuck her head inside the room and said, "Wu, your family just came into the waiting room. They are going to wake Blue up soon. Why don't you go down and join them now."

Wu held out his fist to Will, and Will reached out for a fist bump. "You get better, dude, so I can trash you on the basketball court."

"Dream on, friend," replied Will.

After Wu left, Rose, who had slumped down in a chair, let out a gigantic yawn and said, "Wu stayed with us here all night. He let me use his leg for a pillow." "*AND THEY BROUGHT US BLANKETS.*"

"Wow, you stayed up all night Rosie?" said Will.

"Yep!" she said, her eyes closing.

"*MORE LIKE MOST OF THE NIGHT. SHE GOT A FEW HOURS SLEEP,*" voxed his mom.

"*MOM! YOU SHOULD HAVE GOTTEN SOME SLEEP,*" voxed Will.

"Don't worry about us son," his dad replied. "We have enough adrenaline running in our system to last for days! You, on the other hand, have endured a lot of trauma and need to rest and let your body heal."

"But what about Blue? Is she really going to be okay?"

"She is going to be fine, and she will probably be in to see you before you are in to see her. So be patient my friend and just sit back and rest." His dad paused and then added, "You know Wu was right. Your actions did save Blue's life. As I told you, 'audentes fortuna iuvat!'"

Will had completely forgotten about his dad's last words the night before. "Something about fortune?"

"Yes, my friend. 'Fortune favors the bold!'"

***

Blue was awake, tired, sore, and worried. But mostly worried. She didn't know what was in store for her now. She felt like maybe she should just stay in the hospital forever, but the sight of Ma Beth erased that feeling. When Blue saw her walk in the room, it felt like coming home.

Ma Beth smiled. "And here is our bright Blue again. You look so much better."

"Thanks, I feel a lot better." She wanted to continue and say, "now that you are here," but she couldn't. She was almost there, but not quite yet.

"The rest of the family is in the waiting room and anxious to see you."

"And is Will here?" asked Blue.

Ma Beth's brows creased. She didn't speak for a second and then she said, "He is. You know Will got hurt last night? He is in the hospital, too." She must have seen the panic in Blue's eyes because she quickly added, "Don't worry, he's going to be all right!"

Blue felt a little dizzy, "What do you mean he was hurt? What happened?"

"Blue," said Ma Beth, "I will tell you everything we know so far. However, some of it may be shocking. Do you think you can handle that?"

Blue nodded her head, though she really didn't know. She still was feeling like she just woke up and wasn't thinking completely clearly, but the one thing she did know clearly is that not knowing might drive her crazy.

"Okay, here we go. Will found the house where you were being held last night. He texted Chief Hannah with the address. When Chief Hannah arrived, she saw a man leaving the house at the address, and she asked him to stop, so she could ask him a few questions. That man turned out to be the man that kidnapped you."

"Bronco," said Blue.

"Yes, Bronco. Apparently he did stop but then he pulled out a gun and fired at her . . ."

Blue inhaled sharply.

Ma Beth added quickly, ". . . Chief Hannah was not hurt! The man shot out the headlights on her police car, so she couldn't follow him. After he fired his gun, he ran to his car and drove away. Chief Hannah radioed the other police officers to go after him. Then Chief Hannah went to investigate the house, and she found you unconscious on the floor. You must have been unconscious for quite some time. When she found you, you weren't tied up anymore because Will had set you free."

"Will!" She couldn't believe it. She remembered the vox scream that had exploded out of her eyes just after Bronco gave her the massive dose of heroin. Will must have heard it. It was almost supernatural to think of him hearing that one call. She hadn't done it consciously—it was totally reflexive. Now she shuddered to think what would have happened if her body hadn't thrown out that last desperate lifeline.

"Yes. Will didn't wait for the police. He went into the house and found you alone. Will said that when he found you, you weren't breathing. He said you were pale, and your lips and fingernails were turning blue. He removed the tape from your mouth and then got you breathing again and then unbound you. He saved your life!" Ma Beth was holding Blue's hand, watching intently. "Are you okay? Shall I go on?"

Blue was looking down at her hands. She saw where the zip ties had left dark purple bruises on her wrists. She knew that she had almost died. She knew when that was, it was when she felt like she was sinking—she was remembering now—she had felt like it was okay to die. Will saved her from sinking to the bottom. The warm breath she had felt, it must have been . . .

"Blue?" asked Ma Beth again.

Blue nodded slowly and said, "Keep going . . . please."

"Okay. Just remember that everything is okay now, and that even though this is upsetting, it has a good ending. Okay? Are you ready?"

Blue nodded. She was afraid, but ready.

"Okay. What we think happened was that Will found you when you were alone and that the man, Bronco, came into the house and discovered Will as he was untying you." She didn't say what was in her mind, but Blue heard it anyway. "*THAT BASTARD LEFT YOU THERE TO DIE!*" Ma Beth paused to compose herself. She continued, "When he came back and found that Will was untying you . . ."

Ma Beth paused and looked intently into Blue's eyes and then said carefully, "He shot Will."

The next thing Blue knew, there was a ringing in her ears and she was looking up through a gray haze into a Nurse's face, and the Nurse was saying, "Talk to me Blue. Look at my eyes. Can you hear me? Talk to me!"

Blue said, "I'm okay, I'm okay. Really I'm okay."

"Good," said the Nurse, "but I want you to stay lying down. You fainted there for a minute. Stay lying down and if you can do that I will let you two keep talking. Deal?"

"Okay," said Blue.

"Okay then," said the Nurse, and she left.

Ma Beth said, "Blue, Will is okay. He was hurt badly, but they brought him to the hospital, and he is going to recover. You can see him soon. He had some surgery last night and everything went well. He should make a full recovery. Do you hear? He is going to be okay."

Blue could hear, but she couldn't reply. She laid there looking at the ceiling. A bane, a Jonah, a nightmare, that's all she was to these people. She could never go back and live with them. She was going to climb back into Mrs. Jamison's car again, and she would keep doing that forever and ever and ever, and her nightmare would revisit her every time she started to feel comfortable again. She started to close her eyes and wish for the mindless haziness of the heroin to come back to her.

Before she could complete this wish, a soft warm hand gently stroked her forehead. She opened her eyes and looked at the kindest and wisest face she had ever seen. It had a beautiful smile and it said to her, "You are safe now my dear girl. Perish any thought that you are to blame for any of this. The world is filled with challenges and evils. When you stand up to them you can't always control the outcome, but the choice to stand up to them is always the right one."

Ma Beth kissed Blue on the forehead and held her. Blue felt the warmth of Ma Beth's touch surround her, like sunshine emerging from behind a cloud.

37

SUMMER'S END

"Bronco, or I should say, Bob Kelly, has vanished. I say Bob Kelly, but we know for certain that's not his real name. We are using it for now because that is what he was known as around here. We don't have a single lead yet on what his real identity might be or where he might be right now. Key evidence would be finding his car, but that hasn't happened and he has not been spotted—at least no credible sightings. The guy was smart, I mean really smart."

Chief Hannah had come to interview Will for her police report.

"That's all I can tell you at the moment. And now I have to ask you a few questions. Not many. Just enough to help us find some clues, so we can find him. You can refuse to answer any time, but it would really help us out if you could tell us as much as you can."

"Okay," said Will. "I'm just not sure if there is anything I can add to what you already know."

It was Will's second day in the hospital and he was ready to be released. He wasn't happy about it, though. He was feeling pretty safe and comfortable there in his hospital bed. He wasn't worried about Bronco being at large, he was worried instead about the press at large. The news crews were chomping at the bit to interview Will and Blue. Apparently, their hellish night was a big sensation in the news. Fortunately, their doctors, not to mention their parents, were not allowing it yet. But he knew that couldn't last.

"You'd be surprised what comes up when you ask the right questions. Thanks to Blue's drawings and descriptions, we have some distinguishing features for the police artist, but we wanted to ask you if you remembered any outstanding features that would help us identify him."

"Yes, he had one outstanding feature, and that was he was a cold-blooded bastard," replied Will. He was surprised at his own bitterness. His mom gave him a stern look. "I'm sorry, but just bringing him up makes me boil. No, I can't think of anything, I mean he was so average looking and his beard hid half his face anyway."

Chief Hannah nodded. "Yes, like I say, he was smart. It's easier to add a beard to a face reconstruction drawing than to take one away. A beard can hide facial structure. And a bearded guy in Vermont? That describes about a quarter of the population. He's probably shaved it by now. What about names? Do you remember him being referred to as any other name than Bronco, or Bob, or Bob Kelly?"

"No, sorry, nothing but those names."

"How about his car? Did you notice anything inside the car when you were close to it? Any luggage or items that were visible?"

"I did see a backpack. It was red with black straps and black reinforcements. It looked like a light hiking pack or mountaineering pack—not like a cheap book pack. It had a hip belt on it, I think. He was also carrying a brown shoulder bag, like a messenger bag. That's where he pulled his gun from."

Chief Hannah wrote some notes down. "Okay, this is helpful. As you know, this case is quite a sensation, and if he ditched the pack somewhere, there are so many people following the case on the news, someone could find it and give us more information. Believe it or not, just that one tip could break things wide open. You never know. That's all I'm going to ask right now, on the record."

"Now what I really wanted to come here for, off the record, is to see how you are. You know, you gave us all quite a scare." Her hardened officer features softened into a look of genuine concern and almost . . . tenderness?

"I gave myself quite a scare. The doctor said I am going to make a full recovery, though." Will paused with a grimace as a surge of pain hit him. "It doesn't feel like it right now, that's for sure. He also said I almost didn't make it. He said you saved my life, and well . . ." Will looked down. He felt awkward, not quite sure what you say to someone who saved your life. Finally, he looked back up and said, "Well, thanks. I mean . . . thanks a lot!"

"You're welcome. I was just trying to do my job, but I want you to know that I was scared out of my wits, and I almost screwed it up. You see, I didn't notice how much you were bleeding until it was . . . well I should have noticed it sooner and gotten pressure on your wound."

"Yeah, but you were there. If you weren't, I'd be dead. Blue would be dead."

"Hold on there, friend. You were the one who texted me with the address. You saved yourself, and I am afraid you will just have to take credit for saving Blue yourself, too. I would not have gotten there in time."

Chief Hannah paused and stared at Will. The pause was long enough that it started to worry him.

She finally broke her silence. "Look, what I really want to tell you is this. Your wound will heal, but everything you have gone through will stick with you the rest of your life. You also have to accept the fact that you are a hero. You saved someone's life and nearly lost your own. There are people out there that will love you for that and, oddly enough, people out there who will hate you for that. I'm telling you this, because as soon as you step out the door of this hospital, it won't be the world you were in before this happened. Just always remember to hang in there and be true to yourself and your family, okay?"

"Okay," said Will in a puzzled tone. "This is sounding pretty heavy. Is it really that bad?"

Chief Hannah looked down for a minute and said, "Yeah, sorry. It probably won't be as grim as I make it sound, but it can be tricky for people like you. I know this from experience."

"What do you mean people like me?" said Will, now truly puzzled.

She looked him steadily in the eye. "*I MEAN . . . PEOPLE LIKE YOU, AND YOUR FAMILY, AND BLUE!*"

Will sat dumbfounded. He looked at his mother. She just nodded at him.

"*MOM, DID YOU KNOW THIS?*" He looked back at Chief Hannah. "*CAN YOU HEAR ME?*"

His mother replied to the question, "She can't hear you. She's not like us, but she knows we can hear her. Summer and I went to college together. She became a close friend" "*I TAUGHT HER ABOUT VOX.*"

"I'm sorry I kept it from you," said Chief Hannah. "I want to respect and protect your privacy. In fact, I wouldn't have even told you now except I had to ask you this question. Your mom told me about Blue. You heard her cry out, a vox cry, didn't you? That's how you found her?"

Will was still shocked, but he answered. "Well, I heard something, and it had to be Blue, but the sound was . . ." he shivered. "It was . . . it was something I don't want to hear again." It was like the cry of a dying animal, is what he was thinking. He looked at his mom. "*HOW MUCH DOES SHE KNOW ABOUT VOX? DOES SHE KNOW WE CAN PLAY BACK ANY SOUND?*"

His mom nodded.

He looked back at Chief Hannah. "I can't really do it with voice. It's something . . . it's just something only we can hear."

"I get it, Will. You don't have to explain. I only know a little about what your world is like. Just don't let what you can 'hear' get to you, okay?"

All three of them were quiet. Finally, Chief Hannah broke the silence. "I needed to know. I am just going to put down that you spotted Bronco by chance. That's all that needs to be said. okay? Agreed?"

"Yeah, I agree," he said.

"Look, Will, dealing with the press, dealing with friends at school, dealing with anything you feel you can't go to your parents for, I want to be your ally. I'm offering that to you."

Will looked at her. "Does Blue know? Will you be her ally, too?"

"No Will, she doesn't know. I swore to keep your secret. Only you can decide who you want to tell. Maybe you have chosen to tell some friends. Just be careful. Besides, Blue has a better ally, though may not know it yet," and Chief Hannah looked directly at Will's mother.

His mother smiled.

Chief Hannah looked back at Will and patted him on his good shoulder. "*TAKE THIS TO YOUR GRAVE . . . JUST NOT RIGHT AWAY!*"

"Very funny. And thanks," said Will. "You guys make it sound like getting shot is easier than dealing with the publicity."

"Well, I guess you'll find out and just have to let us know afterward, right?" said Chief Hannah. "*JUST DON'T FORGET, YOU ARE NOT ALONE!*" "Now I gotta go. Thanks, Will, and good luck. We are going to get this Bronco Bob. He's smart but we're not letting him get away with it."

Chief Hannah left with a nod and a wink.

Will felt oddly better about the thought of leaving the hospital, though it sounded daunting. He was still stunned by the revelation that Chief Hannah knew about their vox, and that she could control her *chiss* the way she did, almost like she was a vox herself. But she couldn't hear. It was weird talking back and forth that way. Jesus, how many others could do it that he didn't know about?

"*MOM, HOW MANY OTHERS LIKE CHIEF HANNAH ARE THERE OUT*

THERE? YOU TOLD US TO KEEP IT SECRET BUT YOU GO OUT AND TELL PEOPLE?"

His mom looked him steadily in the eye and replied, *"YOU AND ROSE NEEDED TO LEARN THE DISCIPLINE OF HOLDING A SECRET. I THINK YOU HAVE LEARNED, BUT ROSE IS STILL A LITTLE YOUNG. AND THOUGH YOU HAVE LEARNED THE DISCIPLINE, YOU DON'T YET KNOW HOW VERY SEVERE THE CONSEQUENCES CAN BE IF THE WRONG PEOPLE LEARN ABOUT US. SHARING CAN BE A WONDERFUL THING, BUT ONLY DO IT WHEN YOU HAVE ABSOLUTE TRUST."* She paused and looked away as if she was trying to avoid looking someone behind him. He almost turned around to see what it was, but before he could, she turned back to him intently. *"TELLING THE WRONG PERSON CAN TURN INTO A NIGHTMARE."*

A wave of discomfort hit Will and he felt disoriented for a moment. He'd never quite felt anything like that before and he wondered at first if it was a side effect of the drugs. But as he looked at his mom's eyes, he realized this discomfort was coming from her. There was more conveyed in her vox than words. Will could actually feel himself tensing up at a memory of something horrible. But it wasn't his memory.

"YOU TOLD THE WRONG PERSON ONCE. YOU CREATED A NIGHTMARE."
She nodded.

"MOM, JUST NOW, IT WAS WEIRD. I FELT . . ."

"I know. You are growing up. Your brain is developing in ways that are more social now." *"VOX OCULIS DEVELOPS AND MATURES, TOO."*

"YOU MEAN THAT, JUST NOW, THAT WAS YOU? THAT WAS REAL?"

"YES, THAT WAS ME. YOU HAVE QUESTIONS, I KNOW, BUT RIGHT NOW IS NOT THE TIME. WHEN YOU ARE READY, YOU SHOULD BRING IT UP WITH YOUR FATHER."

This was a lot to think about. He wasn't sure whether to tell his mom that he'd already trusted someone with their secret. Someone he would trust his life with. And the emotion that rocked him just then, it was vox? Why was he only learning about this now? And if he could pick up his mom's emotions, could Blue pick them up now, too? She wasn't as old as he was, but she was a girl. Girls seemed to mature earlier in every way than boys, at least all of them except Blue. She was such a tomboy. God, this was too much to process right now. But it did bring up something else that was weighing on his mind.

"Mom, I haven't seen Blue yet. What's going on? Everyone says she is fine, but why hasn't she come to visit? Is there something else I should know about?"

His mom had a thoughtful look on her face. "Well, what you should know is that Blue has seen you, and she got quite upset. You were asleep at the time, but I think the sight of you in a hospital bed with that bloody bandage and bruising on your arm and chest and tubes and monitors . . . it was a bit much for her." "*God, it was bit much for me.*" Will felt a quiver in his chest. Now he wasn't sure if that was from him or from his mom.

"She's still in a pretty fragile state herself right now. She was a captive for almost 24 hours, as you know, but she is also feeling very, very guilty about you."

Will thought about how Blue had looked when he found her. She had been bound to that chair, alone, in fear for her life the whole time—not knowing where she was or what her fate was. And yet, this was Blue, the tough, invincible kid.

"Fragile?" he said. "I have a hard time imagining Blue as fragile. She is tough as nails."

"On the outside," said his mom. "Inside she is pretty tough, too, but we are all human. We all have our limits. We all have a breaking point. An experience like this can push anyone to their limit. Just be kind and be aware that she is feeling guilty, and though you may not blame her, she blames herself."

"She's not to blame!" he said. "*I'm to blame. I should have gone with her that night. This wouldn't have happened.*"

"*As your mother, I have to strongly disagree. Neither of you should have gone out that night. Nothing will change my mind about that. That being said . . .*" His mom paused and then continued "I THINK YOU SHOULD SHARE THAT WITH HER. SEE WHERE IT GOES."

"But when can I see her?"

"You mean Blue?" came a voice from the doorway. Wu was standing there and Blue was standing next to him. She was in street clothes, so they must have released her from the hospital. She was looking down at the floor.

"CLICK, CLICK, CLICK . . . HEY LITTLE FOX!" She heard. She caught the reflection off the floor. He could tell.

Blue looked slowly up at him. He just had time to suppress the expression of shock as she revealed her face. Her cheek was black and blue, she had a red lump and scab on her forehead, and she still had a crust of a scab in the corner of her nose. Her skin was blotched with red spots around her mouth. She looked beat-up.

Still, he couldn't suppress a smile. She was alive.

She walked shyly over to his bed and touched his good hand. She stared at him nervously and intently and said, "I AM SO, SO SORRY! I CAN'T BELIEVE I DID THIS TO YOU!"

Will was oblivious to her apology. He was under the spell of the enormity of the simple joy of seeing someone alive who you thought was gone forever. He didn't realize until that moment how close he had grown to this crazy creature and how much he would have missed her. He took his hand out of hers and pulled her to him in an awkward hospital-bed one-arm hug. It didn't matter that it was awkward, it just felt good to feel a real live Blue.

"God, Blue!" he said. "We were so afraid! You're back! Don't go away again! Okay?"

"Okay," she whispered.

He finally released her and looked her in the eye. "ARE YOU OKAY?"

She looked down for a moment but then looked back up at him with a sober face and said, "I'M FINE."

Will heard her vox and tried to smile, but he felt a tiny, faint spark of anxiety that he knew wasn't coming from him.

38

DINNER AT THE O'DAYS

They all gathered in the family room. It was almost time for the 10 o'clock news. Earlier that evening they had feasted on Ma Beth's cooking. All ten of them had managed to cram around the dining room table, the Woods and the O'Days, for a celebratory feast, now that Will and Blue were both home from the hospital.

Will was still taking it all in. Just being in a warm room with good food in his stomach and his friends and family around him made him feel like everything was finished. Blue was back safely, his summer job at the college was over, and he was home from the hospital. There were no more obligations. Everything was back to normal and it was a great feeling. And yet, it wasn't the same normal that he'd known at the beginning of the summer.

It was a new normal. Something inside of him had gone through a major shift. It felt like he'd had an upgrade. The old Will seemed like an innocent boy, and the new Will saw the world from a much sharper perspective. It was a harsher world, but at the same time a more interesting one. And painful. He moved his left shoulder gingerly to feel a little bit of what this new harsh world had done to him. His arm was in a sling, his chest and shoulder had dozens of stitches, and even though his chest tube had been removed, breathing deeply was still painful. Still, he felt alive. More alive than he ever had. And the scars would be there for the rest of his life as a reminder of this change in his life. They were also testimony to the fact that he had taken the first big hard knock and survived. He could survive. And Blue had survived.

He looked over to where Blue was standing. She was in front of a side table, which was crammed with flowers and cards from neighbors and friends. Will walked over to where she stood. She was holding a card that Rose had made during the search. It had a simple drawing of Blue's face. In large colorful words, it said, "Come back to us Blue, we all love you!"

"It makes a poem," Will said. He recited the words in a lyrical rhythm, "Come back to us Blue . . . We all love you!"

Blue put the card back down and looked up at Will. It looked like she was fighting hard to keep any emotions from showing.

"Hey. You okay?"

She just looked back down. Will wasn't sure how to react. Blue had been distant and withdrawn since coming home from the hospital. She was back in her own world much like the world she had been in when he first saw her face in the third-floor window months earlier. It wasn't the same world, though, and she was different. Different for the same reason he had changed, of course. Who wouldn't be changed by that? But not in the same way. It seemed like she was in limbo, like she hadn't started healing as he had.

Suddenly there was a faint high pitched ring in Will's head *"Eeeee!"* and then Sam announced, "News is on in two minutes!" He had turned the TV on and had the new remote control in his hand. He looked down at it and then glanced towards Blue and Will guiltily and put the remote down and mouthed the word, "Sorry!" while his eyes leaked, *"Oops!"*

The TV came to life and everyone found a place to watch it in the crowded room. Will stood behind the couch where his mother and Ma Beth were sitting. Sam and Rose were on the floor in front of the couch. Pa Bill was in his easy chair, and Nate, Wu, and Blue gathered with Will behind the couch. Most of them chatted about the interviews and wondered how it would all come across on TV. Pa Bill bemoaned how the reporters these days always sought the most drama and managed to make people look their most foolish by editing the footage in an unfair way.

Will was silent. He watched the images flashing by on the TV screen. The sound was turned down as the national and international headlines led the broadcast. They were full of reports of suicide bombings and wildfires and car accidents—a silent montage of tragedy and suffering. It made his and Blue's experience seem trivial in comparison. The feeling of warmth and security started to drain out of him, replaced by a feeling of anxiety. Suddenly he didn't feel like watching the interviews. He was ready to turn away from the TV and leave the room, and then he felt a hand slip into his. It was Blue. She gripped his hand tightly. He turned to look at her, but her eyes were locked on the screen. Her face had an expression that seemed out of place for Blue. It looked like fear. He turned back to the TV. He could deal with it. He wasn't going to just leave her there like that.

He forced himself to watch the images again, but instead of getting sucked into the misery of the world playing out on the glowing screen, his thoughts were drawn to the sensation of warmth radiating from the body of the girl standing next to him. That warmth, along with the pressure of her arm against his, was like a balm, infusing him with a sense of calm and stability. He realized his anxiety was dissipating. He felt Blue's hand relax. She seemed to calm down, too. It was as if a bubble of serenity had descended to protect them both. As they stood there together hand-in-hand preparing for the media's distorted version of their ordeal, his mind tried to make sense of what just happened. He had grown accustomed to Blue's unpredictable behavior, but he never imagined she would feel the need to reach out to someone. Then again, he never imagined that maybe he needed someone to reach out to him.

Sam jumped forward and turned up the volume.

"And finally, a happy ending to a local story we have been following for the past few days. It's a story that started last Friday with the report of a missing teen. As you already know, that story quickly became much more. It soon evolved into a story of abduction, drugs, violence, and now, it turns out, some acts of amazing heroism! We at Channel 6 News have kept you up to date with each new development over the past few days, and now we can finally put names and faces to the people involved and fill in the missing pieces of this incredible tale! Bill, you were there when Chief Hannah briefed the press. Tell us what you learned!"

"Well, Linda, it was quite an announcement Chief Hannah made today, and we were there to record it! Here's what she had to say!"

The image switched to a crowded room where Chief Hannah was standing at a small podium with a microphone.

"As you already know, at 10 a.m. last Saturday morning, we received a missing person call from William O'Day saying that their foster daughter, Blue DuBois, a fourteen-year-old, had been missing since about 10 p.m. on Friday night. He and his family had searched the home and neighborhood and found no sign of her and decided to call the police for assistance. We arrived and interviewed the family and neighbors and determined that foul play may have been involved."

Blue DuBois! Will was shocked. He realized he never knew what Blue's real last name was.

A voice from the crowd of reporters shouted out, *"Chief Hannah, what was it that made you suspect foul play?"*

"See, I told you," muttered Pa Bill.

"SHHH!" hissed Ma Beth.

"I cannot tell you details about that at this time because it is still under investigation."

"So was this a kidnapping?" shouted another reporter from the crowd.

"Yes, this was a forced abduction. Miss DuBois was abducted and

forced into a car against her will and taken to a vacant house on Pine street, where she was bound and gagged for the period of time between approximately midnight Friday until 8:30 p.m. Saturday night."

Will became aware that Blue was gripping his hand tightly again. He gave her hand a reassuring squeeze back.

The camera switched to the newsroom where the anchor continued, *"Bill, my understanding is that Chief Hannah responded to a searcher's text that he had found where Blue was being held."*

"That's right, Linda. That searcher was Will Woods, the son of West-bury College professor, Dr. Daniel Woods, and he had actually entered the house where Blue was being held and was trying to rescue her. He was shot and injured by the kidnapper, who then escaped in his own vehicle but not before shooting at Chief Hannah's car and disabling it from pursuit!"

"Wow, Bill, that's a frightening story!"

"It is a frightening story, but I want to make sure our viewers know that everyone is okay. Chief Hannah was not injured and Will Woods will make a full recovery. And of course, Miss DuBois was rescued and is recovering now, too."

"I understand you got to interview Blue and her rescuer!"

"I sure did Linda, and I can tell you these are two amazing kids."

The scene switched to the hallway of the police department where the reporter was asking Will questions. Will thought he looked a bit dorky on the screen and not as mature as he wished he'd looked.

"Will, can you tell me about that night. What happened after you texted Chief Hannah? What made you go into that house that night?"

"Well, I, uh, I guess I'm not really sure." Will groaned internally. He sounded like an idiot. But then the boy on the screen started to gain some confidence and restarted, *"I mean, at first I wasn't sure exactly what to do, but then it just came to me. We'd been looking all day for Blue and everyone was frustrated because it was getting late and dark, and everyone was worried. But then I saw the guy, Bronco, coming out of that house. I knew that if there was any chance of finding Blue, I*

had to go look in that house. Bronco left the house to go into an apartment next door so I ran in, and there she was, in a back bedroom. She was tied up and she wasn't breathing, so I tore the tape off her face and got her breathing again and then tried to free her from the chair. It was hard. She was really well bound, and it took too long and Bronco came back. Everything else just happened and it was like a nightmare after that. If it wasn't for Chief Hannah, I probably would be dead."

"So you must have been scared. Did you know at the time how seriously you were injured?"

"It was weird when I was shot. I wasn't sure at first that I'd really been shot, but then the pain started, and the bleeding. Was I scared? Well, yeah I must have been scared, but I didn't really think about it while it was happening. I was scared for Blue. I thought for sure he would shoot her, but someone else came into the house and Bronco chased after him instead."

"Who? Who came into the house?"

"I have no idea, some guy who just ran off, but I'd like to thank him because he probably saved our lives too!"

Blue and Will and Chief Hannah had decided to skirt the whole issue of Jack. Will was glad. He really did think he owed one to Jack.

"Well, we're all glad to see that you're going to be okay. And I think everyone is grateful for what you did to save Blue's life. You are a hero!"

"Look, I'm not a hero. I wish people would stop saying that. I just tried to do the right thing and I got shot. I'm glad to help, but I sure could have done without the whole shooting thing!"

The reporter just laughed and so did everyone in the room at the O'Days

"That's telling him, Will," said Sam.

"That's my brother!" said Rose.

"I also got to speak with Blue DuBois, and I can tell you she is one tough little lady." The screen faded back to the police station where the reporter was interviewing Blue. The Blue on the screen was the tough survivor Will had gotten to know that summer, but the Blue clinging to his hand tonight was not that Blue.

"So Blue, it must have been very frightening for you! How do you feel now that it is all over?" asked the reporter.

"I was very scared, but I was angry, too. I think being angry helped a lot. This guy was scary but I wasn't going to let him get to me."

"Did you ever feel like you would never get rescued?"

"Come on, what kind of question is that to ask? I'm sorry I let them interview you Blue!" said Pa Bill angrily.

"Hush Bill!" said Ma Beth.

"I . . . I tried not to think about it. I never lost hope, at least not until the heroin."

"How do you know it was heroin, Blue?"

Blue shot her patented glare at the reporter. *"You don't even know? This guy was a drug dealer in town! He's been getting kids drugs for months now! That's why I was angry. I wasn't going to let this guy get me."*

"Well, I can see that he got more than he bargained for with you! I am glad everything turned out okay, and that you're safe now."

"It didn't turn out okay because he's still out there somewhere!"

"Well, I'm sure he won't come back here—not with you in town. That's for sure, Blue!"

Everyone in the O'Day house was clapping and cheering. Will looked at Blue, and she was finally smiling, a bit like herself. She relaxed her tight grip on his hand, but she didn't let go.

The news kept going talking about the search for Bob Kelly, and they showed police drawings of him with and without his beard. And then they showed the drawing of Bronco made by Blue.

"You make those police artists look like amateurs," said Sam.

Ma Beth said, "Sam, be nice." But everyone else was nodding in agreement.

The news mentioned the red backpack and the missing car and then gave numbers for anyone to call with information. This was all stuff everyone in the room already knew, so there wasn't much listening going on anymore. Instead, everyone was discussing theories of where Bronco Bob may have gone, what his chances of being found were, and why his car hadn't been found.

Blue looked up at Will with an expression of slight embarrassment and then let go of his hand. It was like she had woken up from a bad dream, and realized she had been clinging to a stranger.

He tried to reassure her, *"Hey, it's okay."*

She didn't reply, she just looked down.

The discussion and the noise of the TV in the living room suddenly irritated Will for some reason. He decided to retreat back to the kitchen, away from the voices. Blue followed him. They were there only a moment when Wu slipped in to join them.

All three stood silent for a while until Wu finally said, "Blue, I am still mad at you, but you had guts, going after Bronco. Just don't scare us like that again, okay?"

"Okay," said Blue. "Thanks, Wu. You're a good foster brother."

Wu laughed and said, "Hey sister." *"Thank God you're okay."* and he grabbed her and gave her a hug.

Will heard Wu's *chiss*, and from the look on her face, Blue must have, too.

"Wu, there is something we didn't tell you about vox."

Will glanced at Blue. She looked back at him with a raised eyebrow. She didn't say or vox anything but her eyes dropped to the floor for a moment like she was thinking. Then she looked back at Will and nodded.

Wu was watching them. "You're doing it now, aren't you?"

Will looked at Wu and smiled. "Actually, not! But you were."

"What?" said Wu. "What are you talking about?"

"Look, sometimes we can hear other people's thoughts. It's like everyone has a little vestigial vox tissue in their eyes. Sam was right, we can kind of read your mind sometimes. Just now, Blue and I both heard you when you thought 'Thank God you're okay.'"

Wu stood stock still. Will waited for some reaction but Wu's expression was frozen. It almost looked like he wasn't surprised, or maybe he was shocked into a coma. Will looked at Blue, who was looking at Wu, and then he looked back at Wu and saw that his face began to change. Wu screwed his face into an intent look like he was going to stare a hole in the wall. And then Will heard a *chiss* delivered slowly and deliberately, "*I AM GLAD YOU HEARD ME. I DO THANK GOD YOU ARE BOTH ALIVE.*" "Did you hear that?"

Will and Blue looked at each other and then laughed. Blue's laughter startled Will. It was probably only the second or third time he had heard Blue really laugh. The sound seemed to break a spell, and the tension brought on by the newscast finally dissipated. He turned to Wu and said, "Yeah, I think you're getting it. You don't have to make that face for us to hear you, though."

Just then an announcement came from the living room. It was Pa Bill. "Okay, it is time for a toast and then bedtime! Some of us have work in the morning!" Will looked at Wu as they headed to the living room and whispered, "I'll explain it all later. This is going to be interesting, I've never had a friend that knew about us."

In the living room, Ma Beth was passing out cups of seltzer water. Pa Bill held his glass of tea high in the air and announced, "To the Woods and O'Day families! And to the great power of family, friendship, and love! And especially to the safe return of two very special people!" He nodded his head toward Will and Blue and everyone raised their cups and chanted, "Hear hear!" Then there were hugs all around, as the Woods family gathered their things and said their goodbyes.

Will took one last look at Blue and Wu, as he and Rose walked down the sidewalk behind their parents. He saw Blue glare at him from the porch and vox, "*BALANCE! MOVE LIKE A CAT!*" And he thought he might have heard a faint, "*SEE YOU, KNUCKLEHEAD,*" from Wu. Just before he turned away, he saw Blue jab Wu in the ribs with her elbow. He noticed her classic half-smile was back. She seemed to have returned closer to her normal, good self now. He hoped it would stay that way but there was still something else going on inside her. The fact that she had reached out to him showed that she wasn't invincible. She could hide her inner thoughts, and she could control what she said and how she expressed herself, but the grip of her hand and that anxiety that he felt when she looked at him revealed that under that thick skin, she was still fighting demons.

He watched the sidewalk passing below him as he walked. He knew he should be feeling worried about her, but instead all he could think about was the tingle that crept up his arm when she slipped her hand into his and the feeling of warmth emanating from her body as she stood close to him. His hand felt empty now. He looked at it and flexed his fingers. A little shiver went up his arm. He sighed and stuck his hand in his pocket, just so he wouldn't feel the emptiness. He caught up to his parents and fell in behind them. As they walked the last half block to their house, he looked up at the stars and breathed deeply. The moon was just rising, and it seemed that the air had a little September nip to it.

Everyone was in bed, or at least retired to their bedrooms. Blue was lying on her bed with only the night sky lighting her room through the open window. Her mind was rambling again. The events of the past week were over. The get-together tonight was the closing chapter. That was how it was supposed to feel, at least. But it didn't. There was something else going on that hadn't been there before. It showed up as soon as the newscast started. She didn't know where it came from. All she knew was that she suddenly felt like she was going to fall to pieces. The only thing that prevented it was Will's hand. She didn't know how or why, but like so many times before, it seemed like her body knew what to do, much better than her mind. It had seized his hand and gripped it like a lifeline. His hand was strong and from it flowed a sense of stability and security. That feeling was still with her now. She sighed. She didn't want to be dependent on another person for that feeling, and yet it had felt good, holding his hand. Maybe it was okay just this once.

A soft gust of wind ruffled her window curtains. The late summer breeze was warm but tinted with a slight crispness, hinting that fall was coming. She closed her eyes, so she could empty her mind and open it to the familiar sounds that surrounded her now. She felt the softness of her mattress supporting her gently. The breeze from the window played with the loose strands of her hair, making them dance lightly across her face. Her bedroom door was open wide. She was never going to close it again at night. She wanted to absorb every creak and shuffle and voice and laugh from every corner of the house every night from now on. She could hear the muffled sound of Wu telling something to Sam and Sam laughing. She heard the voice of Pa Bill calling down the hall telling them to quiet down. She heard the pipes rush as someone ran water somewhere. The house made its own living breathing sounds. They surrounded her like a warm soft wind, lulling her gently into a sense of peace, allowing her to forget, just for a moment, that her demons were not banished, only at bay.

39

OLD HAUNT

"Same again, Justin?"

The bar was nearly empty, but the air was still thick with cigarette smoke. It was always thick with cigarette smoke, whether there were people there or not. It was a permanent fixture of this bar, like the neon "Schlitz" sign with the flickering "l", or the ancient mirror behind the bar, encrusted with decaying autographed photos of dead, half-famous celebrities.

"Why not," Justin said.

It wasn't his favorite bar, but it was quiet. Quiet was what he wanted right now. Quiet and a fair dose of alcohol.

The bartender poured another whiskey and added a splash of water. He put it down in front of Justin and took the empty glass. It was the fourth, or maybe fifth glass he'd taken from Justin tonight.

"Taking the subway, right?"

"Always looking after me, eh, Stu?" Justin replied.

"Lookin' after me. Gotta keep my license," he said. "Sorry to hear about your car, though. That was a sweet ride."

Justin didn't answer, he just took a sip from the fresh drink. Stu knew better than to hang around, so he moved back down the bar. Justin let his eyes wander up to the small flatscreen TV above the mirror. No sound, just the same channel Stu always played, the Endless-Fucking-News channel. Maybe it was good for business—showing non-stop disaster and death. It seemed to match his mood at the moment, anyway, and he was drinking plenty. Here's to you, Stu. He held his glass up to the TV.

He stared at the images in an alcohol trance. He watched the mouths of the talking heads open and shut. Wah, wah, wah, wah. He watched a flashy news-break graphic do its seizure-inducing dance on the screen. He stared at it, bleary-eyed, foggy, half-comatose. Another image appeared on the screen. For some reason, this one burrowed down into the still-sober part of his brain. When it finally penetrated the alcohol barrier, he felt like he was hit by a cattle prod. He nearly fell off the bar stool.

It was that damn cop.

He focused his eyes on the news ticker at the bottom of the screen.

"UPDATE ON ABDUCTION IN WESTBURY, VT . . . RESCUER AND ABDUCTEE INTERVIEW UP NEXT . . ."

He glanced down the bar. Stu was watching the other flatscreen and faced away from him. He looked back up at the screen. Now it was that damn kid, his arm in a sling.

"I'M NOT A HERO SAYS 15-YEAR-OLD RESCUER . . ."

Bastard. Live witness number one. Rub salt in my wounds, why don't you. He's not my real problem, though. It was that she-demon, the mind-reader, the one that knew his secrets. How many, he wasn't sure, and that was his problem.

Her image flashed on the screen. A little beat-up looking. At least that was satisfying. She looked at the camera and he nearly ducked. Steady, you idiot, he thought. She can't see you and there is no way she could read your mind through a TV.

"I WASN'T GOING TO LET THIS GUY GET TO ME, SAYS ABDUCTEE, WHO WAS DRUGGED AND BOUND FOR MORE THAN 24 HOURS . . ."

Fucking little witch.

"Stu, I'm ready to settle up." He'd had enough. It was time to go home and come up with a plan. He had unfinished business and he'd put it off for long enough.

"Just a minute, I want to finish this."

"What kind of bartender are you? The TV is for the customers."

"Yadda, yadda, what's your hurry. Hey take a look at this police sketch . . . no it's not a police sketch, it's a sketch by that girl!"

Justin looked back up at the screen. He might as well have been looking in the bar mirror. It was as if he'd sat for a portrait. At least a portrait before he'd shaved his beard off. Jesus. Fucking. Christ.

"Jeez, Justin, this guy, Bronco sure looks a lot like you! You got a brother in Vermont?" said Stu, finally turning from the TV and walking down to where Justin was sitting.

But Justin was gone.

Stu stood there with raised eyebrows. "You're welcome!" He snapped up the wad of bills that Justin left on the bar, counted five twenties, and nodded appreciatively. He put two of the twenties in his pocket. "And you are welcome back any time if you keep tipping like that, Justin my boy."

But Justin had no intention of coming back.

At least, not as Justin.

Or Bronco . . . .

ACKNOWLEDGMENTS

Creative work cannot happen without a community of supporters, and below is a list of those who helped bring *Vox Oculis: Not Alone* alive. They deserve a medal of valor for enduring the early (very) rough drafts and shining a bright light on the (many) errors of my ways:

Tom Smith
Kerry Lozito
Collin Parker
Deb Brinkman
Jeff Tonn
Holly Magnani
Elizabeth Cady Martin

ABOUT THE AUTHOR

Photo Credit: Dorothy Schnure

Frederic Martin lives and writes in and about Vermont. He was awarded the 2018 Vermont Writer's Prize for his short story *Maybe Lake Carmi*. *Not Alone* is his debut novel and book one of the *Vox Oculis* YA science fiction series.